THE ESFAH SAGAS:

RISE & FALL OF THE OBSIDIAN GROTTO

BY
CHRISTOPHER D. SCHMITZ

A DRAGON DICE NOVEL

CHRISTOPHER D. SCHMITZ

PUBLISHED BY TREESHAKER BOOKS

The Esfah Sagas

Rise and Fall of the Obsidian Grotto
Cast of Fate

The Relic Quests
Ashes of Ailushurai
Rise of the Champions (coming 2021)
Drakuwar (coming soon)

The Cyrean Songs
Chill Wind
Eye of the Storm
Secrets of the Shadowlands (coming 2021)

STAY UP TO DATE ON THE WORLD OF ESFAH!

Get a free copy of book 1 in the Esfah Sagas by visiting:

www.subscribepage.com/getfreedragondicenovels

Subscribers who sign up for this no-spam email list will get free books, exclusive content, and more! You'll get a digital copy of *Rise & Fall of the Obsidian Grotto* immediately… if you would like more details or want to follow the author, you can find his details at the end of this book.

BACKGROUND

Dragon Dice™ was originally created by Lester Smith and produced by TSR in 1995. It is an Origins Award winning strategy game where players create mythical armies using dice to represent each troop and is one of several collectible dice games that emerged in the 1990s. The game combines strategy and skill as well as a little luck.

After several years, TSR, now owned by Wizards of the Coast, had put Dragon Dice™ on hold to work on other projects. In October of 2000, SFR Inc. purchased the rights to Dragon Dice™.

Most of the races and monsters in original TSR Dragon Dice were created by Lester Smith and include some creatures unique to a fantasy setting and others that are familiar to the Dungeons & Dragons role-playing game. While the world of Esfah, where Dragon Dice™ takes place, has many similarities to that of Dungeons & Dragons, it is distinctly different in many respects. In some ways, there are greater unknowns and its history is both newer and older all at once.

Around the end of 1995 I was a teenager and avid board gamer who had a burger-slinging job (which gave me a disposable income) and a car (that took most of my disposable income.) In addition to many other games I played as part of a regular quartet of gamers, Dragon Dice™ was one that we all enjoyed.

I fondly remember how the four of us would cut out of elective classes, study halls, and independent learning periods to meet up for gaming sessions. Dragon Dice™ came in a pocketable carrying bag which made it perfect for that.

We also had a mutual acquaintance. An older gentleman in town owned a new and used book store that also carried a limited supply of gaming products. Though he did not stock Dragon Dice™, he did have a copy of *Cast of Fate*, the first

Dragon Dice™ novel which included a special promo die. I snapped it up right away as the most avid reader of the foursome (which lent itself to me becoming the dedicated DM for our role-playing game sessions and solidified my path as a story-teller.) The included promotional die was our bright and shiny object for months.

Cast of Fate by Allen Varney was not the only book set in the world of Esfah, though it remains one of the few. As I write and publish more and more fiction (both Fantasy and Science Fiction,) I tend to write the stories that I've always wanted to... and I've always wanted to have a voice in a shared universe. Creating a story within the Dragon Dice™ universe is something I've always wanted to do, so I give a special thanks to SFR, a company composed of true and like-minded fans who have kept alive a product that was one of the gems of the 1990s.

-- Chris

FOREWORD

In eons past, when time was young and creation malleable, the four powers of Nature -- earth, air, fire, and water -- the children of Nature, the Mother goddess, and each gods in their own right, brought forth two races of beings to care for their fledgling world, Esfah, which was created by the All-Father, Tarvanehl. One race, the Selumari or coral elves, was created to husband the fluid forces of air and water. The other race, the Vagha, a dwarvish race, embodied the stability of earth and the tempering power of fire. Together, these two peoples worked to nurture their infant world into something glorious and beautiful.

But Nature had a nemesis in Death, the spirit of entropy. In imitation of Nature, Death brought into being its own races: the Morehl, or lava elves, who worshiped fire and destruction, and the Trogs, a race of goblins, who sprang from earth and corruption. From the moment of their creation, the Morehl and Trogs sowed conflict, defiling the very world that gave them life and corrupting the other races who tended it. War sparked over land and possessions. Soon, hordes of dispossessed Selumari, Vagha, Morehl, and Trogs swept back and forth across the lands of Esfah, locked in endless battle.

In their struggles for supremacy over the fledgling world, the First Races pressed other magical beings into their service. The Morehl were the first to do so, bringing up fire-breathing Hellhounds and web-casting Driders from the deepest caverns below Esfah. The Trogs followed suit, leading Trolls, Harpies, and other monsters into battle. In response, the Selumari called forth Coral Giants from the ocean and swarms of Sprites from the skies. The Vagha enlisted Gargoyles, Androsphinxes, and other creatures of the crags.

Conflict raged across the face of Esfah and Death delighted in the carnage.

Back and forth across the world, darkness battled against light. Each side escalated the conflict, seeking victory, and the battles grew ever savage and desperate. New races arose, each pressed into the fray of the bloody struggle that seemed to have no end in sight.

Saddened by the bloodshed, Nature, the goddess-mother Ghaeial, dealt death to preserve life. Death, the bastard child of Ghaeial and Selurehl, the god known as Void. Death reveled in the chaos, terror, and pain that war brought.

A time of champions arose to safeguard the realm. Wars continued and an entire age passed. Pockets of tenuous peace grew from apathy—Death engineered a new trick to soften the resolve of Nature's troops, and seemed to have abandoned his playground for the comforts of the Abyss--but his attention has never truly waned.

Esfah has never known true peace. It is not in the planet's makeup: this is where the children of gods war on their behalf. Both old and new races struggle ever onward--creatures inspired to greater ends, forever in search of either an end to the bloodshed, or carnage renewed, as each is bent towards his or her own ends.

Esfah cannot know peace. The god known as Death will not allow it. Only a few know his true name--and to speak it aloud is to court Death himself.

For a short video overview of Esfah's origins, visit
https://youtu.be/JhF8RPFkF9I

CREATION'S SECOND SONG

In the beginning, there was only quiet. Coldness and silence penetrated all within the Void and its god, Selurehl. Nothing other than the frigid quiet was known, except by those beyond Selurehl's domain. Only Tarvanehl, the Father of All, he who is called Father Time, and his younger brother Turambar, the master of Fate, knew other.

Before Turambar gave over his domain to his three daughters, lo, before they were sang into existence, there existed only the three brothers: Tarvanehl, who fixed all things within the void, Turambar, who often coaxed the eldest to action, and Selurehl, who disliked every perfect sphere of creation his brothers deposited in his Void and which he froze with his frigid silence.

With the eldest brother watching, Turambar pushed those first orbs of creation into motion. When those first ones collided after many millennia, which passed as if a day to the gods, they exploded into a cacophony of sounds and stirred to cosmic motion with the first blast of song. It shook the Void and called the worlds into motion. Circling Soll, two sisters danced around the bright jewel of the sky, spinning in silent motion.

Selurehl watched, ever frustrated by his brothers, until his domain quieted again.

But Turambar had been so pleased with the sound that he continued to guide the sisters' destinies, and he encouraged Tarvanehl, likewise. It was to Esfah that the Father whispered, and his voice awakened her. Across the night sky, Esfah's sister Leguin heard them but faintly and roused from slumber to sleepily watch Nature emerge as an awakened goddess: Mother Ghaeial. Esfah. Ghaeial erupted in song—for she knew no other way to exist but with brilliant vibrance and joyous noises, remembering the whispers of the one who woke her as a goddess-wife.

Ghaeial's voice soared into the expanse, drawing the attention of the other spheres of Tarvanehl's creation and threatening to rouse them in similar fashion. Selurehl drew close to end her proclamation, but her songs of genesis had already begun.

Tarvanehl smiled upon her and desired her to sing and bear his children. The goddess's voice rumbled low as tectonic notes roared and undergirded the soprano whistle of her winds, and she birthed two gods of the elements, Eldurim and Ailuril. Her passions rose with fiery zeal, spewing lava from her core and spawning Firiel. Her song reached a crescendo with Auguarehl and it trickled to a gentle babble as life's song faded to a sustained vibrato.

I need not tell you what happened next—of the four gods' creation of the elder races - much has been written in *The Tale of Creation* and elsewhere. But of Esfah's quiet sister, only those with oracular sight know the truth. Leguin can be seen shimmering above the horizon at dusk and dawn, but only the sages remember how she awoke to life in a harmony song subtler than Esfah's, whose choir was four strong.

Selurehl could not tolerate this noise—but could seek no recourse amongst his brothers. And so he fell upon Ghaeial. Interjecting his will, he reached for her with his withered hand and shook her, disrupting Nature's song with corrupting touch.

Her songs turned to a shrieking dirge at his gnarled, chill taint, and Selurehl took perverse delight in those cries more than he appreciated the silence and his abuse towards Tarvanehl's beloved spawned [name redacted**] the bastard god known as Death. Selurehl despoiled his brother's beloved Nature and then returned to the coldness of Void to watch his own son come into being.

Turambar watched from Leguin's embrace—both desiring to help his brother's lover, but afraid Selurehl might similarly ravage his precious Leguin.

Strife came to the children of Nature—and the five siblings' quarrels came to bloodshed. [In the third year of the First Age*] three things came to Esfah: the Dragons, by Ghaeial's own tears; the Misbegotten One—the god Death; and the First Daybringer Comet.

In response to his siblings who comforted their mother and threatened the youngest brother, Death composed his own lyric. His song reached his father's ears and pleaded for obliteratingly certain effect. Selurehl gladly flung an instrument of apocalypse; he cast a meteor with unerring aim. Half as large as pale Rhaudian, [Death]** rejoiced at the twisting mass that would quickly end all of Esfah's song.

With her children in danger, Nature sang again, more fervently than ever. Her song pierced the cold and reached Tarvanehl's ears—but Turambar was closer, watching curiously from his post with his hidden lover. The song's beauty moved him so much that he intervened before the comet could strike, splintering it into the chain which passes on a loop through the cosmos, circumnavigating the heavens every twenty-three years to remind Selurehl that song will always defeat the silence. (It is for this reason that those who worship Ghaeial celebrate Turambar's Day at the comet's arrival.)*

While the first meteor shower rained harmlessly upon Esfah, large pieces struck the sleepy sister and scarred her face, rousing her to wakefulness similar to her sister. Leguin screamed with surprise, but her voice was pure and pleasant, and Turambar blessed her. Three pieces fell from her and entered the void near bright Soll. They eventually lodged upon the face of Rhaudian as the daughters of Turambar, who he left to watch over Esfah—to shape and guide their cousins' fates, intervening if necessary. They can be easily spotted on a full moon's night.

Now a parent in his own right, Turambar gifted Mother Ghaeial, setting a crown upon her head to remind her that she was not alone. Turambar and his family promised to help guide Nature's children to the last generation, binding his line with hers. Upon this crown, he set a powerful diadem, Turambar's Elemental Relic, in which he wove his desire to prosper his sister-niece's children and the music they make when they resist Selurehl's entropic desire for the void to consume all: for the grand silence his son [Death]** seeks to actualize.

Some say the relic was a flute that could control the elements. Others say it was a gem to reflect the glory of the Mother. Still others refuse to believe at all—deafened by callousness and [Death's]** spirit as he works to further his father's will.

Only the sages know the Relic's true nature and purpose. It must remain hidden.

After this intervention came the *Fall of Turambar,* when Selurehl created a muse to trick him into leaving behind his godhood-status and become music itself (which is why Turambar is known as the deity of song) and yet even then he wields great power to move a person's heart through music. That tale of trickery is recorded in *Fall of Turambar,* but before his metamorphosis, Turambar gave the Three Singing Sisters the power of fate and control over the destinies of all Esfah's children. They are the Sisters of Fate.

(There existed other songs of Turambar and of Leguin, who he loved as Tarvanehl loved Esfah, but most were lost when the libraries of Yentosh burned during the Dawn of War in 19FA. Only fragments exist.)*

Book of the Land: The Singer Sister and The Quiet One (attributed to the Vaghan sage, Tal the Righteous, who lived in 359 First Age)

* this addition added by Kholkoro Wicebrow in her commentary on the *Book of the Land, 1122 Second Age*

** *Death's name has been substituted in these texts; as the old proverb goes, "to speak Death's name is to invoke him." --K. Wicebrow.*

LOVE, BLOOD & FIRE
PT. I
THE FAME OF DAVIAN WHISPERWYND

Year 19 of the First Age

Smoke rose above the wreckage of Daur-Bor-Nin. The proud city had fallen in spectacular fashion. Smoldering husks of structures that once housed elves and dwarves alike had crumbled beneath their own weight. Their collapse scattered embers into the air.

Hunks of stone lay like headstones wherever they had fallen. Even the foundations of the stronger buildings had been toppled. The grand tower of the Daur-Bor-Nin University, where the Grand Sage of the eldarim taught his wisdom and knowledge to new students in the Library of Yentosh, had been toppled.

On the nearby hillock, Davian Whisperwynd stood alongside a handful of his fellow warriors and mourned the heavy losses. "So much for the first free city," he stated quietly.

He bowed his head and offered a prayer to the gods, Aguarehl and Ailuril. His long locks of silver with green highlights cascaded around his blue-skinned face.

Davian and his company had responded to calls for aid from the selumari living there, the blue-skinned elves that were part of his race. They'd made the trek in their airship, the wreckage of which lay burning in the heart of the city. It was a long walk back to their home in the city of Maris-ta-Sehlim, which meant in their tongue, "the city of the good folk."

Selusis, Davian's closest friend, put a hand on the warrior's shoulder and tried to cheer him up. "They are calling you one of the heroes, you know. How valiantly you fought against the enemies... you must have single-handedly slew a hundred of them... and those creatures they rode?" Selusis shuddered.

Many of the giant spiders and scorpions they rode upon lay dead. Even a few wyverns had fallen in the battle which had raged for more than a tenday. Finally, reinforcements arrived from both the coral elf city of Maris-ta-Sehlim and from the closest vaghan cities in the west, dwarven strongholds including Oxforge.

Davian's eyes lingered on a wyvern corpse. They looked like dragonkin, but the eldarim experts had assured him they were something else entirely and not related to the drakufreet as far as they could ascertain.

Davian nodded his head and stood tall, trying to shake off his sorrow. He towered nearly a full head above most elves of his kind, not that the selumari people were short by any means. He brooded, *these red-skinned traitors may be elves... but they are not selumari. They called themselves the 'morehl,' gladly accepting the term 'bad elves.'*

"I did not intend to be a hero," Davian mumbled. "I only meant to save those who needed it most."

His companions nodded as they watched the smoldering remains from the overlook. They felt much the same way as Davian.

Below them, the eldarim of the city, folk who looked like elves, save that their sturdier bodies came in a wider variety of skin tones and their ears were not pointed, scrounged for whatever they could salvage. The vagha people, what the dwarves called themselves, had begun to form up into groups by their families; many of them had already begun journeying west where they had kin in the Daurhedges, south towards the Mezzoscarp, and east to the mountains of the sa'Eldurim Massif. A collection of the three races huddled tearfully nearby with a pile of tomes they'd managed to save from the flames.

The sages only rescued a fraction of their writings; Yentosh is ruined.

"There is nothing left, here," Davian acknowledged. "Not for any of them." Even though Daur-Bor-Nin was not his home, he had liked the idea of a free city where the races and their myriad cultures intermixed.

Jarroch, another of their company lamented, "Without the airship, it will take us at least another hundred leagues or more out of our way to return home, nearly 350 leagues in total," he estimated.

Davian sighed, "It will take a full tenday just to get back home by foot, and that's provided we don't encounter any of more of those beasts that have been crawling out of the sloughs of Brackishomme lately."

Davian looked out across the fields of battle and noted that so many of the dead were those same vile creatures which had been attacking the outliers of Maris-ta-Sehlim. The goblins had been in some kind of alliance with the red-skinned elves all along.

Jarroch worked his jaw. "Maybe we're lucky and the swamps have emptied of them. There are certainly a lot of them lying here, dead?" His voice brimmed with optimism, though none suspected the swamps near the Maris Coast would breed anything but these wretched fiends they'd begun to call trogs.

Davian asked, "What do you think, Selusis?"

"Morehl," the elf hissed and spat, still staring at the fallen enemies whose crimson blood steamed slightly as it came in contact with the air. "These red-skinned elves arrived only two years ago, claiming to be just like the selumari—that was an obvious lie, in light of what happened here: it was all a ruse meant to let our guard down." His face tightened as he gave it more thought. "There are morehl living in Maris-ta-Sehlim… I'm for going home as soon as possible. There's not any more good we can do here in the Crechelands—especially since most of our provisions were destroyed with the airship."

"What do you suppose all this means for us?" Jarroch wondered, surveying the wanton damage.

"The Dawn of War, of course. Neither selumari nor vagha can let this attack pass," Davian muttered. "This will certainly be only the first war among many."

"I think we should find the best way possible to join the fight against these wicked beasts and kill every last one of them," Selusis hissed, gathering up his pack and preparing for the journey home. "And you, the great warrior Davian Whisperwynd, your services will be in high demand. I think any of us will be glad to fight by your side again."

The company all chimed in with their assents. Shortly after, they began the long trek home.

Davian and his companions met little trouble on the road back to Maris-ta-Sehlim. Several of the selumari survivors and a few misplaced vagha and eldurim accompanied the warriors as they headed north across the plains and through the muddy trail as it winded through the marsh.

The spongy road through the troglands was plagued by only a little resistance. Several well-placed arrows from Davian's company ensured they traveled unmolested and kept any curious goblin onlookers at bay during the exodus.

After arriving to great fanfare in Maris-ta-Sehlim, Davian and company found it much unchanged, except that whatever local morehl had been in the city had been enslaved. Selumari soldiers had uncovered their coup against the city leaders and put it down before any harm could befall them.

Months followed and Davian led raids against the trogs of the Brackishomme swamp, alleviating immediate concerns to their safety.

Shortly after, those warriors who had followed Davian into battle at Daur-Bor-Nin served alongside him when they answered the call to war against their enemies. They mustered for countless skirmishes as war broke out across Esfah. Fewer of them returned home each time, hardening Davian's resolve.

After two years of battle, Davian tired and returned home to hear stories of his great fame. The stories, primarily embellishments from tales told by survivors of Daur-Bor-Nin who had relocated to Maris-ta-Sehlim, had spread readily. He shrugged off the people's praise, despite Jarroch's insistence that he revel in it.

"Use it for your advantage," Jarroch insisted one night over wine.

Davian practically pouted into his cup. The doors opened to Jarroch's fine, new home, which he'd purchased through smart business moves. Selusis entered, catching up on the conversation.

"He's right, you know," Selusis insisted, pouring a glass for himself. "I've been elected to the city's high council. Only the high minister is a higher position—and one I intend to find myself in. I couldn't have achieved my election without the fame purchased by adventuring alongside you." He winked at Jarroch, "And this one... he was a simple warrior but now a successful entrepreneur—we both owe our success to defeating the morehl at the first free city."

Davian said little. He'd withdrawn further with each meeting of his friends.

Another door opened at the rear and Jarroch's serving woman entered, a young morehl woman dressed in selumari finery, except for the chains on her hands and feet. As with most females, her eyes twinkled when they set upon Davian, who nodded politely, but made an effort not to lead her on.

Davian's eyes, however, did catch Jarroch's. They lingered on the serving wench as she plated their food. A sound like an infant's cry sounded somewhere within Jarroch's house, and the woman hastily rushed off to attend.

"Is that a baby's cry?" Davian asked. "Jarroch, have you fathered a child?"

Jarroch and Selusis traded knowing looks. Finally, Jarroch said, "I'm sure that, whatever that sound is, that was no son of mine."

Davian wanted to know more, but Jarroch evaded his questions.

"You really must be my running mate," Selusis insisted. "You have earned great fame with your sword—think of how much good you could do for Maris-ta-Sehlim from a place of real power: from a political chair? My oldest friend... do I have your support? Will you be my co-chair when I run for minister?"

Davian looked aside and watched the young mother nurse her babe down the hallway. With chained ankles and wrists, she held the babe to the red skin of her breast and fed him.

Ka-Clang! Ka-Clang! A warning bell rang in the distance, startling them all. Selusis spilled his wine, and Jarroch's bastard babe shuddered and cried. The mother did her best to quiet the child as the three selumari snatched their swords and ran in the direction of the danger.

A horde of goblins had emerged from the southern swamps. The outlying homes at Maris-ta-Sehlim were in flames, and the snapping of wardog teeth tore apart the flesh of dead elves.

Trogs swung their crude axes and flung stones from their slings. They snarled and overwhelmed whatever citizens they could.

Davian raised his blade and roared his battle-cry. "For the selumari!"

Selusis and Jarroch raised their weapons to match and shouted the response, "Into the abyss!" and then the three charged into the fray, rallying the elves behind them.

Though it had been a year at least since they'd all three fought together, they worked as a unit and beat back the trog invaders. The surrounding elves harnessed their energy and inspiration, putting down goblins more easily now that the fear of meeting selumari heroes distracted them.

Davian and his friends reached the thickest of the fighting. A hulking beast of a trog with mottled skin like lichen on bog stumps looked up from the abuse he doled out upon a well-known coral elf tailor; splatters of greenish blood marred his face and the tailor's daughter screamed as the brute lorded over them with his great axe made of jagged metals.

"Face me, you fiend!" Davian shouted.

The goblin abandoned the tailor and whirled to roar his challenge. They clashed in the square: Davian the hero and the trog champion. This beast was larger than even Davian, who was well known for his size, but after trading a number of blows, the selumari warrior was clearly the superior fighter. He ducked an axe blow that might have taken his head off and then flashed his blade, separating the creature's hands from his body. The great axe flew off into the distance.

Falling to his knees, the trog roared with painful defiance; the goblin army's resolve broke, and they fled for the safety of the swamp. The wounded creature laughed as his yellow blood pulsed from his wounds. His eyes met the tailor's daughter as she screamed, terrified and holding her father's limp and lifeless body.

"Why? Why do you attack the city?" Selusis interrogated him.

Sneering through his pain, and ignoring the selumari's demands for information, he merely hissed, "We will not stop coming. We will never stop. The god of Death demands we wipe out all children of the other gods. Our totem spirit, Noxigant, offspring of the dark lord, will make it so!"

The blue-skinned child wailed the entire time. Davian swung his blade and severed the fiend's head from his body, finally quelling the young girl's cries.

A crowd had begun to form as Davian scooped up the child. She sobbed on his shoulder as the selumari crowds gathered.

Selusis seized on the opportunity and addressed them all. "My friends, my kin! If we were more adequately prepared, this might have never happened. Our losses could have been so much fewer. You have all heard tales of Davian Whisperwynd and know that he and I have fought alongside each other. *Davian knows battle...* I know battle. And I have a plan to prosper Maris-ta-Sehlim. Know what I stand for and that I require your vote to build a stronger community when I run for our highest office."

His announcement brought a few cheers. One voice called out, "And what of Davian? Captain of the army?"

"Put him in charge of defense strategy!" another shouted.

Selusis looked hopefully to his friend.

Stoic, Davian shook his head and set the child down. He looked at her. All of twelve years old. She dried her eyes and Davian thrust his sword into the ground where it stood like a battle standard. "No. I am a warrior, not a leader. I would be a terrible figurehead."

Davian grabbed the bulbous head of the goblin commander and threw it into a nearby wagon. "But I make a pledge to my people," he said, looking again at the girl, "I will not set foot again in Maris-ta-Sehlim, my home, until this cart is filled with the heads of our enemies."

He scooped up his sword, untethered the wagon from the pony that had died in the middle of its transport, and pulled the cart beyond town where the citizens watched his departure.

Year 28 of the First Age

Davian Whisperwynd left his cart a couple leagues away. He was deep in the swamp, but goblins had a keen sense of smell and the stacked heads had a distinct odor. His wagon brimmed with the decayed heads of trogs he had killed.

Though he did not break his vow these past seven years and return home, he often stopped travelers to get word of worldwide events and to hear news from his home. Maris-ta-Sehlim had not endured another raid from goblin marauders since he undertook his vow.

Travelers sustained him and delivered supplies in addition to sharing news; they knew his efforts kept the roads safer. And they reminded the city who it was that kept them safe.

He pushed away his pride at the thought. Davian did not do this for pride; his only goals were to prosper the selumari who lived in his home... though he was not opposed to those benefits extending to the few vagha or eldarim who lived there. Or to the new race that had appeared a few years ago; travelers called them humans.

Davian had not met a human. Perhaps he would, someday, after his vow had been made complete. He assumed the citizens of Maris-ta-Sehlim would embrace them if they were good. *All lives have value*, he'd come to believe during his solitary journeys. He disliked the trogs and morehl, but had to acknowledge that they had at least *some* intrinsic value.

Over these past many years, he'd become something of an expert on the goblins. He'd even learned their language, a beastly sort of grunting compared to the eloquent elvish tongue. Davian learned that his efforts had made an impact on *them*, as well; recently he sat outside a goblin hut and listened to a trog sow warn her brood against going out alone into the bogs where she thought it unsafe.

[The blue elf who whispers in the wind might get you and take your head,] she insisted before blowing out a crude candle in the mud hovel where Davian hid outside.

That had been two days ago, and Davian had chosen to spare that village. Even though the head of a goblin wife took up just as much space as that of any other trog, he felt it dishonest to wipe out such helpless prey purely to add to his pile, even though he knew this brood would be mature enough to be a menace in a matter of two years. It only took trogs about six years to reach fighting age.

Davian still wore the mud that he'd caked himself with that night. He regularly used it to cover his blue flesh and camouflage him in the thick of the swamps. Currently, he stalked through the peat mats that squelched his footsteps as he approached a set of mud huts in the marsh. Even after so many years, he never grew accustomed to their distinct stench. It made his stomach turn until he acquired a temporary nose-blindness to it.

He crept into the edge of the tiny village and noted yelling from within, like the howls of a trapped feline. Davian peeked around the nearest hut's corner and spotted her: a goblin wife.

There were five of the shacks, each with a variety of inquisitive faces peeking out. Goblins typically birthed litters of eight each spring. Within a few years time, this tiny cluster of hovels could grow exponentially.

A goblin wife laid in the middle of the huts, growling, scratching, and wailing. She was an ugly thing and caught in the throes of childbirth. With a final scream, she pushed out the last of her disgusting pups.

Davian relaxed his fists from the grip of his weapon. It did not seem right to kill her in such a state. He nearly left when he heard the raucous singing beyond the huts. A group of hunters dragged a few wild goats towards their home, arguing over who had made the actual kills.

He counted them. Five. One for each hut. He remembered that goblins were polygamous. These males likely shared the one wife until the next brood was old enough, or until they found and abducted another female from somewhere else. The size and makeup suggested these were probably the leftover children from a village he'd razed years ago when he first began his singular war against the Brackishomme.

Five trogs. He frowned, cracking the mud caked on his jaw. It would take six to finish filling the cart. Davian cocked his jaw. Five would have to do. Perhaps he would encounter a rogue goblin upon the road.

He pulled his blade and charged into the center, leaping over the surprised and exhausted goblin sow.

Davian struck down the first trog with ease, and the others were quicker to draw their axes; none of them proved much of a challenge, and he hacked down three more with ease.

The last of the trogs panicked and dropped his weapon. He tightened his fists and drew an orb of darkness in clear midday, threatening to fling the arcane spell at Davian with lethal intent.

This one has a strong aptitude with magic, Davian thought as he brought his sword to bear. With a quick and lethal stroke, he cut the beast down before it could fling the spell at him. *It is good that I end his bloodline before he can breed again.* He shuddered; death magic in the hands of untrained goblins could prove disastrous for his people on a large scale.

With the five lying dead, Davian recognized that none of them had shown much experience with real combat. His private war had been effective enough that he'd knocked out the ruling class of blooded warriors. It would take them years to recover… years in which Maris-ta-Sehlim would be safe.

Davian spotted a pitcher of water nearby and sniffed it. It seemed clean enough, and he used it to wash the blood and mud from his skin, revealing the blue underneath. He felt more like himself again beneath the streaks of remaining grime. He took a few spare moments to rinse out his hair as well and make himself look more like a proper selumari, and less like a trog wild-man.

The elf who had terrorized the goblins of Brackishomme looked on the goblin wife with pity. Her breaths came in ragged gasps and whimpers. She gathered her pups to her side protectively and refused to look at her other brood and alert the hunter that they were hidden all around.

As beastly as she was, Davian knew she felt sorrow for her dead kin; she likely feared for her extended litter as well as her own well-being. He ignored her glaring eyes as he cleaned his blade of the goblin blood.

Using his feet, Davian rolled the heads into a pile and removed a stringer from his belt. He pushed the sharp end through the thick cartilage of each ear, tying them together for easier hauling.

"Noxigant will come! He will throw down your city and smash it to bits!" the goblin wife roared, spitting curses at him.

[Noxigant is a myth, like the rest of your corrupt religion. There are only four gods in Esfah, and their bastard brother Death is not worthy of note.] Davian replied in the goblin language. He'd come to learn in his study of them that the god was prophesied to come to the peoples and help them make war upon their enemies. Death would arrive as the four Faces of Death, of which Noxigant was one. These heralds would come to only the strongest of the goblin clans: proof made positive through the blood of the clan's enemies.

She appeared startled at first, hearing the hunter speak her tongue, but then she unloaded on him with a hail of curses. [Death has shown us his four faces—and they will be unleashed upon the world. Perhaps they have not yet come—but Noxigant will aid us! And until that day, my children will ready themselves to make war upon your precious city.]

Davian finished stringing the final head and then sighed. He knew she spoke the truth, and that she had forced his hand—he could not let her train up a brood with such dedicated hate. He drew his sword and, a few moments later, filled out the length of his stringer with the final tally to complete his seven-year task.

After slogging through the remaining distance of Brackishomme separating him from his wagon, he tossed the last bundle of heads upon those heaped high in his cart. He moved to its front and smiled. *Soon, he would be in his home.*

Not long ago, an eldarim herdsman had offered him the use of a dragonkin to pull the laden wagon. Davian released the scaled creature from the yoke and let it slip off and into the wilds, free. The path to Maris-ta-Sehlim was mostly downhill from here, and he could manage the unwieldy cart on his own.

The wheels of Davian's wagon creaked and groaned as he pulled his burden into the town square. A hush fell across the crowd, which gathered around him. Many eyes filled with both admiration and fear met his gaze, and then turned to the disgusting wagon he'd dragged into town.

Davian opened his mouth as if to speak and then chose not to. Abutting the town square, Selusis came bounding down the stair to congratulate him on the task well-done. A young elf joined him, hanging on his arm. Davian recognized her as the tailor's daughter, now grown up; she wore finery that indicated social position.

Selusis made reintroductions. "Bellara has become quite the advocate for peace and safety these last several years." Selusis looked at her affectionately. "And soon she will be my wife."

Davian bobbed his head towards the hideous cart. "Peace? How then does this sight strike you? Does it offend?"

Bellara shook her head. "Quite the contrary. In order for peace to come, and if it is to last, those that worship Death must be eradicated entirely. If only more selumari had grit such as yours, Davian Whisperwynd."

Davian stared at Selusis a moment. He looked much softer than when they'd last seen each other, seven years prior.

"Come," Selusis insisted. "You must dine with us and tell me all about your time in the wilderness."

Davian tried to protest, but Bellara linked her arm in his and escorted him up the steps. The famed warrior relented, "Just so long as I may take a bath, first."

"I shall make it so," Selusis said as they entered the home. He clapped his hands, and a morehl came running like a dog. He held his chains in his hands to keep them from jangling too loudly against the smoothed coral tiles. "Fetch my friend a hot bath," he insisted. "And make it quick or you'll feel my switch again."

The slave ran off silently and got to work.

Davian's lips tightened to a thin slit as he watched him go. The warrior accepted a goblet of wine and stood at a large bay window that overlooked Maris-ta-Sehlim; he watched while he waited for supper and the bath to be readied.

Elves went about their daily business in the court below. Despite the stench, they looked aside admirably at the mounded pile of goblin heads parked in their midst. An occasional morehl, in chains and sent on some errand by his or her master, glanced sidelong at the cart with revulsion.

"How many?" Selusis asked. He stood by his friend's side, sipping his own wine. "There must be at least five hundred of them."

Davian took a slow sip. "Eight hundred and twenty-eight."

Selusis's eyebrows arched, but Davian spotted something. He hissed, "Hold, now. What is that?"

He pointed to an elven child who was dressed like a pauper. The child walked with his eyes downcast; they refused to meet anyone else's gaze. He looked like any other young elf except that his skin was gray. Members of the crowd shoved him as he meandered through, keeping his head down.

Selusis chuckled. "He is a degenerate, a mudblood. Nothing worthy of mentioning."

"Mudblood, is that what they are calling the humans?"

Selusis nearly spat out his drink. "I'm sorry. I forgot that you have been away so long. No. We've not yet received any human visitors to our city. That one is frehlasuhl, a gray elf. They are a bastard breed, Davian, products of selumari and morehl unions." He said it with such disdain that Davian knew such a thing had been forbidden. "There are a handful within the city."

"And Jarroch?"

Selusis shrugged. "Still wealthy and successful. And as foppish as you think me to be, no doubt."

"But his child. Does he feel the same way?" Davian asked.

Selusis quirked his mouth and sipped his wine. "Jarroch has no children. Not any legitimate ones he'd lay claim to, anyway."

Davian set his jaw and turned back to the window. He found the crowd still shoving and harassing the mudblood boy, preventing him from leaving the main square. A red-skinned woman wearing chains shrieked and ran to his aid. Davian recognized her as Jarroch's concubine slave.

"He's just a little boy—my child has no say in what he is!" she screamed, trying to defend him, thrashing at nearby selumari, using her doubled length of chains like a whip. She struck several coral elves before they realized she was there.

Davian flew from the house with Selusis on his heels. "It's no use," he called after the warrior.

The crowd immediately turned savage and began beating her, enraged that a morehl slave would dare strike a selumari. She collapsed before Davian could reach her. The crowd dispersed before the renowned warrior. Smiling, the selumari assumed he had come to deal the final blow. Instead, he scooped her up, though she was already fading fast from her severe wounds.

A light of recognition lit in her eyes and she recognized Davian from their meeting years prior. And then she died in his arms. Davian looked at her face, certain that this was Jarroch's slave girl.

"I told you," Selusis said. "These are not people. They are animals—and one must not keep a feral animal as a pet—and pets that turn feral must be put down. This is the law. It's how we prevent another Daur-Bor-Nin."

Davian growled wordlessly. He turned his eyes up to the rotting collection of heads. *If a trog mother, who is little more than an animal, feels sorrow, pain, and happiness, then don't the morehl as well? They are elves, too, aren't they?*

He laid the woman against the cart and stood, locking eyes on the grey skinned boy. Barely eight years of age and thoroughly thrashed, he panicked when the massive selumari advance towards him.

The child hesitated, taking one final look at his mother who lay propped against the wagon filled with kill-trophies, and then fled before Davian.

With Selusis still following him, Davian hurried through the crowd, pursuing the boy at a brisk pace without sprinting after him. He knew where the whelp was headed, and he did not desire the crowd to snatch up the boy on his behalf and potentially hurt him.

A few moments later, they arrived at Jarroch's home and hot on the boy's heels. The child blasted through the doors and out of sight. Jarroch was at the door before Davian and Selusis reached it.

"My friends, I am glad for your arrival—I just learned the good news. Davian! I heard about your achievement... but come, have you dined yet? You must take some wine, surely..."

"The boy," Davian snapped, spotting the child cowering behind Jarroch. "The people killed his mother," he said sadly.

Jarroch shrugged. "A pity. She was good help. Now I shall have to find another."

Davian stared incredulous at his friend. "But... but she was your... the child? What of your son?"

Jarroch glared at the gray-skinned boy from the corner of his eyes. "That abomination is no son of mine."

The child recoiled, and hid from the elves gathered near the door.

What has hatred done to my people? Davian wondered. He refused to look his long-time friend in the face, afraid for what he might do in his anger and for the way his fingers had tightened around the grip of his sheathed blade. He hissed a curse of disgust below his breath, turned, and left.

"Davian! Davian, where are you going?" Selusis called after his friend, chasing after the warrior.

Davian did not reply. He simply kept moving towards the edge of town. Onlookers watched as their champion stormed angrily towards the outskirts.

Finally, he stopped at the very edge of the city's boundary. Davian turned around. "I have more stomach for the plight of goblins than I do anymore for these people."

"Surely, you don't mean such a thing. Come now, Davian. Be serious. Trogs and half-breeds are below the selumari."

"Do you now claim to speak for Ghaeial, mother of the gods?"

Selusis defended, "Well, no, but…"

"But you murder the offspring of her children's creation," Davian interrupted. Passion flooded his voice. "I am no friend to Death and his worshipers. The cart in your square and my reputation among the trogs attest to that—but there is an inherent value to all life, and to see it mistreated thusly by those claiming to be its defenders…" he trailed off with hot words lingering heavy between them.

"Are you finished?" Selusis asked. "Your words would have carried more weight if you had taken my earlier suggestion, years ago. You could have been seated on the council. You could have steered public opinion a different direction, but you claimed it was no place for a warrior and instead chose the sword."

"I *am* a warrior!" he howled. His nostrils flared, and he snatched his sword and shook it in his friend's face. "But perhaps you are right. *This is what I know,* and the sword is bound to my fate, but I vow to you and all the gods that I will not take up the sword again for any purpose—not even if willed by the three goddesses of fate."

No sooner had he uttered those words than a peal of thunder split the sky like an omen. Selusis looked up after the thunderclap, but no clouds marked the horizon.

"I would be wary of defying the gods, my friend, especially not the daughters of Turambar; the other gods are more fickle than Ghaeial's children, and they may very well answer your challenge. Why would you make such a rash vow? Please, take it back while the god-sisters of fate might still forgive it."

Davian shot his friend a wild look.

Selusis knew his friend would not recant. "Fine, but, please, come back with me. Surely the bath is drawn and supper is ready. I promise to listen to your thoughts on the matter, only let us get back."

Instead of a response, Davian turned and began heading south. "Davian? Davian!" Selusis called after him.

Clouds began to form ominously now. A storm seemed likely.

The elf kept waking, undeterred. He grumbled below his breath, "*Maris-ta-Sehlim. Ha.* The city does not deserve her name. It might as well be Maris-ta-Morehlimar." He shook his head. *City of the wicked elves.*

"You can't be serious," Selusis scoffed, refusing to chase him any further. He called after his friend. "After all, you made that vow and you've still got your sword."

Davian did not look back. Instead, he held his sheathed blade out and made a show of dropping it. Davian continued walking until he was out of sight.

Selusis hung his head and collected it in hopes that his friend would someday retrieve it, but that day never came.

Thus, Davian Whisperwynd left Maris-ta-Sehlim and never returned, only reporting the rest of his tale to a wandering sage shortly before his death, some years later.

THE RISE OF THE OBSIDIAN GROTTO
PT. I
THE DARK DEAL

Year 96 of the First Age

Screams echoed across the plains one hundred and fifty leagues west of the Obsidian Grotto, the lava elf stronghold built into the northern tip of the Crooked Spine mountain range of Esfah's Birthlands.

Krak-kow!

The lava-elf's carbine erupted in a flash of light and the haze of blue smoke as he pulled the trigger and cackled. "Another," the red-skinned elf demanded, tossing the long-gun to his subordinate so that it could be reloaded. "I love the way their little heads explode in the distance." Another attendant handed Shedakor a freshly charged weapon as he leaned over a fallen log and took aim. Shedakor sighted down his weapon with coal black eyes.

Kra-kah! The muzzle flashed and the butt of the gun rocked with recoil.

In the distance, another orange-haired head broke apart into darker shades of red. The field was littered with the bodies of their dwarven enemies. Shedakor was in charge of the morehl's military forces and had spied out a campaign to push back the borders of the Obsidian Grotto, the region's preeminent lava elf empire.

Shedakor chortled and exchanged the weapon again for another. He'd been picking off stragglers from the back of the dwarven forces for several minutes, littering the grassy field with their bodies.

Five years ago, he'd gained control of his region's military forces after winning a duel against his predecessor. Shedakor hoped to make, after finally destroying their dwarven neighbors, the vagha, the crowning success of his career. What the morehl and the vagha shared in devotion to one of the five main gods of Esfah gave him little pause. The slaughter of the dwarves had begun as little more than a land dispute, but the lava elves were more than happy when it turned violent.

Shedakor grinned and took down another enemy in the distance.

This skirmish might be about more than just land. Certainly some of this conflict is about pride, he mused. Ruthak, the dwarven warlord in command of the vagha forces, had insulted Shedakor's emperor during treaty negotiations a decade ago. Now, ten years later, Shedakor verged on having the last laugh.

Once the forces of the Obsidian Grotto finally quashed Ruthak's army, they would march into the vaghan tunnels and put the sword to the women and children of Valis, the nearest dwarven city. He was all too happy to claim the vaghas' land for the expansion of the morehl empire. Even now, using their flintlocks, Shedakor's cavalry forced the whole of the dwarven army into a massive ravine where he'd stationed hidden troops along the ridges.

Normally, the morehl hated to fight in the open, but with his troops out of the range of vagha axes and with the enemy on the run, the dwarves would not survive the sprint to escape via the old aqueduct before they would fill it with blood and smoke. His shooters would cut them down—every last one.

Shedakor took aim again, muttering a curse and daring Ruthak to show his face; he pulled the trigger. Something caught the smooth ball-shot with a loud clang: a large tower shield.

It glowed golden as the dwarf champion lowered it enough to peer over the top of it. He locked eyes with the sharpshooter.

"General Irenicus," Shedakor hissed as he beckoned for a fresh gun. It wasn't Warlord Ruthak, but General Irenicus was the dwarven general's right hand. *First Irenicus, and then Ruthak,* he promised himself. "One of these days I *will* get an angle around that mystic shield of yours."

The vagha in other parts of the world had standing alliances with the selumari, the blue-skinned coral elves. They'd also become friendly with the gremmlobahnd lately, the gnomes who had begun crafting items on their far away continent of Charnock with a sea between them—and Gnomehome was on the far side of even that. The gnomes had thus far refused to sell their secrets for creating the arcane weapons their forges churned out.

Shedakor's finger pulled the trigger again.

Kra-thak!

His bullet deflected off the magic defenses again. "Eventually, one of these bullets will take you down, Irenicus… I think today will be that day."

The vagha general thrust his battle-horn into the hands of the dwarf he'd just saved as he further warded against Shedakor's bullets. Pealing loudly, the trumpet blasted a signal to the dwarven forces.

Shedakor sneered. He already had an accounting of Ruthak's forces; he knew that over ninety percent of them were right here—about to fall into his trap. That signal horn would only direct them further into the lava elves' trap.

He drew a bead on the horn blower and fired. *Kra-koom-taaang!* Shedakor cursed as the shield caught the edge of the bullet; it caromed off and whizzed past his target's face. The lead ball cracked through the end of the horn and busted the edge with a jagged break, changing the pitch of the horn's note to a feverish, insistent tone.

"Reload me!" He tossed the spent gun to another red elf who failed to catch it. "Another," he demanded of his distracted troops. They stared off into the distance, ignoring their leader.

One of them shook away the daze and handed his leader a fresh weapon. "Don't you hear that? It—it sounds like thunder." The elf looked down at the metal carbine he held at a vertical angle, slightly worried about lightning strikes. They were far from the coast, but selumari sorcerers had been known to call down deadly electricity from the sky when they commanded the elements devoted to their gods—neither of which the morehl respected.

"Don't be ridiculous," Shedakor scoffed. He grinned as the dwarves began their descent into the trapped chasm. "There aren't any coral elves for hundreds of leagues and the sky is clear."

He sighted down the barrel and drew a bead on Irenicus, waiting for the ginger-bearded fool to peek his head out from behind his protection. Shedakor exhaled a breath and held it at the bottom when his aim would remain most true.

The delicate hairs within his ears vibrated with the low rumbling sound that suddenly picked up volume. He'd been too focused on his prey to notice it before—but now it was unmistakable.

Tearing his sight away from Irenicus, he cocked his head. "That's not thunder…"

The next thing he heard were the sounds of lava elves screaming and rotating chariot wheels as unexpected cavalry reinforcements arrived to turn the tides of battle.

Irenicus turned aside and smiled when he spotted Warlord Ruthak approach. He stood alongside the amazon chariot master, Iluchus. She stood a full head and shoulder taller than the mighty Ruthak, whose ruddy beard flagged in the wind.

The humans who lived on the plains were keenly aware of the invading morehl who'd been a blight on their lands. They'd proven all too eager to ally with the dwarves of Valis.

With the lava elves drawn out and into the open, they would be easy prey for the incredible speed with which the human warriors could attack. Whether by spear or by blade, the morehl would quickly fall and be sent back to the Grotto where they would lick their wounds.

Irenicus looked up and saw his enemies already turning to flee. There was nowhere for them to flee to, not given the speed and strength of the humans' chariots, and the dwarf estimated that at least half the red elves' numbers would fall. He did not know the total strength of Emperor Kurlahk's military, but suspected this was a significant portion of it.

All around him, Irenicus's troops began to rally. They raised up a cheer and joined in the pursuit of the routed, red elves.

"Ha!" Ruthak clapped Irenicus heartily on the shoulder. "We sent those bastards back to the Void," he chortled through a sour vaghan brew. Still chuckling, frothy splutters of ale lodged in the thick braids where his mustache wove into the red beard sprouting from his chin. "You shouldda seen the looks on those gurks' faces."

Ruthak poured another mug from the cask perched on a stack of supplies on the battlefield. A human supply caravan had pulled into the middle of the military encampment to provision the soldiers in the aftermath of the battle. Smoking bodies littered the plains where the hot morehl blood seeped into the steppes.

"Your plan worked perfectly, sir," Irenicus beamed and sipped his cup more conservatively.

"A-course it did," Ruthak said. "Not that it was an intricate plan by any means. Shedakor is too cocky to command and his pride blinded him. His soldiers paid the price for it."

One of Iluchus's troops pulled near on her chariot. She flashed the dwarf a curt nod of respect. "The morehl are routed and the area is secure," she reported. "Our amazons have set a perimeter of soldiers with their drakufreet companions for defense." She accepted a mug of the ale from Ruthak as he offered it to her mid-sentence and then returned the gesture by handing over her hip flask.

They both took a deep swig of the others' drink. Both mouths twisted into a grimace of displeasure, making the other laugh and trade back. "We will escort your army back to Valis in the morning. Is there another way I can assist you, Warlord Ruthak?"

"Aye!" Ruthak grinned at Irenicus, flashing a smile, and gulped the rest of his mug. He climbed aboard her chariot and began writing up a note. He beckoned for Irenicus, "Go and fetch some wax so I can seal this message for Gundraokh Shatterfist."

"The King?" Irenicus began rummaging through the nearby supplies.

Ruthak grinned. "A battle report and an invitation to visit Valis. He must come and drink with us after so marvelous a victory."

"I thought you said that Shedakor's undoing was his pride?" Irenicus cocked an eyebrow as he turned over a candle.

Ruthak waved away the concern. "Victors are allowed a stipend of pride." He winked and drew upon a portion of the elemental power his connection to Firiel, the god of fire, provided; all of Firiel's children had at least some ability to draw upon the flame. The candle lit and Ruthak turned it to deposit drippings on the parchment. He sealed it with his signet ring and gave it to the charioteer. "Please see that your fastest courier gets this to the king in Gundakhor."

She nodded as the warlord stepped out of the vehicle, and then she rode away.

Irenicus handed his commander a freshly filled mug. "How long has it been since the King visited?"

"Ten years at least," he chugged half his mug and wiped the foam out of his whiskers. "He's long overdue... nasty business, being king. I'd rather make Warchief than take the crown any day; an axe handle is far more comfortable in my fist than a throne under me ass. I dunno how the great Gundraokh Shatterfist handles it."

Irenicus knew of what he meant: the capital and the southern dwarf cities endured frequent goblin attacks. "I've one idea how he copes," Irenicus grinned, and finally slammed the rest of his cup.

"Here's to that!" Ruthak poured them both another and they raised them to each other in salute. "We'll be back in Valis in a few days—and hopefully the King will visit in a tenday thereafter."

Hair prickled on the back of the elf's red-skinned arm. Shedakor descended deeper into the pit. His loss upon the Duar'Bondeen Steppes demanded an immediate answer and he hadn't even planned to return and give a report to Emperor Kurlahk without a plan in place to overthrow his enemies.

Shedakor's gut turned. It wasn't the heat or humidity of the winding tunnel that bothered him; all morehl, lava elves, were quite used to those conditions—he preferred them even. It was the reputation of the creature he approached that unnerved him.

Somewhere deep below him, hammer strikes clanged with steel on anvil. Someone worked a forge in the unknown shadows. *Clang. Clang.*

Nearing the bowels of the abyss he paused and steeled his nerves. He did not want it ever said that something had rattled the renowned elf champion; Shedakor's legacy and honor was worth more than his life to him. It had been the combination of his bravery and skill that had earned him the command of the Obsidian Grotto's forces; that and one well-placed shot between the eyes of the previous commander. Not even their emperor wielded the kind of power that came with the respect Shedakor earned from those under him and he would not sacrifice his reputation over some mere quakes in his belly.

Clang. He took a few more steps ever downward. *Clang.*

He stepped off the last stair, and his feet crunched upon the bleached bones that littered the floor. They cracked with each of his steps as he neared the mouth of the cave and the fiend who lived there. Drapes of fine silk obscured her dwelling. Lights flickered on the other side of the fibrous curtain, casting shadows of the mighty Sshkkryyahr's monstrous silhouette.

Clang.

Shedakor walked confidently into the home of Sshkkryyahr the drider, careful not to move a hand anywhere near the butts of any of the four flintlock pistols holstered on his waist or the two additional ones affixed to his torso. He knew the slightest misunderstanding might end with his demise.

Clang.

The silk curtains parted as he entered and looked upon her. Were she a morehl, Shedakor would have thought her the most beautiful creature he had ever seen. But Sshkkryyahr only resembled a lava elf from the waist upwards; her hips joined to the body of a giant spider. She wore no clothes and Shedakor had to force himself to keep from staring at her as he staved off lusty thoughts.

Clang. A pale, skinny eldarim stood in an alcove at the far of the cave. Wrapped in black sackcloth, he laid a hand upon the gnome that he supervised.

He laid down his hammer and lifted his goggles as the slave master yanked on his cord attached to the torc fixed around his neck. "Come, gremmlobahnd," he ordered, referring to his species rather than a name. The gnome followed his master and they departed.

The drider fixed her black eyes upon the brave morehl and scanned him head to foot. Sshkkryyahr curled a lip and exposed her sharp teeth in a kind of predatory smile.

"Mighty Sshkkryyahr," Shedakor greeted as he bent a knee in respect. He did not lower his gaze. Monsters could prove treacherous creatures, at least until a bargain was struck. "I come seeking your assistance." He scanned the drider appreciatively.

She was nude from the waist up and long locks of hair tumbled down to obscure her breasts. Were it not for the jagged teeth of a carnivore, she could have seduced him on the spot… but even now, Shedakor wasn't certain he could remain impervious to her. The drider was a monster, but she was a chief officer in the cult of death—more than even the head spell casters of the Obsidian Grotto, she worshiped the god of death.

Sshkkryyahr looked at Shedakor lustily. "You come with honeyed words, sharpshooter. I have heard tales of your deeds," she returned the flattery, and then her words turned jaded. "Your most recent battle did not go well, according to rumors that reach me even in the depths of my lair."

Shedakor grimaced, but spoke frankly. "I assume you were told rightly. We had nearly pushed the dwarven warlord Ruthak out of the region and claimed Valis as our own. But he enlisted the aid of the would-be queen of the Amazon folk in the nearby plains."

Several of the skeletons strewn outside her lair were decidedly human in origin. She had certainly become acquainted with their species.

The drider smiled. "I have heard that Iluchus is as formidable as she is beautiful. But then, you know better than I."

Frowning, the morehl continued. "We'd pushed the dwarves into the ravine where the washout meets the plains. They should have been easy prey for our marksmen… but then the chariots fell upon us. They came so fast and their spears darkened the sky like a storm-front. Despite bringing up a second force, Iluchus's cavalry routed our troops who had nowhere to seek cover."

Sshkkryyahr merely stared at her supplicant.

"I have been told that you could offer assistance?"

The drider moved about her lair with uncanny speed as she closed the gap. She lowered her carapace so that she was at eye level with the crimson elf and the monster caressed his cheek with the smooth backside of one talon. The razor-keen edge played seductively across his exposed skin, promising greater sensations of either pain or pleasure at whatever the drider's whims would be.

His gaze met hers, and Shedakor felt as if he'd fallen into the warm pool of her deep, coal-black eyes.

"We can certainly come to some sort of arrangement," she cooed. "But it will cost you something in return. No magic comes without cost… and neither does the help of an elder creature such as I."

Shedakor sighed. He'd expected there would be some kind of toll and he'd already tried to calculate what he might be willing to give—what the emperor of Obsidian Grotto would give, that is. "What do you require?"

"You control the forces of your master, Emperor Kurlahk?"

He nodded measuredly.

"Excellent." Her voice hissed with serpentine danger. "I only require one thing. You must desecrate the altar in the Temple of Firiel. I will not assist the Obsidian Grotto while it remains intact."

Shedakor cocked an eyebrow. He was not particularly religious, but he still respected the power of the priestly caste.

She rose taller on her spiny legs. "You do still worship the fire goddess in your realm, do you not?"

He nodded. "In addition to Lord Death, yes. But the spell casters…"

"Do not worry about your sorcerers and mages. I do not seek their ire, and I do not require you to abandon the magic your kind pulls from the flames."

"Then what?" All morehl kind was birthed of Death and Flame, but only madmen worshiped Death—Firiel was the goddess the morehl faithful turned to when they sought hope. But Death was a capricious master—at least one might supplicate the fire goddess when one was in dire need; Death demanded sole worship of his adherents and was fickle with any response.

Sshkkryyahr grinned. "You must instead *worship* only *Death*. Rip the arcane power from Firiel's heart as you like. Twist and bend the elements to your will, morehl. But do not worship or revere the third-born of Tarvanehl—your devotion belongs to the void-child, *Death*, if you want my assistance."

She leaned forward again and whispered the secret name of the Death-god into Shedakor's ear. Her hot breath felt seductive on his neck. Speaking the name aloud was forbidden by the gods—and to do so risked the wrath of them and rumors persisted that speaking Death's name could summon him to the speaker's doom. Something about her closeness and the brazen use of Death's name stirred an especially erotic impulse in Shedakor.

"It-it will be done," he swallowed hard, pushing down the lust that rose in his loins. He noticed the obsessive scrawls drawn upon every surface of Sshkkryyahr's walls. The black name covered everything; ink sigils drawn in her devotion to the dark god sealed her lair with death magic so thick that it made his skin feel oily.

The drider put a finger to Shedakor's lips to quiet him and then licked her own. "Excellent. I will consult the four totem-beings of my master and seek a boon on your behalf. One of these spirits or more will respond—and your pledge to foul and destroy the temple will be the price of your bargain. I will win this war for you, morehl gunslinger. Warlord Ruthak and his dwarves will fall by your hand."

Shedakor nodded, turned on his heels, and strolled away from her cave; something knit his soul to hers with black chains, and he felt a kind of addict's withdrawal for leaving her side. Over the crunching of bones he could hear her invoking the most powerful of the dark spirit beings.

"Malfeus, Noxigant, Ghastamant, and Surfeibese, your humble servant seeks an audience on behalf of your father, the god who must not be named…" and then she named him.

Shedakor ascended the winding stairs. He had a temple to destroy.

Green was everywhere. Even the air smelled of it.

Drokh stood in the doorway of his small, stone block hut. A simple, woven shift covered his dwarven body, and he breathed in deeply as the morning mist dissipated. His companions had not yet arisen, and he watched the empty circle between their four homes for a few long moments and rubbed his bald head, felt the bristles where his scalp had begun a new crop of golden-red.

Entering the yard, he patted his eidolon on the head. The gargoyle shuddered at the touch and awoke; his skin broke away like a peeling eggshell that had formed overnight as he slept. It looked at Drokh curiously, and remained at its post near the door, guarding over his bonded sage.

Drokh found the bucket where Shella had filled it the night before with her magic. She was a selumari, a coral elf, and as intimately connected to the god Aguarehel as any of the other Master Sages were to their gods. Hidden in the Feylands since the destruction of their home nearly eighty years ago when Daur-Bor-Nin fell, they lived in a community of four. The forests and Nature herself protected them from the cruel world beyond.

He did not know why the gods had spared them when so many of their brothers and sisters died in the battle, but he knew that they'd been preserved for some great purpose. *I'll know it when Eldurim tells me,* the vagha told himself. He smiled at the large octopus that peered out from Shella's door; the tako enjoyed the dampness of the air. Drokh collected a pitcher of water from the community supply and sat down to shave his head.

He set a small mirror upon a table outside of his home and retrieved a sharp piece of obsidian glass from Lyta's hut. Her hut was made from the stuff, and Firiel's sage would be glad for him to keep up his practices. Drokh sat down and cleaned his scalp free of the stubble, leaving his sideburns and beard to accent his tattooed baldness. Like the other sages, he bore the symbols of his god upon his skin. None could see him and know him as anything other than a sage of Eldurim.

As soon as he finished cleaning off, a dreadful hand of shadow coiled around his heart. He staggered as if ill and then looked up. Wehge and Shella had likewise stumbled from their huts, made from rose and white coral. The look in their eyes assured him that they had also felt a similar terror.

The three of them traded glances, and then they all turned to face Lyta's home as one. When she did not emerge, they rushed to her door and found her seated on her rump in the middle of her floor. Her eidolon, an androsphinx, laid curled around her, wrapping her with its wings and the paws of its lion body.

She looked up at them with glistening eyes. She'd always felt things more intensely than the others.

"I've not felt such evil since the burning of Yentosh, when we first went into hiding," Lyta stammered.

The other three nodded assents. They all turned to look far off and away—and in the same direction. The gods did not always communicate with words—they were not limited to such primitive language as that, but they all knew that, whatever this evil was, it lay to the south.

"I feel something stirring in the realms of the gods," Wehge said.

Drokh nodded. "I feel it to. I think our greater purpose has been revealed... and whatever this great evil is, it has emanated from one spot—some nucleus of evil."

The others bobbed their heads in agreement and Lyta climbed to her feet. "Whatever this is, we must face it."

They each turned their faces to the south, and something distinct stirred within Shella. "I know this evil. It has a name. Four names—I read them in the Libraries so long ago, before Yentosh burned. The book is long since gone, but I remember the *Lineages of the Gods*. The aspects of Death have been released: Malfeus, Noxigant, Ghastamant, and Surfeibese—his chief spirits of evil. The four totem beings."

Drokh bit his lower lip and puffed a sigh through his nostrils. "Then gather your cloaks and call your eidolons, my friends. We must deal with this evil before it weaves its way into the fabric of Esfah and her children."

Sshkkryyahr stood tall as she walked through the corridors of her lair. The gnome looked up at her with soot staining his cheeks and brow as he worked the forge, making it difficult to tell where his mutton chops ended and the dirt began. A chain draped down his body and trailed into the shadows where the drider knew her minion waited, holding the other end as he supervised the tinkerer as he worked his craft.

She bent down and picked up a handful of spheres from one of the buckets where her slave had deposited them. They were smooth and perfect, like ripe berries—except they would kill rather than sustain whoever had received them. Each one was etched with a damned sigil that glowed ominous and red with the power of death magic. *Cursed bullets.*

"Gremmlobahnd, is this all there is?"

Hesitantly, the gnome nodded. "The—there is still more star metal in the store, but it must be refined first. These buckets represent a third of our supply." He bowed his head with contrition, as if he were somehow responsible for the diminishing volume of the rare metal in their stores.

He didn't look at her, but she did not look at him anyway. Sshkkryyahr's eyes remained locked upon the mystic ball shot that would supply the victory she'd promised to Shedakor. "What if I told you, gnome, that I know where to get a great amount of the stuff. You will be able to create weapons for me and my army that will win me the world in honor of Lord Death?"

The gremmlobahnd lifted his goggles and rubbed his eyes. He could not disguise his displeasure at the thought. Any freedom but death would continue to elude the gnomish crafter unless he'd run out of the mystic eldrymetallum. Until then, he was too valuable to her.

"Y-your army?" he stammered. "I thought there were only you two?"

Sshkkryyahr snarled and smacked him across the face with the back of her hand. She calmed down a moment later. "Soon. My army is still being formed, but you must be ready to provision them." The drider dropped her fistful of bullets back into the bin. "It will be enough. Come, Nekarthis. Leave him. He has much work to do."

The eldarim dutifully emerged from the shadows. He latched the manacle end of the chain to a ring on the nearby anvil. The gremmlobahnd would not be allowed to leave without his supervision. He followed the drider as she descended a stairwell deeper in her warren.

At the bottom, a hall stretched out, lit by torches that revealed myriad cages of wrought iron. Six of them were filled with a trog each. Their putrid stench hung noxious in the air. Both the eldarim and the drider ignored it. Two other cages remained empty, though a clay ocarina laid upon the floor, discarded where it had laid now for decades. Nekarthis's eyes lingered on it only for a few moments and then he pulled them away.

Four of the six goblin prisoners stood still. Silent and alert. The other two raged and lashed at the bars, knowing their jailers were present. They squealed and screamed curses at them. Sshkkryyahr merely grinned and stroked the face of her favorite minion with the back of one talon. "You were once like this. Do you remember?"

She took the key rings from a hook on the wall and twirled one on her finger. "When I found you, you were merely a child, but the magic runs deep in your veins, Nekarthis, and I have shown you the true path. One akin to your father's."

"I am not my father," the eldarim stated blithely.

"You are not. Hielosch is the great Death Bard of Dereh'Liandor—even the gods are moved when he plays and ushers his audience into the abyss." She unlocked the four cells containing the calmed trogs. "These ones now serve Lord Death faithfully. Just like you, Nekarthis. Any can be taught to serve and obey the Dark One... to revere him. Just like you."

She inserted a key into the doors of both the goblins, who raged and screeched. None of them had eaten for weeks and they were ravenous.

"Come now, Nekarthis. It has been too long; play us a song."

The eldarim retrieved the ocarina where it had laid these past many years. As he began to blow and play a mournful tune, Sshkkryyahr turned the keys. Before the frenzied trogs could escape, the four others dashed from their cells and stormed into the two where the others stood. Sshkkryyahr's new minions tore their old kin apart with untold ferocity. Sickly yellow blood splattered the chambers and the trogs feasted upon flesh and entrail, devouring the softest parts first. The dying screeches accented the tune played by the eldarium.

Sshkkryyahr explained over the din. "They have each one been imbued with one of the totem spirits of Death. Malfeus, Noxigant, Ghastamant, and Surfeibese." They turned to look at her one at a time as she named the spirit possessing each trog.

Nekarthis finally came to the end of his tune and his arm hung limp at his side. He felt something, or an invisible someone, bump into him as he blocked most of the hall in the prison quarters. His ocarina slipped from his hand and cracked open, splitting in two.

He turned his head sharply. He whispered, "Father?" Nekarthis wondered if Hielosch had come to ferry the souls of the two murdered trogs to the deadlands. Did their disembodied spirits now hear the sounds of his father's rabab as he dragged a bow across the strings, just as the younger gods had cursed him?

Nekarthis shook off the thought. "What of these totem beasts?"

Sshkkryyahr smiled so wide that a razor sharp tooth caught one of her lips and drew blood. "They shall return home. Each one will stir up religious zeal. Fervor to incited chaos in the name of our dark lord. They are our oracles, and they will bring glory to their master. These are the Faces of Death."

"They will give you the army for your gnomish weapons," the eldarim observed.

Sshkkryyahr shook her head as she escorted him back towards the upper level. "I'm afraid you have much to learn." She scooped up the broken halves of the music maker as she passed. The four totem creatures followed them.

"I have been weaving plans for decades. I would not pair such crude instruments as trogs with the devices the gremmlobahnd can create. My plan is far more intricate and you will see when the tapestry comes together and my web is fully complete."

Nekarthis bowed his head and made room for the trogs. They stepped past him, panting and sweating. Their stomachs, starved for weeks, now distended with cannibal gluttony.

"Go now," Sshkkryyahr commanded. "I will have use of you in the future and you will answer to my call." She made a mystic sign in the air, and the four trogs dashed out from the drider's lair, fleeing into the distance, and returning to the swamps and marshes that had spawned them.

Shedakor walked towards the heart of the Obsidian Grotto. A throng of people followed him; both civilians and members of the military flocked into his wake. He'd become a hero of the people, even despite his recent defeat on the Daur'Bondeen Steppes.

Word had reached Shedakor that the Emperor had left for the pleasure houses in a neighboring community which owed their fealty to the Grotto. He recognized it as an opportunity to shift the tides of history.

With Emperor Kurlahk currently indisposed, Shedakor knew the time was right to uphold his part of the bargain with the drider. Resistance would be lessened in the absence of authority.

A small contingent of morehl praetorian guards stood in a line in the intersection within the subterranean streets of the Grotto, barring their path. The crowd whelmed behind Shedakor but he halted in front of the royal branch of the military.

"Halt!" yelled some upstart whose name Shedakor did not know. "General Shedakor? What is the meaning of this? Is it an insurrection?"

The marksman scowled at the elf. "With the King out of the city? That would be the worst coup in the history of all revolts! Do you think me so foolish?"

An unruly murmur roiled in the crowd behind him.

"You can go no further until you explain yourself," he insisted.

Shedakor sighed. "I am here to tear down and desecrate the temple of Firiel."

The sentry's eyebrows rose. He hadn't expected such blunt truthfulness. "I, uh, can't let you do that. The gods will punish us?"

Shedakor cut him off. "Do you worship the gods, boy?"

The elf nodded hesitantly, unsure where this was headed and keenly aware of the angry crowd gathered behind the popular general.

"Is Death the most powerful or the least?"

"That's uh…"

"If the Death god guaranteed the morehl a victory over the vagha, should we forsake his sister Firiel, should we not do it?"

"That's a question for the priests and the King," the whelp argued.

"I've already had the Priests of Firiel killed," Shedakor stated nonchalantly. In the distance, a temple worker fled down the street, escaping one of Shedakor's assassins. "Well. Except for that one."

He snapped a pistol to bear and fired, killing the priest of Firiel who collapsed almost three hundred cubits away.

"I'm telling Charbann," the low-ranking praetorian insisted. "Do not think this will go unnoticed."

"Your friends may tell him," Shedakor said; he knew the captain of the praetorian guard by name and reputation, though not in person. "But it will not matter. You will already be dead and I will already have handed the king a victory over the vagha."

The guard stared at Shedakor with a flinty glare, and then the shooter snap-fired with another of his pistols. The praetorian sentry's head blasted wide open in a flash of light and blue smoke.

A roar of approval went up from the morehl behind him, and they surged forward, sprinting towards the temple in order to tear down any vestige of Firiel's honor within the city.

Wisely, the other members of the Praetorian guard stepped aside and let it happen. Shedakor tipped his head to them and watched the temple collapse a block away as his countrymen smashed the building to rubble and painted the ruins with the broken circle, a symbol of Death.

Shedakor smiled and then turned to depart. He wanted to get back to Sshkkryyahr right away and tell her that he had succeeded. The time had come for her to deliver the vaghan city of Valis into his hands.

Sshkkryyahr crept upon the gremmlobahnd in his cell. He shifted and awoke at her presence. He cowered in his hovel. The poor creature had seen her feast before and feared she'd come to him with carnivorous intent.

Instead she held out two halves of a broken ocarina. "Slave. I need you to remake this instrument. Craft it special for Nekarthis and do not make him aware."

The gnome accepted the pieces with trembling hands. "I… I will do as commanded." The tone of his voice indicated his confusion at the eldarim's boon from such a harsh mistress.

"You will find that there are benefits to being my loyal servant," Sshkkryyahr said. "Your best work will be rewarded. And I have not overlooked the faithfulness of my servant Nekarthis."

The gnome bowed his head. "I… I want to do my best," he promised. "But I fear that the supply of eldrymetallum will run low. It will soon be gone."

"There will be more. Very soon," the drider insisted. She turned and exited the slave's chambers and ascended to the central undercroft of her lair. Shedakor was there waiting for her.

Sshkkryyahr raised her eyebrow at his presence. Nekarthis stood there, staring at the morehl in silence and guarding the crates of engraved bullets that sat waiting for the lava elves.

"My part in our bargain is completed," Shedakor said. "The temple of Firiel is no more. The Obsidian Grotto worships only Death, now."

Sshkkryyahr cocked her head and cooed. "Excellent. Then you may take your prize." She scooped up a handful of the round projectiles and deposited them in a leather bag and tightened its drawstring. "I will assume you'll want to test these." She put them in his hands and covered hers around them and the precious bundle.

"I have a battle plan already arranged. My troops will come by shortly to retrieve the rest. The way is long and we will travel under darkness. Within a tenday, Valis will fall," Shedakor hissed.

Sshkkryyahr grinned deviously. "That, my dear morehl, is something I would very much like to see."

Shedakor touched a finger to her chin. This time it was his turn to play the flirt. "Then see it you shall. I go now with my scouts to ride on ahead of the military, but I've always wanted to see the prowess of a drider in combat."

She crooked the edge of her mouth. "You shall see that, and so much more."

Two dwarves guffawed with hearty belly laughs up ahead.

Shedakor peered through the scrubby undergrowth and waited, grinning. Sending his spies ahead shortly after the defeat upon the plains had paid off. He knew all the pieces in play and their positions. Just on the other side of the grove walked a cluster of drunk vagha: Ruthak led the way, prattling raucously about how they'd so recently dismantled the morehl forces.

"It'll be months before the redskins will be able to mount an effective attack again," one declared.

"Th'only shame," Ruthak howled with a drunken lilt, "is that King Shatterfist could not make it to our celebration." His tone took a pouty note. "Next year, he promised."

Shedakor's eyes narrowed to slits. *Gundraokh Shatterfist? If he had been here, that would have made this a glorious battle indeed. I could have cut of the head of all of Gundakhor!*

"Well then! We'll just hafta kill a few thousand more o' the morehl before now and then—maybe Shedakor's head on a platter will get the king out of his castle."

More laughs. The warlord's entourage chortled as they threw back flagons and bottles.

"Closer... closer..." Shedakor whispered to himself. The five expendable morehl scouts hung on his heels and stood still as statues on either side. They awaited his signal in the shadows.

The vagha took another thirty steps and stopped right in front of the crouching lava elf warriors where they hid amongst the shrubbery. Ruthak whirled drunkenly. "Oy! Hold up," he demanded and then leaned against the limestone berm that hedged in the far side of the path, propping himself up with one arm.

Shedakor stayed his companions with a hand as his enemy unclasped his belt and began pissing on the escarpment wall, swinging his waist in loops as he wrote words on the stone.

"Hey," he called. "How do you spell Shedakor?" Ruthak laughed as he maneuvered his hips to write the name.

"Now!" Shedakor howled. The morehl pistol-men leapt into action.

Dwarves spun on their heels. Shocked, they fumbled for their weapons.

Lava elf flintlock hammers snapped and then boomed with ominous reports. With nowhere to flee for cover, lead and steel shot tore Ruthak's guards apart.

The ever-sober General Irenicus leapt in front of his warlord to protect Ruthak with his magic shield.

Shedakor grinned as he stared at the warlord and his general.

Irenicus blasted a rally note from his signal horn, and lights went up in the nearby guard towers. Lamps intensified, and they used directed mirrors to shine wide beams as brilliant as Soll's rays. Irenicus held his tower shield at the ready and crouched ever so slightly, ready to react to any gunfire from the morehl general.

"Move aside," Shedakor demanded. "This war ends now. I am taking Valis and killing Ruthak."

"Aye," Irenicus spat. "You're half-right, anyways. Any second now. It'll be over... *when we take yer cocky little head from your shoulders.* More guards will arrive in a moment."

"Do you mean *yours or mine?*" Shedakor narrowed his eyes, trying to goad a reaction out of the dwarf.

The general returned the glower. "You don't have enough troops to attack us in our home. Not after the recent losses you took on the steppes... not with our defenses."

"Give me Ruthak. His life is mine," Shedakor hissed.

"Not as long as I have my shield," Irenicus fired back.

Shedakor tossed a round piece of shot to the dirt in front of Irenicus as his loyal morehl reloaded their pistols and took defensive positions twenty paces down the path on either side.

Heavy footsteps tromped against the cobblestone in the nearby shadows. The cursed bullet that had landed in the dirt glowed with a villainous glimmer, illuminating Irenicus's feet with a light somehow both red and black at the same time. Shedakor gloated, "Maybe you're right and Valis will resist me. But I have these. A boon from Lord Death."

Irenicus clutched his shield at the ready and howled as Shedakor yanked pistol after pistol from their holsters and fired them in rapid succession, putting six neat holes through the general's mystical artifact. The dwarf's body leaked blood and Irenicus collapsed from his wounds, dropping the ineffective shield; its arcane, yellow glow had dissipated and smoke poured through holes in the busted item.

Ruthak growled in pain as he slunk to the ground behind his fallen comrade, clutching at superficial wounds. He spewed curse words as he slid to his rump atop the piss-soaked soil. The battle-hardened warrior drooled blood and spittle from his lips; it clotted in his beard as he roared a challenge. Even wounded he could prove a formidable foe—perhaps now even more so. In close combat, even a wounded Ruthak could likely win the day. The warlord might die in the end, but he'd drag the morehl into the abyss alongside of him.

Shedakor had no intention of letting that happen. He smiled and walked backwards into the grove, dissipating into the shadows. There wouldn't be time to reload his weapons before Ruthak's reinforcements arrived to cut down the morehl strike team.

The crafty lava elf could have risked his life to end the war in their favor, but now that he knew how deadly these cursed bullets were, he had no reason to take foolish chances. The vagha would fall, and soon.

With one final grin, he flashed the white teeth of his smile and bowed mockingly to the stout warlord. Shedakor disappeared fully into the night. This new alliance with Sshkkryyahr had proved most advantageous indeed.

Depleted though his forces were, he knew that *now* was time to press the attack.

THE RISE OF THE OBSIDIAN GROTTO
PT. 2
WRATH OF THE DRIDER

Deep within the dwarven stronghold of Valis, Tonga stirred the fire with his stick. The red glow intensified and cast the stone walls and ceiling in shades of crimson. He and his friends sat together inside the military barracks and waited for their official night watch shift to begin. Cinder and ash leapt above them like fireflies and illuminated the bearded faces of his two companions, Fhurg and Mowgathon, although technically, Mowgathon was his *brother's* friend. Churloch, his brother, had died in a recent vagha-morehl war. Tonga frowned slightly through his red beard as he poked the embers.

"I heard that General Irenicus was murdered a day ago by those durngam lava elves," Fhurg spat.

Mowgathon crooked his jaw and added, "Rumor is that Shedakor himself finally got the drop on him."

"So close to our homes?" Tonga asked.

Mowgathon nodded. All creatures of Esfah could draw upon magic to varying degrees—like sips from a stream—but some, such as Mowgathon, were particularly gifted at it and could dive and swim in it. The thaumaturge's furred headdress, a symbol of his appointment as a spellcaster, bobbed slightly as he agreed. "They've penetrated so deeply into our homeland in just a few days... they must have consorted with some new source of dark magic. Something far different from the blessings of Firiel."

Tonga frowned and glanced down at his war-axe. He hadn't seen actual combat yet; he was still young and had been content to remain home to tend the family forge as their most promising metal crafter. All vagha families were required to contribute one son to the military, and that had been his brother Churloch. Tonga's family paid the ultimate price—but once Tonga learned Churloch was sent to the Eternal Lands in a hail of morehl bullets, nothing could stop him from taking his place on the battle lines.

"First Churloch and now Irenicus," Tonga fumed. He and Fhurg had been part of the last team of recruits trained under the famed general and had grown close enough to think of Irenicus as a mentor. Tonga and Fhurg had met during their training, just as Churloch and Mowgathon had.

"They will be avenged. By Firiel, I swear it," Tonga grumbled. They all had plenty of reason to hate the lava elves; not a soul in Valis had escaped loss on their behalf.

Fhurg nodded and looked up at the moonport. Even so far down in the earth, the subterranean device used a mirrored tube to measure time by the moon's passage. "I have a dark feeling about tonight. We might spill morehl blood before Rhaudian sets on her second cycle."

"Mowgathon, you can read the destinies? Will we avenge our loved ones tonight?" Tonga asked.

The spellcrafter bit his lower lip. "Prognostication is far from an exact art. Too many variables… best I could hope for is a premonition. And ye might as well ask your mother fer the intuition in her bones. It's about as accurate."

Tonga blew a hot blast through his nose, unhappy with the report. "I'm tired of waiting in the dark. Our watch doesn't start for two more hours." He stirred the flames again. Neither he nor his companions could sleep and they were scheduled for the latest shift of the night.

"We could go watch Rhaudian," Fhurg had offered earlier. It would get them out of the bowels of the dwarven caves, at least. "It's supposed to be a blood moon tonight."

"A grim omen," Mowgathon said.

Tonga stood. "Well, let's go then."

His companions rose and followed him through the winding tunnels. The lower levels of Valis felt bored and organic, as if some unknown creature had melted or chewed its way through the bowels of the bedrock. Something else had been here before the vagha put down roots nearly a century ago.

Tonga brushed a hand against the walls as they smoothed out into the polished edges and artistic cuts more consistent with dwarven craftsmanship. They passed through an expansive undercroft and into the main halls of Valis, the region's biggest vaghan city this far east of Gundakhor. A temple erected in honor of the fire goddess rang the hourly bell.

The three passed and noted the hour. They still had plenty of time to watch the ominous moon before they had to report to their post for tower duty upon the palisade walls above ground.

Shedakor walked confidently into the spacious tent in the heart of a secret morehl encampment. His forearms were splattered with blood and likewise his feet were darkened from the shins downward by the dying sprays of his enemies.

Sshkkryyahr perked up at the metallic scents of prey. The edges of her nostrils flared with the tantalizing odors.

The lava elf general strode boldly into her presence. "It was as you said, Sshkkryyahr. We annihilated our enemies in their defensive outposts. A few drakufreet under the care of our spellcrafters remain within to keep the signal fires active. The vagha will not know that we have breached their defensive line until it is too late."

"Excellent," Sshkkryyahr hissed as she drew closer to the assassin. Mere days ago his army had verged on fracturing. Now, they were poised to deliver a killing stroke and end this war—all because of *her,* and the cursed bullets she had provided them with. There was no shield made by any race, not even by the gremmlobahnd, that could stop those bullets. "There is one more thing," she teased.

Shedakor raised an eyebrow and his posture poised for defense. His eagerness to deploy the army was clearly written across his face. A distrusting glimmer lit within his eyes: he suspected that the monster's deal had been too good to be true.

She crept closer to the elf and felt the heat radiating off of his fiery, red skin. "Such wariness," she smirked as she lowered herself on long, spindly legs so that she was at Shedakor's height. "I would think you did not trust me."

He put his hands on his hips and stared at her, still waiting for her to speak plainly.

"I am an ambitious creature," she admitted. "There are things that I desire—grand and lofty things." She tapped his chin with a taloned finger and stroked the elf's skin from dimple to navel. "In order to fulfill my needs, I will require a strong consort. One who will not hesitate to help me take what I want." She purred, "Such a position will have its own benefits and privileges, of course."

Shedakor's black eyes widened with sudden understanding as the drider walked sidelong around him as if he were little more than prey. The implications of such a union with the half-elf, half-spider flooded his mind, but it was clustered too fuzzy with lust for flesh and battle both to make sense of his feelings.

Sshkkryyahr blocked the way between him and the door. "I have *very specific needs*," she teased. "We are stronger *together*."

With a tug of a rope she closed the drapes to her tent's entry and sealed them within, giving them privacy.

"The war can wait a little while... partner." She eyed him lasciviously and then wrapped her appendages and lips around him and made him hers.

The dwarven sages, Drokh and Lyta, walked in the lead as they traveled through the thick forest of the Feylands. Shella and Wehge, both selumari, walked behind their vagha friends. The two coral elves had their own side conversations, as did the dwarves.

Bringing up the rear came their four eidolons. The strange menagerie moved with an oddly cumbersome gait, but there was no doubt that the four of them combined could lay waste to an entire army if it attacked the sages they protected.

Drokh's gargoyle walked with a shifting amble. Lyta's androsphinx trotted alongside, and Wehge's sprite swarm flitted around them both like a brilliant wind. The most awkward of them was the tako. Shella's monstrous companion was a span and a half taller than the selumari and resembled a giant octopus wearing a chitinous suit of armor it had grown from its body. Made of shell and coral, the removable husk protected its softer parts. Eight thick ropes of corded muscle protruded down from its base and it walked upon those powerful tentacles with such smoothness that the tako's body seemed to glide along as if it hovered.

The forest had passed like a green blur these past several days. The sages and their companions had only stopped to eat and to rest, drawn ever onward by the distant evil they had felt birthed when they'd been in their sanctum.

Lyta paused mid stride and stopped. Drokh turned to face her and the coral elves nearly bumped into the dwarven sage of Firiel, not realizing she had halted.

"What is it?" Shella asked.

"Don't you feel it?"

Drokh scowled as he returned to the Lyta's side. "Aye. I feel it. The evil is no longer south. It is spreading... branching out. The evil ones are on the move... all four of them separating."

Lyta tightened her jaw. They couldn't be certain that the combined faces of evil would be any less difficult if they faced them one at a time or all at once—and now they had no choice but to chase the enemy far afield and across the expanse of the planet. If their task had not grown easier with this new development, it would certainly take much longer to accomplish. What might have taken them a couple months, finding and binding these rogue aspects of the Death god, might take a decade.

She sighed and then continued walking. The only thing they knew for certain was that they'd have to keep moving in order to face this threat.

"We can do nothing by remaining in the Feylands," Lyta sighed. She put one foot in front of the other and the others followed.

Tonga and his friends sprinted as fast as they could through the maze of barricades. They smashed the oil bulbs along the palisades which dripped on the candle mounts and lit the signal flares. A morehl attack had come late in the evening, about two bells into their shift, and it was their duty to rouse the troops.

"How did they get through our watch-posts undetected?" Mowgathon cried as they hurried. "The signal fires are still lit." He pointed to the horizon. The flames would have been snuffed if the spotters saw invaders—and they would have gone out if the watchmen died.

The vagha had long ago erected a network of towers so they could either signal danger—or more importantly, warn of trouble. Should any of their signal lights go out, they'd know disaster befell an outpost. Tonga, Fhurg, and Mowgathon worked one such tower—one on the edge of the city—as watchers. They'd abandoned their position now and hurried towards the sounds of flintlocks once they heard them on the far-side of the palisade walls that hemmed in Valis; the bulk of the city lay beneath the hill.

Gunpowder reports and bursts of light signaled where they were needed most.

"The army can't be that large for them to have snuck past the watchers!" Fhurg quickened his pace, eager to help repel the invaders and spill lava elf blood.

They'd no sooner cleared the last storehouse on the besieged side of the stockades when they collided with the retreating dwarven forces who had manned that section of wall.

"We're over run," one of them cried, trying to turn back the eager reinforcements.

The commander grabbed Fhurg by his arm and pointed across the way to the coops where they kept their messenger birds. "You've got to send a message to Iluchus. Call for help!" Fhurg wasn't the fastest dwarf, he was merely the closest when the order had been given. "Send the message. We'll need the humans' help if we're to survive this one."

Sprinting forward towards the posts of the main gates in the hillside, the commander shouted his orders. "Fall back— retreat and defend the main hall!" He locked eyes momentarily with the three dwarves and nodded. Then he raced further into the heart of Valis by the main gates.

Mowgathon turned to look at the breach in the palisade, still unsure that it could be so bad. *"We were winning this war just yesterday, weren't we?"* he muttered.

Red-skinned morehl advanced through the busted barrier, stepping over the bodies of fallen vagha and pouring into the main cloister. They advanced and pumped cursed bullets into dwarves whose armor and shields did nothing to stop them. As the lava elves unloaded one set of missiles, the next wave of fusiliers stepped around them to do likewise while the previous troops reloaded. They advanced with relentless progress, like the grinding of gears in the mine works.

Mowgathon realized his friends had already run after the messenger birds. He turned and sprinted towards them as they hastily scrawled pleas for assistance onto scraps of parchment.

The cages broke open as they grabbed for a bird each; the doves fluttered in a frenzied, living cloud as thick as a smoke plume—and just as visible to the invaders. The two each had a fowl in hand and feverishly tied their message scrolls to them when a morehl contingent found them.

"Run!" Mowgathon howled. Everything seemed to move in slow motion as the spellcrafter watched his enemies level their flintlocks at his friends. Reacting purely on instinct he drew power from the source deep within him—he harnessed his arcane connection to the gods and the heart of Esfah. His connection to Eldurim, the earth god, was especially strong, but he could only summon enough power to aide one of them.

Blue smoke and concussive shock waves erupted from the enemy. Their cursed bullets tore Fhurg to pieces. He collapsed into a gurgling red mess.

Tonga screamed as his bird exploded into gore within his hands even as his skin hardened to stone from Mowgathon's spell. Bullets glanced off his reinforced exterior, leaving only tiny nicks and scratches as Tonga scrambled away from the flood of invaders.

"Come on! Fhurg is gone," Tonga screamed at Mowgathon as he shook the shocked dwarf back to attention. They sprinted for the main halls. Tonga glanced back to watch his dead friend's body relax; his hand opened and released the carrier. His lone dove sprang into the air and fluttered into the distance.

The morehl invaders did not notice it. They were too keen to pursue the routed vagha.

"Mowgathon! Mowgathon?" Tonga stopped fully and turned to locate his friend whose footsteps faltered.

The caster locked eyes with Tonga. "Run," he insisted with a fading voice. Blood leaked from a hole in Mowgathon's chest where a bullet had pierced and exited his body. Tonga had never even heard the shot. Mowgathon pitched headlong and collapsed into the dirt.

Tonga's stony skin reverted back to normal when the spellcrafter fell. He blinked back tears and dashed for safety as fast he could, ducking beneath the wicked, elvish gunfire.

But the message has gone out… surely the amazons will come to our aide.

Dwarves huddled within the cavern of the greater cloister at Valis. The massive hall stretched for acres and acres. Myriad doors, all locked and reinforced with sturdy beams, barred any access to the secure zone where the most vulnerable of the vagha had gathered for safety.

Horrible scraping noises reverberated through the air and caught the women and children's breaths in their throats. The cracking and clawing sounds sounded eerily similar to marrow being scraped from bone.

Ringing the edges of the community, the pulverized warrior class stood guard in case the morehl broke through. They could do nothing until either a new plan was formulated or help came to rescue them.

Members of the faithful offered prayers to the vagha's patron gods. They prayed for intercession, miraculous victory, or for Iluchus to receive a summons for help. Without Tonga's party reporting in, none were sure any message had even been sent.

"Don't worry," an older vagha comforted a child and squeezed his shoulders. "No enemy has ever passed those gates. What's your name?"

The child looked up at her. His eyes traced the age lines in her face. "Freir." He said. "You are old."

She smiled. Freir's matter-of-factness was a welcome alternative to the booming, grinding sounds of the predators trying to penetrate their defenses. "I should be," she chuckled. "I was one of the first dwarves."

Freir's eyes widened.

"I still remember coming here when this place was new... it was not so long ago, I think. Who knows how long a ripe old age truly is for we vagha?"

A loud crack echoed through the cavern.

"What was it like... in the beginning?"

She smiled at Freir and put a hand on the child's shoulders. "I still remember the gods. Eldurim and Firiel walked the face of Esfah in those days. They made us and they cared for us, you know. Shortly after they came, those two formed dwarf-kind. I only remember awakening as if I had already and always existed—as if waking from a dream..."

The doors suddenly collapsed inward and invaders poured into the gap, interrupting the old woman. Crying out as they fell, the front line of lava elves collapsed under a flurry of readied crossbow quarrels.

With a burst of acrid, blue smoke the enemy returned fire as they closed the gap. Towering above the other intruders, a drider stormed through the gate. Her jagged legs stamped down upon any dwarf who challenged her; they sliced and pierced the brave warriors as if each leg were tipped with swords.

Freir gasped at the noise of the combat. The cave seemed to amplify every scream within its confines, keeping it close enough that the audience, especially the helpless ones, heard and felt every terrifying nuance.

Across the way, the young dwarf caught sight of their leader, the mighty warlord Ruthak. He fought even wounded as the others rallied around him.

Ruthak's face fell when he locked eyes on the monster that cut a line for him. Vagha bodies hung upon her spiny legs as if they'd been stuck upon meat hooks and she wielded a long pike from the morehl half of her body, lancing any dwarves that scurried below her where her legs could not reach them.

The warlord gulped and ordered a full retreat as mob after mob of his men fell to elven zealots. A horn blew, and the chaotic herd of dwarves surged towards the Great Hall: the next, deeper inner chamber of Valis. The citizens had protocols already establish in case of an emergency.

Freir looked around frantically for the old woman. As the boy followed the crowd, his panicked eyes located her. She laid dead near the enemy lines—they'd already breached so deeply that she'd fallen to a morehl rapier.

He bit his lip and followed the crowd. Freir hoped the woman was right about Eldurim and Firel caring for them… the citizens of Valis could use some divine protection about now.

Tonga scrambled through the winding halls and crashed through a door and into a narrow chamber that smelled like fire, lard, and ground wheat. Under any other circumstances he would have happily strayed in this bakery. He ducked his head and kept a low profile while scrambling from furnace to furnace on his way to the next section of kitchens beyond. Tonga had hoped to catch up with the army and report that the message had been sent to Iluchus, but he'd needed to find an alternate route since they'd barricaded the main passages before he could get to them.

He'd never been in this part of Valis before. Before joining the army he'd been a metalcrafter and never had any reason to see the kitchens. A sense of wonder fell over him as he pushed open a set of doors and saw the expansive galley. Rows of tables stretched to the far side; utensils and cooking tools hung or laid neatly at workstations.

"This must be where they prepare the great feasts." His inner artisan appreciated the orderly nature of it all. "If we get out of this alive, I'm going to learn to bake a loaf of bread," he mused to himself.

A nearby door swung open, and Tonga instinctively slid to his rump. He slowed his lungs and his breath burned in his chest as two morehl scouts entered the huge room. They worked through the nearby kitchenettes with a blade in one hand and a flintlock clutched in the other.

They drew near where Tonga crouched and the dwarf tightened his grip on his axe as he tensed his muscles. There were only two of them—but the dwarf would still have been anxious with only one. He hoped the element of surprise would give him enough of an edge to put them both down.

As the lava elves searched the adjacent row, they stood just opposite of the cook station Tonga hid behind. The dwarf crept around to the other side of the station as they stepped into the aisle where they could've spotted him. Their steely gazes surveyed the area and then they turned to continue past.

Tonga breathed a sigh of relief and then his toe kicked a stray ladle that had been abandoned on the floor. *Not so neat and orderly after all!* He cursed beneath his breath, and the enemies whirled towards his position.

Snatching a knife from the cutting block as he stood, Tonga pushed aside a hanging rack and instinctively threw it at the further enemy. It lodged in the elf's neck and the wound spat hot, red blood while leaking mist like steam.

The second morehl discharged his gun at point blank range. A pan hanging from the utensil rack swung perfectly to catch the bullet as it returned to its original spot like a pendulum. Luckily it hadn't been one of those magic bullets which proved capable of cutting through vaghan shield and armor alike.

Maybe they have limited supplies? Maybe these elves are so low on the totem pole that they weren't given them?

Both the shooter and Tonga stared in momentary disbelief. Tonga reacted first; he heaved his ax and sunk it deep into the scout's chest.

He scrambled for the exit before anyone could respond to the noise from the skirmish. The doors flung open as he burst out and into the promenade that encircled the Great Hall.

Tonga skidded to a stop as soon as he passed the doors. A thousand lava elves that had camped around the blocked gates to the Great Hall turned to stare at him. He stood there for a split second and stared at the army in surprise.

"Nope!" he flung himself back the way he'd come before any of their marksmen could gun him down.

Crashing back through the kitchen, Tonga searched for another way to find the vagha army when he spotted a scullion door: a smaller passageway that led to the Great Hall for food service workers. He raced towards it and found it locked, but he could hear noises on the other side.

Tonga banged on the door and screamed, "Let me in—hurry, before the lava elves get me!"

Voices argued on the other side, insisting the door remain closed.

He pounded and howled again. "By Firiel, I swear if you don't open the door they will find and kill me!"

"It could be the morehl trap," a vaghan voice urged on the other side said. "They worship Firiel too."

"I would swear on my mother's floral bonnet if it helped—but if I swear by Eldurim, you'd just say all morehl are liars…"

More arguing. Tonga was certain this door would remain locked and that he'd be dead any moment.

Another scullion door peeked open a little further down the way and a child's eyes looked out from it. Tonga rushed forward and slid through even as new lava elf scouts entered the galley in search of him.

Slamming the door shut, Tonga glowered at the dwarves a little further down who had left him to die. He slid a brace against the door to keep it blocked and then squeezed the child.

"Thank you. I'd be dead right now if not for you. My name is Tonga. I have to find Warlord Ruthak."

"I know where he is," the boy piped up. "And my name is Freir."

Sshkkryyahr angled her head aside as Shedakor and the rest of the morehl army turned to face the bearded intruder. A lone dwarf stumbled into the area where they'd mustered their army, blocking them within the Great Hall. She began heading in the opposite direction as a cluster of lava elves gave chase to the startled vagha.

"Where are you going?" Shedakor demanded.

The drider rose up slightly taller on her legs and turned her head to stare down at him. Her spiny appendages still bore the remnant gore of their defeated enemies.

Shedakor grimaced, keenly aware that he'd overstepped the chain of command with his tone. He may have controlled the forces of the Obsidian Grotto, the Emperor's army, but Shedakor did not control *her*. Swallowing hard, he stepped back and tightened his lips. He repeated his question in a gentler tone, still wondering where she meant to go. "We have them cowed behind these massive doors. As soon as we break them down, we will take Valis. The war will be over."

Even now the troops scrambled to construct a pair of battering rams.

"I have my own mission, *and he has his.*" Sshkkryyahr stared into the distance. Only now did Shedakor spot the drider's pale-skinned eldarim servant. Shedakor hadn't even realized Sshkkryyahr had brought him. The silent eldrim bowed his head and slinked away into the dark. "Firiel's temple is that way." She began walking; hate burned in her eyes.

"Mission?" He followed her a pace behind.

"Given to me by the god with the ineffable name… *Death*. I go to desecrate the dwarven fire temple. I must blot out the names of Death's bastard siblings and prove myself worthy of invoking his name." Sshkkryyahr nodded to the gates which sheltered their prey. "If the war is truly won after you breach these doors, why waste effort chasing one wayward soldier down? Send a handful of scouts, but break this door down and be done with it. I will return once Firiel's temple lies in ruins."

"Then take this." Shedakor angled towards a cart in the rear of their forces and placed two large crocks of gunpowder in her arms. Putting a long fuse into her hands he said, "Light it and leave. It will speed up the process."

She grinned deviously and propped the bombs beneath her ample breasts. Sshkkryyahr was familiar with the destructive power of the elves' black powder; she skittered away with a grin.

Shedakor watched her go. It would not take her long, and they'd surely feel the explosion once she accomplished her mission. The lava elf had no idea what the eldarim was up to, but he did not feel threatened by him… not after Sshkkryyahr's assurances in her tent. Taking Valis was everything to Shedakor—and he would accomplish that task in short order.

Tonga hustled through the crowd with Freir panting and trailing after him. They found Ruthak near the front of the army; the trepidation on the warlord's face worried Tonga more

RISE & FALL OF THE OBSIDIAN GROTTO

than the blood seeping from the wounds that their leader had already taken a day prior.

After looking around futilely for the commander who had given Fhurg his orders, Tonga reported to the first dwarf of rank he could locate and explained his need to speak with Warlord Ruthak.

Freir stared up in awe at the leader once he and Tonga finally received an audience with the military head.

"The message was sent. Iluchus has been hailed," Tonga explained. "At least one dove made it out to our human allies."

Ruthak nodded but seemed disinterested. A fidgety adviser who stood nearby held a scroll drawn upon with ink markings. It looked like some kind of infrastructure map.

"A cry for help... sent to the human cavalry." Tonga pressed the good news, hoping for a different response; he desperately needed Ruthak to confirm his reasons to hope. "Any hour now we can expect Iluchus and her chariots to render aid."

The warlord twisted his mouth. "It has been a long night. Valis will not survive to the morning." Ruthak, surrounded by his decimated army, looked over the sea of people huddled in the great hall. "We must abandon our land if we hope to survive. We can exit through the drains and flee west to the sa'Eldurim Massif by skirting the stone ring around the Feylands. Our brothers in Gundakhor will surely take us in."

Tonga furrowed his brows. "I helped craft the barrier grates after the trogs invaded through those tunnels six years ago. It would take two days to evacuate everyone through that route."

"Good. You can help us dismantle the grates then, and make good our escape."

Tonga set his jaw and glared at the warlord talking about retreat plans. "My friends died so we could send a bird to Iluchus and request aid—she may yet arrive before the citizens of Valis can escape." He stared at Ruthak, bewildered that their leader hadn't understood basic tactics.

Ruthak stood tall. His glare withered the younger dwarf and Tonga finally understood. *The army* was leaving; *Valis* was staying… the army was abandoning its citizens.

"If we wait any longer, we'll all be dead," Ruthak stared at Tonga coldly. "Better that those of us who can fight our way out do that. We must leave the rest to the inevitable. Better that some of us survive than all of us die trapped like rats. The vagha army can live for vengeance later."

"But… but Iluchus…"

Ruthak snapped at him. "Have you ever seen a chariot underground, Footman Tonga?"

Tonga worked his jaw, flabbergasted. He had never actually seen a human chariot. "No."

"Iluchus could be outside right now—and when she sees that we are overrun on the surface, she will have no choice but retreat. The stockades are in ruins. Where will she leave her horses while she sends her Amazons to die below-ground on our behalf in a war that she cannot win?"

The sharp words finally shut Tonga up. *Even if support came, they could not help us. That left only divine intervention.*

Ruthak's adviser muttered in a voice barely more than a whisper, "We won't even have time to retrieve anything from the vaults. Besides, it's too dangerous to the army should the beast have an episode, if we brought it with us."

The warlord's attention returned to the logistics of a retreat.

Tonga took a step backwards, realizing the scroll the adviser carried was a map of the dwarven plumbing tunnels. He still believed they had to fight to the last dwarf. "No. You can't do this. Valis—these people—need protecting."

"Aye," the warlord sighed. "And that's what the gods are for. If we belong to 'em, let them fight for us."

The cavern suddenly rumbled with a low growl and jarred with tectonic shifts that rained dust and debris from overhead. Both dwarves held their breath amid the unmistakable sounds of a cave-in somewhere outside the gates and near Firiel's temple.

Tonga finally dared breathe again. He looked across the troop of soldiers and realized those troops with families that lived in Valis had quietly gathered them to their sides.

"Footman, either fall in with the army and prepare to march or stay behind and die with the rest," Ruthak ordered. "You may bring your child," he said, trying not to sound heartless as he nodded to Freir.

Taking another step back, Tonga bumped into the boy. The soldier set his face and glared daggers at Ruthak. He'd clearly resolved to stay.

Ruthak tilted his brow towards Tonga. "So be it. Axes up, everyone!" The warlord gave the order to move out. Within minutes, the army departed leaving behind only Tonga and Freir to defend the citizens.

Tonga turned and met the very worried eyes of the common folk of Valis. All that remained were the untrained, unskilled, and very young.

Boom.

Like ominous thunder the battering ram boomed through the massive chamber. With the vagha huddled in clusters inside the Great Hall, all eyes turned to Tonga.

He worked his jaw utterly clueless for a few moments. The dwarf looked over his kinsmen and his heart sank. He knew deep down that they could not beat this army. They barely had a weapon between every five of them. With each new beat of the ram against the main barriers he could hear stones crack and splinter beneath the blunt force—even if the doors held, their moorings wouldn't. Lava elves would be upon them any moment.

Boom.

Tonga shouted over the pallid, nervous crowd. "Children of Eldurim and Firiel. I am afraid that death is coming for us through those gates. We are abandoned by our protectors *but not by our gods*. Each of us has been imbued with power and talents from our makers—it may be only a small glimmer, but it is enough. Eldurim has given us magic over the earth and Firiel over fire. Even without weapons, *we are powerful*. Are you not the children of the gods?"

Heads nodded and beards wagged. Several howled their assents; none wanted to die without putting up a fight.

Boom.

"Draw on that inner connection, like the spellcrafters do. We may not be theurgists, but we are *many*. Together we wield the power of the gods. Dig into your hearts and pull out that divine spark—lend your magics to mine!"

More cheers. Tonga watched his countrymen. Some concentrated; some bowed in silence; others moved with swaying motions as they sought to locate that arcane spark.

Boom. Crack.

"Together, Valis… together we are mighty. Valis is not a *place*… it is a *people—an enduring spirit*. The enemy can take our lands. They can take our lives. But *Valis* can never fall. Now let us do what those cowards in the army would not do and *fight*. Fight until we see each other again in the Eternal Lands! Lend me your magic, Valis!"

Tonga felt a surge of power—an overwhelming sensation that Mowgathon had once described to him. This seemed so much stronger than what the dead spellcaster had told him of—he felt as if he were about to burst from the inside; power like hot light coursed through his veins.

Boom. Craaackk. The gates busted wide, and morehl flooded into the Great Hall. What few crossbows remained in Valis fired into the whelming horde as it charged forward.

Tonga screamed as the power pulsed through him like a conduit. He channeled it to the edges of his people, sheathing them in stony skin just as the enemies' flintlocks opened fire.

Cursed bullets ricocheted off the men and women of Valis.

Dipping into the red fury of Firiel's blessing, Tonga spewed a cloud of fire across the elven shooters. Fire elves were normally resistant to flame, but not to such a kiss from the fire god as Tonga commanded; they crumbled to cinder and ash, bewildered looks on their faces scorched away to bone and blackened by holy wrath.

The vagha cheered and leapt into the fray. Stony fists grabbed for their attackers and Tonga twisted his hands, controlling the stone above and below; he used the earth itself to smash the morehl into smoldering red paste.

Cackling as she leapt from stone pillar to pillar, an enormous beast crawled along the ceiling and drew the dwarves' gaze upwards. The drider rushed into the fray from a vantage and dumped a swath of webbing upon the front lines of Valis.

Startled by the creature, Tonga's concentration faltered, as did that of his countrymen. He felt his purchase on the spark fail, and his control over the magics dissipated.

Morehl firearms raised as Valis' protection crumbled like dust.

"No!" Tonga screamed. "Run!" He grabbed Freir's hand and fled even as the hall filled with shrill reports and gun smoke. Cursed bullets tore the citizens of Valis to pieces.

Tonga felt one rip through his shoulder and two others grazed him, only opening superficial wounds. He ran until he reached the edge of the Great Hall. Freir collapsed behind him forcing Tonga to pause and haul the child back to his feet.

Freir bled from his cheek but was otherwise unharmed. Perhaps two dozen others had followed and managed to reach the perimeter.

Behind them, the dark cluster of morehl and vagha were barely visible through the blue-gray haze. Ball shot whizzed past Tonga's head as a sniper tried to target them at a distance. "Into the tunnels!" Tonga ordered. The remnant of Valis followed him even as the Obsidian Grotto army, led by Shedakor and Sshkkryyahr the drider, began their pursuit like hunters chasing game for sport.

Tonga sprinted through the passageways until the smooth, hewn surfaces turned to the organic, rough surfaces of the lower levels. He rounded a bend and found the tunnel had been collapsed by Ruthak's forces as they passed. They could not even join with the vaghan army if they wanted to.

"Back! Go back the other way," Tonga pushed the group. They took a different path, but the sounds of the lava elf pursuit swelled ominously behind them.

Tonga hurried down a path and tried to think of a plan, but he could not. He didn't know of any other exits that would let them slip past the invading army that Ruthak would not have collapsed to secure his escape. In truth, Tonga was merely stalling, and the others had begun to suspect as much as they rounded the endless bends under the hill.

"Where are we going?" Freir asked between ragged gasps of air.

Taking another turn that led further into the bowels of the earth Tonga hissed, "The vault. There are weapons there. We can't win this fight—but maybe we can kill as many of these durngam lava elves as possible before they send us to meet the gods."

Tonga paused in front of the tall doors to the vault. The term "vault" was more of a reference to the depths and its usage than anything else. The doors did not even lock; they weren't made of metal but of timbers and they swung easily on greased hinges.

Weapons and other tools hung on the walls. Banks of locked, stone hatches lined the two walls. Compartments had been mined and then these hatches erected to keep the treasury secure.

Just down the hall from the vault were the mining tunnels where laborers unearthed precious metals and gems stored behind the hatches. They'd already seen the piles of useless refuse that had been pulled out of the depths, a kind of worthless purple-tinted stone that pocked the seams of gold that criss-crossed the depths below Valis.

Tonga scoffed when he saw the locked banks. "What good is gold at a time like this?" He moved towards one large door that was twice the height as any vagha and the same dimensions wide. It sounded like chains rattled behind it, and he stuck his head down into a food trough to try to peek at what hid behind the door.

A bulbous eye met his face, and the pupil dilated. The creature roared. When the echo subsided, the tromping of morehl footsteps down the corridor alerted them that only minutes remained before their doom arrived.

"We've got company," a dwarf yelled.

Tonga looked back and found that his group of survivors had all equipped themselves with weapons and stood with their backs against the wall to hide from sight. They would spring upon the lava elves when the opportune moment arrived.

With his impromptu guardian distracted, Freir stepped away from Tonga and slid into the food trough. He laid down, able to crawl into the pen.

Tonga whirled back. "Freir—get out of there! We don't know what that thing is…"

"It's an umber hulk!" the boy yelled, crawling though and into the next room with the locked door. "I've seen one drawn in a picture book."

"We need all the help we can get. Can you let it out?"

"I can open the door from inside, but it's chained up with a lock."

Tonga looked back to the weapons rack near the vault's entry. A key ring hung on a hook. Before he could signal a closer dwarf to grab them, the enemy arrived with gun and rapier in hand.

The first wave of morehl entered, and the vagha fell upon them with axes. The element of surprise earned them several morehl heads, but they were in the open now and exposed. Morehl soldiers fought back, pitching the chamber into chaos.

Tonga sprinted forward and snatched the keys even as a pair of lava elves clawed for him. He risked a glance beyond his assailants and spotted the drider coming closer, walking at a leisurely pace. Beside her strode a regal looking elf in a gunslinger's vest: Shedakor.

Breaking away from the thugs who tried to grab him, Tonga spun and chucked the keys across the room. They landed in the trough and slid into the basin where Freir could reach them.

Lava elf attackers finally got a hold of Tonga and dragged him to the ground. One pinned him to the floor while the other casually held the point of his blade to the dwarf's throat. The capricious morehl used his weapon to play with his prey's beard, trying to whittle it down, delivering an insult before striking a killing blow.

The rear door suddenly burst open, and a bug-like creature bellowed a challenge. It rushed forward with massive arms that were covered by chitinous plates.

Before any morehl could respond, the umber hulk charged upon the red-skinned intruders. It whirled and smashed them wherever it could, splattering them like grubs underfoot.

Tonga scrambled to his feet and ducked beneath the monstrosity. He found his way to Freir's side and huddled next to the boy.

For a moment, they dared hope that they could fight their way out.

Shedakor lunged over the troop in front of him and stabbed a beleaguered dwarf with his rapier. He left the blade where it stuck and pulled his flintlock. Whirling, he yanked another pistol from his hip and snap-fired on another dwarf. Ahead of him, the umber hulk locked eyes on Sshkkryyahr who fought at his side. It shrieked and charged for her, not noticing anything else in the vault but its equal enemy.

He fired the other weapon and blasted the umber hulk. It scrunched its face and snorted the pain away. The beast was an elder monster, and even the cursed bullet had caromed off its chitinous plates.

Another elder monster, the drider hissed and took up the beast's challenge. She dashed towards him, and they collided into a heap of rage, all legs and claws. Their whirlwind of commotion dragged anybody near them into the fray. Those who veered too close, either morehl or vagha, screamed as the embattled monsters rolled over them with fatal results.

Shedakor ducked behind one of his own minions just as a dwarf drew a bead on him with his crossbow. The unsuspecting shield-mate collapsed with a feathered bolt jammed through his eye socket. As soon as he hit the floor, Shedakor had his weapon drawn, and he blasted the dwarf before he could reload the crossbow.

The morehl assassin snatched his fallen minion's gun and drew pistol after pistol, discharging them into the room. His bullets took out five more of the remaining vagha, leaving only two. A younger dwarf of fighting age and a child. Shedakor squinted and looked him over; he could swear this was the same dwarf who had stumbled into their battle lines as they tried to tear open the gates to the Great Hall. He dismissed the thought. It would all be moot in a few seconds and Valis would be cleared.

He yanked another pistol and took aim at the last remaining warrior. Perhaps he'd watch Sshkkryyahr devour the child. Shedakor sighted down the barrel and pulled the trigger on his flintlock.

Click. His pistols had each been emptied in the fight and needed reloading. He narrowed his black eyes to coal-like slits and began refilling them with his powder horn. That task would take mere seconds in his experienced hands.

Tonga and Freir backed up slowly as Shedakor's weapon failed to fire. They had nowhere to retreat to—their fate was in the hands of the gods now… and the umber hulk.

Sshkkryyahr and her mortal enemy crashed and collided, knocking each other from one side of the vault to the other. The impact of their collisions busted open the doors of the safes. Gold and other valuables poured out from them, spilling across the floor and scattering wide in the tumult.

The umber hulk punched the drider so hard, that it knocked the enemy clear across the room. After skidding to the opposite side of the chamber, Sshkkryyahr took a step and collapsed. She tried to rise again upon her wobbly legs, but she could not.

Emboldened by his blood-lust, the insectoid beast charged at her, roaring and ready to deliver a killing blow when Sshkkryyahr suddenly sprang to her feet and scaled the walls vertically. The umber hulk careened into the stone surface, smacking into it at full force; the ferocity of the impact cracked the beast's natural armor with a sickening, wet sound.

Sshkkryyahr gooped the monster into place against the wall from overhead, entangling the umber hulk in sticky webs, and dropped down behind it. The tricky creature snatched one of the busted doors that hung free against a demolished safe. Gemstones rained free and scattered across the floor as she used the object as a melee weapon. Sshkkryyahr smashed her prey's head with it over and over, until it busted open like the rind of a ripe hullifruit.

The umber hulk went limp. Its body remained upright, firmly webbed to the wall.

Sshkkryyahr laughed gleefully and began digging into the busted enemy's skull, heaving sloppy glops of gore and gray matter into her mouth. It trickled down her chest in grisly clumps as she cackled and feasted.

With the danger to the lava elf army eliminated, the remaining few morehl walked across the room victoriously. They surrounded the last two remaining dwarves with flintlocks drawn. Shedakor grinned mischievously, clutching a reloaded pistol in each fist.

Freir stood rigid, trying to sound defiant and brave. "We already sent a message to Iluchus. The amazons will never let you keep Valis."

Shedakor's mouth twisted into something like a smile. "Then the humans will share your fate."

Tonga covered Freir's eyes with his dirty, calloused hands and then closed his own eyes tight while holding his head high. The humans had not arrived in time, or else they hadn't entered the battle as Ruthak predicted, but at least Tonga knew that he hadn't run from the fight. His efforts had proved too little, too late.

The army may have displayed cowardice, but the warlord had been right. Valis would fall after all.

Flintlock hammers cracked the air, and the room filled with the blue smoke of morehl victory.

The sages had paused at a stream deep within the woods to refresh. Lyta waded a few steps through the rushes and then staggered.

Drokh caught her. "Are you okay? What's the matter?"

Shella and Wehge looked at them from across the stream. Concern was written upon their faces.

"I feel… it's a premonition. A shadow of things that have passed or of things to come. I cannot tell which, yet, but evil grows stronger."

The other sages set their friend amongst them.

"Rest, now," Wehge said. "We shall need all our strength for what is to come."

The morehl cheered on the slopes of Valis. They drank dwarven ale, even though they hated the taste, and dragged bodies of slain vagha to the surface where birds and carrion beasts could clean the bones of flesh. The skeletons would be used to decorate morehl structures as trophies claimed in battle. Temples dedicated to Lord Death frequently inverted their dead enemies and buried only the heads to dishonor them; the tradition had recently crossed over to the homes of the morehl faithful as well.

Strolling through the revelry, Sshkkryyahr spotted her secretive minion. "You have it, Nekarthis?"

The pale eldarim bowed with a nod. "It is secure; the slaves have opened the mines below the vault." He kept his voice low. "Neither the vagha nor the morehl have any idea of the true importance of Valis."

"Show me," the drider demanded.

Nekarthis reached into the folds of his black sackcloth and produced a nugget that looked to have been forge-blasted. Tendrils of mangled material glowed with a purple sheen, and the whole of it glinted with a metallic luster.

Sshkkryyahr licked it seductively, verifying it by taste. She grinned and purred, "Eldrymetallum... star metal. Deposited in the dirt from above while the gods still bickered over their birth order, and the eldarim were still crawling out from the protoplasmic soup of Ghaeial's afterbirth."

Nekarthis bowed his head. "Your servants will begin its extraction immediately to replenish the stores used to forge your army's cursed bullets."

Sshkkryyahr did not bother to look at him. "You have done good, servant of the dark. Is there much of it?"

"The foolish dwarves did not know what it was. Piles of it lay discarded where they delved for other precious metals. Wisdom suggests there are vast veins of it beneath the city, but only the gremmlobahnd understand how to work it. We will need more of them to work the forges."

"You know some hunters up to the task?"

Nekarthis said, "I have a few charges who can acquire the talents we require."

Sshkkryyahr bobbed her head. "Make it happen, and see to it that our forge is moved to the Grotto."

The Eldarim nodded.

Wandering slightly away, the drider cackled at the moon. "With these weapons they will craft us, not even the gods will be capable of stopping me." She turned back to glare at her minion. "Make sure the cargo is retrieved quickly and secretly. So long as Valis's true worth remains undiscovered, it will be easier to defend. We must not let Gundakhor think claiming this mountain was anything more than a land squabble—and they must believe the land worthless."

Nekarthis bowed, and then disappeared as if he had never been present to begin with.

THE RISE OF THE OBSIDIAN GROTTO
PT. 3
ILUCHUS'S LAMENTATION

On the north-most stretch of the Crooked Spine range, and deep within the heart of the Obsidian Grotto, Emperor Kurlahk sat upon the gleaming black throne of his realm. Charbann, the king's broad-shouldered bodyguard, stood behind the throne.

His red skin contrasted with the massive ebon chair made decades ago by artisans and drakufreet slaves. Crafting the jagged, black glass cathedra had claimed the lives of many dragonkin whose fires had been burnt out in the process, but they were far easier to control than full-sized dragons. Besides, lava elves believed that any life not born of morehl blood was of inherently lesser value. Foreign lives were readily spent like coins in their realm.

Kurlahk leaned forward eagerly when the doors of his throne room opened; news of the victory had reached him in advance of his general's arrival. The Emperor's champions were en route for an audience. Warlord Ruthak and his dwarven forces reached the refuge of Gundakhor, the next closest community of their vagha peers. The dwarf had insulted him years ago, but Kurlahk had taken his home. He honestly believed that he'd take the dwarf's head eventually.

Shedakor and Sshkkryyahr, his drider consort, strolled into the emperor's sanctum. The drider towered above the gunslinger; her feminine lava elf half perched naked atop the giant spider portion below. She may have looked morehl, but she was an elder monster and had little need for clothes. By contrast, Shedakor wore his finest vest, a crushed velvet piece, and leather harnesses to hold his six well-used flintlock pistols. The Emperor wore a robe of similar fabric.

Kurlahk practically buzzed as they approached. "Welcome, welcome conquerors," he greeted. "You have won Valis for me. The land is finally unified under my control..."

"For now," Sshkkryyahr interjected, her eyes lingering upon the fine cloth adorning Emperor Kurlahk's figure.

The emperor narrowed his gaze at her and then at Shedakor. He was not used to disagreement. "What does that mean?"

Shedakor sighed as if he and the drider had discussed this regularly during their return voyage—and they apparently didn't see eye to eye. "Nothing, Emperor," he said. "We can handle whatever..."

"The dwarves had an alliance with the humans of the plains—they have interfered in your battles before. The amazon Queen Iluchus commands a strong cavalry, and the vagha sent a message to them for help before we sieged and took the city," Sshkkryyahr said. "Gundakhor *will come* and take Valis back from you."

Shedakor noted, "We've hidden a contingent of soldiers within the city. Any human counterattack will meet with several nasty surprises."

"With the vagha of Valis destroyed, their alliance with Iluchus is ended," Kurlahk insisted. "Surely they would not risk their lives for paltry vengeance done on the dwarves' behalf?"

Shedakor nodded as if he agreed with the Emperor, but Sshkkryyahr shook her head. "These are not morehl. They think differently than lava elves."

She paused and clicked her teeth; her eyes swept over the muscular captain of the praetorian guard who stood watch over the throne and noted the fancy sword on his hip. Sshkkryyahr found the words to explain her reasoning. "They will not let you keep it because expanding your holdings upsets the balance of power if you command so much territory. They know that Valis could become a stronghold within one generation and you will be able to properly defend it, populate it, and enforce a stranglehold on the region. Iluchus is no fool—she will attack before you have a chance to reinforce it. She will come while you are still recovering from this war you have just won."

"The humans will not fight underground," Shedakor argued.

"I agree," Sshkkryyahr said, "but they could easily blockade the hill and cut your forces off until they are starved."

Emperor Kurlahk sat back and drummed his fingers on the smooth armrest. Finally he nodded. "You may be right... but we cannot strike at the humans directly, and we cannot *yet* properly defend what we have taken without weakening the home defenses at the Obsidian Grotto."

"Correct," Sshkkryyahr hissed. "But I may have a solution."

He bid her continue.

"Make Valis a vassal state. Give it to a trustworthy ally."

Shedakor scoffed. The emperor likewise curled a lip.

"We are morehl. We trust nobody."

"That is not exactly what I meant," Sshkkryyahr clarified. "I have already approached an acquaintance who can manage Valis and fill it with a corps of the thing you lack most: magicians skilled in bending the elements to match your vision."

Kurlahk leaned forward, interested in her proposal.

Sshkkryyahr explained, "Valis would pay an annual tribute as a vassal state. This sorcerer will bring his warlocks and cultists to take over the city and support you and your armies with arcane support when necessary to continue your campaigns. With their help, you could defeat Iluchus and eventually overthrow even Gundakhor."

The emperor nodded; his eyes lit at the notion of expanding west into the great dwarven strongholds. "If it can be done, then make it so. I would prefer to sit atop the ruins of Gundakhor when next I watch the Daybringer return."

"Twenty-two years is an easily doable timeline," the drider agreed, thinking about the next time the comet would pass. "The Grotto might very well control all of Esfah by then."

"This plan goes well beyond wiping out Ruthak and the dwarven city," Shedakor reminded his lord, hinting that he may be biting off more than he could swallow.

"Correct," Emperor Kurlahk said. "But fortune favors the bold—and if we do *nothing*, we may soon find Iluchus on our doorstep."

"I need *him*, too." Sshkkryyahr grinned and pointed to the muscular morehl standing near the throne as the emperor's personal guard.

"Charbann?" he clarified. "Whatever for?"

"Yes, him," she said, eying him appreciatively. "He will do nicely. Our forces are somewhat depleted, and we will require some additional, capable hands to turn back the amazon queen when she arrives."

Shedakor saw the way Sshkkryyahr looked at Charbann and glowered at this new rival for the drider's interest. He noted the warrior's gilded blade; it identified him as the heir to a prominent family in the region, but he said nothing.

"You may have him," Kurlahk nodded, indifferent on the matter. "Turn back the humans and finish this battle."

"One more thing?" The drider took several steps closer to the emperor whose long, wine-colored robes trailed after him. Charbann, along with several of the Imperial Guard, stiffened at her approach. Emperor Kurlahk calmed them with a hand motion.

"May I?" Sshkkryyahr asked, beckoning with a hand. "I do appreciate such a fine weave."

Kurlahk beamed. "The textiles of the Obsidian Grotto are second to none. By all means. Our weavers are unparalleled."

She grinned as she let the fabric flow through her fingers. "I would love to create something so fine… but I have need of your artisans as well. I have something else in mind. Send ten of them to the frontier. I may have use of them."

The emperor flashed her a look of carefully masked confusion and then returned to his chair. "Of course. I will send them at once."

Sshkkryyahr bowed low and beckoned for Charbann to follow. She and Shedakor made their exit with the bodyguard in tow.

Sshkkryyahr walked through the halls in the facility she'd taken over in the Obsidian Grotto. The walls were sleek and flat, not polished as if they'd been crafted by eldarim perfectionists, but smooth. *They must possess dwarven slaves within the Grotto.*

She found her captive gremmlobahnd at his post working metals from a small mound of eldrymetallum that they'd collected from the mines of Valis; it was only a part of the first haul. Two other gnomes worked in similar fashion, bound to anvils near the smithy. One refined the metal, and the other cast bullets for the morehl's cause.

The gnome looked up as the drider towered over him. "Tell me, gremmlobahnd, do you have a name?"

A tense moment passed. "Y-yes," he said. His face brightened, optimistic that the one thing he had left to him might finally have some value. "My name is…"

"You should forget it," Sshkkryyahr snapped. "You and your kin will never leave these forges without hearing the song of the Deathbard carrying you to my master."

Nekarthis stepped out from the shadows as the gnome wilted. "We are on schedule," the eldarim said, dipping a hand into a crate filled with cursed bullets. He pointed to the crestfallen gnome who worked the eldritch metal into different forms of blades and shields much like the fallen vagha general Irenicus had owned. "Our supply chain from Valis is strong."

Sshkkryyahr smiled. "And your hunters?"

"They have captured half a dozen others like this one." He motioned to the gnome crafter.

A dwarven slave entered the chamber, pushing a cart laden with raw eldrymetallum lumps. He kept his head down, fearful of alerting his captors to his presence. One of the other gremmlobahnd helped him unload the mystic ore.

"You have done well, Nekarthis," the drider said. "I seek to reward you." Sshkkryyahr held out a hand to demand something from the gnome.

The nameless one produced a cloth bundle from near his anvil and unwrapped it to reveal Nekarthis's ocarina. The broken instrument had been sand-packed to create a form and then false-cast in pure star metal which burned away the original and created a duplicate. The slight ridge where the fracture had been was visible, and the only difference.

Nekarthis picked up the instrument. A sense of unexpected wonder passed across his face. "My father gave this to me before he…" He pressed it to his lips and sounded a note, increasing in volume and intensity as he worked his way through a tune.

Across the room, the vaghan slave groaned, shuddered, and then fell stone dead.

The eldarim hung it over his neck and thanked his matron.

"Only one of your blood, the eldari line of the Deathbard, may play this," the gremmlobahnd instructed. "It is a relic of great potential… but its power will defend its own."

Nekarthis seemed to heed the gnome's advice, but he yanked his chain and pointed back to the anvil. "Get back to work."

The gremmlobahnd bent over his station and resumed his duties.

"We will have a dozen gnomish tinkerers soon," Nekarthis said. "And the Faces of Death will be prepared by the time we make our true move against Esfah."

"Lord Death's banner will fly in every community from Gundakhor to Maris-ta-Sehlim… and beyond," Sshkkryyahr hissed as she turned to leave her minion to complete his tasks.

"He will be honored," Nekarthis repeated.

Iluchus leapt to her feet, enraged when she heard the news. Toned muscles bulged beneath her armor as she flexed and clenched her jaw.

"What do you mean 'Valis is gone?'"

The scout doubled over with exhaustion. With his hands on his knees, he chugged from the water skin Iluchus offered him. She'd thought it best to send a footman as a scout; horses were more easily spotted on the plains.

Finally, the runner wiped his mouth. "Well, not *gone*. I mean, it is still there, but the vagha were wiped out. The palisade walls and the main gate appear broken; only a small contingent of morehl occupy it."

The amazon queen roared and grabbed her javelin. "Then we must take it back before it is reinforced."

Men and women in her court, warriors all, howled their approval.

One man called out, "They call the Emperor's general Shedakor the *morehl who never misses*."

Laughing him down, a few others heckled him about his apparent fear.

"It's not for fear that I say this," he defended. "I am thrilled that it shall be our javelins that kill him in battle."

A cheer went up.

An old man rose from his seat near the ceremonial chair that marked Iluchus's seat of power. He cleared his throat and silenced the room with a mere gesture. Visech was one of the few remaining First Men, part of the original human race dropped fully formed onto Esfah by the Father-God Tarvanehl seventy-five years prior. His wisdom rarely went unheeded.

All eyes turned to Visech as he spoke; even Iluchus's face softened. "It may *appear* to be sparsely defended, but appearances are not always what they seem," he advised. "The lava elves are cruel and calculating—they may have burned out the dwarves, but they would not leave unguarded such a defensible foothold in their expanding kingdom. I should suspect a trap."

"What do you advise, Visech?" she asked.

"Beware low hanging fruit on montimbanco trees," he quoted the proverb. Nods circulated the royal tent. Aside from a tiny difference in their leaves, montimbanco trees looked almost identical to their hullifruit cousin. Virtually the same in every respect, the imposter's fruit was poisonous enough to kill a man within an hour.

Iluchus tightened her fingers around the haft of her weapon. "Then we will act as we do when we find a montimbanco sapling: we shall chop it down before it is strong." She locked eyes with her adviser and added, "But wisely... patiently, and in due time."

Sshkkryyahr stood a little taller as Charbann entered her tent. Shedakor took a half step closer to his consort and flashed a possessive glare at the former member of Emperor Kurlahk's praetorian guard. After leaving Nekarthis in charge of the gnomish foundry-work, the drider and her morehl companions had returned to their army along with what reinforcements could be spared without weakening the Obsidian Grotto's defense force.

"I have assembled a team for you, Charbann," Sshkkryyahr said.

The newcomer bowed. "What is my mission?"

"I need you to locate an old friend. You and your team of scouts should travel southeast, into the Nhur-Ghale Forest. Torl and his people live between the Narcea River and Bent Morass. You must be quick to find him. Plans are already in motion and the distance is great."

Charbann nodded.

Shedakor relaxed somewhat at the notion of his potential rival leaving for some foreign land.

Sshkkryyahr explained, "Torl is a rakshasa of the Black Forest, a blighted holdout on the edge of the troglands. His home is in the canopy of a massive wood said to have sprouted from the corrupted seeds of *the Great Tree*," her inflection indicated the prophecy given when Death entered the world. "*This* tree bloomed from a corrupted seed. A fallen child—one like *us*, a product of both Nature *and* Death."

Charbann asked, "I thought the Black Forest was a cult?"

"It is," Sshkkryyahr replied. "It is a *people* and not only a place. Now go. Don't return without Torl. Tell him the drider needs him and he will profit mightily from the journey."

Iluchus collapsed her spyglass and tossed it into the pouch hanging at the front of her chariot. She stepped out of the carriage and onto the ground where she grabbed a fist full of soil.

The amazon queen smelled the earthy tones and grinned. It was perfect: not so moist that the wheels would sink and not so dry that her soldiers would send up dust billows. Neither scenario would have created significant problems, but either would necessitate that her plan of attack change.

She glanced up to Visech who rode alongside in her armored chariot. He nodded measuredly at her assessment. "This should be a swift and easy kill, provided they do not see us coming?"

Iluchus bobbed her head. "Just like last time."

Using hand signs, she communicated to her troops and then stepped back onto the deck of her vehicle. With a crack of the reins, her chariot raced ahead towards the morehl patrol in the distance.

Iluchus's warriors fell in behind her, rolling into rank and creating a massive wedge of warriors in attack formation. Armored chariots stacked two deep and shaped like migrating birds created a shield wall that protected the javelin wielding footmen who sprinted behind them.

The lava elves spotted the queen in the distance and formed up against her, setting a rigid defense. With their smaller numbers, the morehl party was not likely to win, but could at least chisel down the attackers and make them pay for venturing into the lava elves' newly acquired lands.

As the humans closed in, and before reaching javelin or musket range, another source of thundering hooves boomed. Iluchus grinned.

Two teams of amazon chargers burst through the flanks of the morehl and criss-crossed through the lava elf forces, tearing them up from the weak side, striking where they had set no shields. Iluchus knew the morehl would be focused on them and had sent her fastest men on horseback to strike where the red elves would be weak.

Cast into panic and disarray, the elves broke formation as some tried to find targets on either flank and some reset their defenses against them—but the chargers did not return.

Iluchus and her soldiers reached a fatal range and released their javelins. Piercing death rained down and wiped out the scattered morehl.

The warrior queen sped ahead and rode through the carnage. Her wheels dragged thin tracks of smoking morehl blood through the heather.

Visech smiled, obviously feeling as spry as any of the young fighters who followed the warrior queen. "That's the third conflict in a row that the enemy has failed to inflict a casualty," he said approvingly.

"I had a good teacher," she winked at him. "You know there is more than one way to destroy a montimbanco tree."

The old man raised a bushy eyebrow.

Iluchus answered the unspoken question. "When you can't strike the root, you do it one branch at a time."

He grinned at his protégé, and the queen exited her chariot with a pair of flags. She stood atop a heap of enemy bodies and waved them, knowing her people watched for the signal. Others would relay the message that directed them to their next destination.

The amazons were at war—and staying mobile kept them one step ahead of the enemy.

"I told you that our patrols are too small," Shedakor snarled. "We've lost two more in as many days."

Sshkkryyahr's face remained unchanged. She let the lava elf vent.

"We need to double their strength, at least… and we need to increase their frequency, too."

"For what purpose? What is your end game?" Sshkkryyahr asked.

Shedakor blinked at her, bordering on disbelief. Exasperation was clear in his voice. "To not needlessly slaughter my kinsmen. To not lose control of our borders at the fringe. We are wasting the lives of soldiers by sending them out in such small numbers..."

"That is not an end game," the drider said coolly.

Her consort growled something unintelligible.

"You are *reacting*," Sshkkryyahr hissed. "Reacting to an opponent's moves is not a winning strategy. It only bides time."

Shedakor crossed his arms. "Morehl soldiers are dying—and we're no closer to locating Iluchus or her community despite the number of lives lost. Every time our scouts believe they find a human caravan settlement they pull up tent pegs and slip away before we can mobilize an attack force!"

"*They are fast*, if nothing else," she stated admirably.

"And that's why we must double the size of our patrols. It will help us mobilize larger numbers of forces faster."

Sshkkryyahr stared down her nose at him. "Do you truly think you can exceed the speed of the amazonian chariots in open flatlands or defeat them in a battle upon the plains? Didn't you attempt that once before?" She raised her eyebrows. The real question—the one behind her words—was clear. *Are you a fool, Shedakor?*

"We've got to do *something*," he insisted.

"And we are. We are moving pawns. There is a master plan." She looked down at the map that tracked the movements of her networked scouts and morehl patrols. Slate stones with chalk symbols drawn across the smooth counters represented their forces.

Shedakor frowned at the layout. He eyed a slate tile marking their most recent casualties and plucked it from the board. The gunslinger spat to wet it and wiped the marker clean before dropping it back onto a pile of blanks; that patrol no longer existed.

As he stared at the map Sshkkryyahr reassured him, "There are parts of this plan which you do not yet understand."

Laid to the side of the map, Shedakor noticed several stones he did not recognize. They had new symbols written on them. And they waited to be placed.

"There are new pieces yet to enter the game?"

Sshkkryyahr inclined her head. "In due time," she hissed softly. "As soon as the timing is right... once Charbann finally returns."

Visech stooped down and poked at the dirt. Tufts of prairie grass burnt around him and his queen. The broken bodies of morehl corpses smoldered where their blood had spilled. A massive hellhound, taken down by amazon warriors, belched smoke into the sky where its wounds had opened.

The old man planted his rump into the dirt next to Iluchus and wiped away the blood from his brow. He leaned against the queen's busted chariot; it hung at an odd angle, tilted upon its busted wheel with spokes broken and bent askew.

Fighting had been fiercer near the old boundary between the vagha of Valis and the Obsidian Grotto.

"You were victorious again, your majesty."

Iluchus scowled and bit her lip. "Yes, but at a greater cost." Her eyes lingered upon a pile of human casualties.

A crew of amazon tinkers hurried to their location. They carried tools and a replacement wheel for the royal vehicle.

"True. This battle was more costly than the others thus far," Visech eyed the defeated monster that laid dead on the battlefield. "It is a testament to how effective your strategies have been up until now."

Iluchus snorted a hot blast through her nostrils. "Up until now," she repeated, looking across the field with dark eyes. She recognized the faces of many of their dead.

Visech slapped her half-heartedly on the shoulder. "This is to be expected. There will be some losses—and still more to come as we cut deeper into the heart of lava elf territory."

She eyed him dispassionately, knowing he was right... wishing he were wrong. Iluchus was grateful for the old man's wisdom; it kept her grounded.

"You are not lopping off mere branches any longer." He pulled his queen's falchion from its sheath and swung it like a hatchet. It sank into the side of Iluchus's chariot, embedded.

She shot him a strange look and grabbed the handle to remove it. The weapon had stuck firm. She wrenched on it for a few moments but it held fast.

"No more branches," Visech repeated. "You are whittling away at the main trunk, now. Sometimes the best way to fell a tree is with help—even changing your tools if necessary. He winked, leading his pupil to think for herself.

She quoted an old proverb. "If the ax doesn't work, find a saw?"

Visech nodded with approval.

"We are not far from the Gwich'in," Iluchus observed.

The old man smiled. "I am sure they could help remove this blight from the land."

Tapping the side of the chariot, the workers signaled that the craft was again drivable.

Iluchus took the closest one and clasped his forearm. "Work with haste," she said. "We must move out as soon as possible. We cannot afford long delays in this part of the Steppes."

He nodded and joined the others. Using hand gestures, he signaled the large cart at the edge of the battlefield. The wagon containing parts moved towards the center to speed repairs on whatever wrecks remained salvageable or for the others to scavenge parts off of those that weren't.

Visech joined Iluchus in the chariot which the queen drove on a circuit.

She informed her generals of their next move. "Meet us at Potshari," she told them one after another. "Visech and I will go on ahead. Bring the rest of the people with you. We should not divide ourselves for long."

A short while later, Iluchus and Visech sped into the outskirts of Potshari, home of the Gwich'in: the people of the land. Tanned faces looked out and watched her arrival from their permanent dwellings made of clay. Unlike Iluchus's warrior tribe, the Gwich'in were not mobile. They'd molded Potshari into a center of worship and knowledge; the Gwich'in focused their efforts on learning the arcane and natural knowledges of Esfah. They fell under Iluchus's rule, but she respected their sequester enough to leave them to their self-selected seclusion. Now, her need had grown too great not to tap them. Besides, the land they were in had fallen under the morehl's claims. The fact that the elves hadn't yet attacked was a wonder.

Iluchus pulled the reins and quieted her horse in the center of Potshari.

Visech stepped out and immediately locked eyes with an old woman who still bore the marks of beauty despite her advanced age.

A spark of understanding lit on the woman's face and she stepped forward to embrace Visech. "It has been many years," she said quietly.

The woman stepped back and observed decorum. "Queen Iluchus," she greeted. "I am Cheyamna, the oracle of the Gwich'in."

"Good," Iluchus said flatly. "You and I have much to discuss." She quickly brought Cheyamna up to speed on the situation between their people and the morehl. "We have need of support."

"I'm not sure how much the Gwich'in can help," Cheyamna began making excuses. "We are a peaceful people.

Most of our magics are meant for healing or growing or making art."

Iluchus stood tall and looked down at the old woman sternly. "We stand together as humans," she said flatly. "If my forces fail, you will fall next. Potsherd is already well within the perimeter of lands the morehl now claim belong to them."

Cheyamna smiled. "They have not found us. They will not... because of our magic. For all their bluster, the Obsidian Grotto lacks folk trained in the arcane arts. They have maybe a small handful of them, perhaps, but mainly suited to illusions and tricks for their royal court."

Visech fixed her eyes on his old friend. "Your disguises will not hold forever. How long will it be before the enemy broadens their tactics beyond artillery? Emperor Kurlahk does not appoint fools—as soon as they tally the damage we've inflicted, the army will change its methods. They may even attack Potshari preemptively, in fact, just to ensure you cannot join our efforts against them."

Cheyamna wordlessly worked her mouth and then she bowed. Visech was rarely wrong; even the Gwich'in knew that. "I will assemble our seers; some of those with shamanic skills who can draw upon the elements will surely volunteer to aide you."

Visech bowed to her. "With your help, perhaps we can end this war before it spirals into something far worse."

The oracle looked to the horizon and spotted a cloud in the distance. Dirt billowed skyward, stirred up by more than a thousand sets of hooves.

Iluchus smiled. The greater amazon army would join them soon. She finally felt they had what it would take to chop down this particular montimbanco.

"Ahh, they have finally arrived," Sshkkryyahr said, reacting to the hubbub outside. She skittered through the tent flaps and left Shedakor to hurry after her.

Torl and his companions entered the camp. They hovered a few hand-spans above the ground, riding upon the flying tiles of carpets the Black Forest sorcerers were known to construct in their obscure community: a cloister of death-worshiping arcanists who lived in and on the wicked tree planted deep within the Nhur-Ghale.

Behind Torl and his mixed company of morehl and trog cultists, an additional carpet carried Charbann and his scouts. Most of them looked relieved to be back among their own kind, and only a few from that party had failed to return. Charbann stepped off of his floating rug, an ornate tapestry depicting a magic seed sprouting into the great Blight Tree that housed the magi of Nhur-Ghale.

Sshkkryyahr tilted her head towards Charbann as he arrived. She did not disguise the glimmer in her eye and let her eyes swing from examining at the impressive weapon hanging at his hip to his physique—especially the region between his hips. "It is good to see you have returned successfully."

He nodded, but added, "I'll be glad to return to the comforts of the Grotto as soon as possible."

Shedakor gritted his teeth at his consort's flirtatious display.

"Then let's win this war," the drider said to the rakshasa. "Torl. My people have brought you up to speed on what we need from you?"

Shedakor cast an askew look in her direction. *"Our people,"* he muttered too quietly to be heard as Sshkkryyahr led the way back to their tent. He, Torl, and Charbann followed her lead.

Torl nodded his felinoid head, showing off his tusk-like incisors. Few morehl from the Obsidian Grotto had ever seen a rakshasa, which looked like a cross between a human and a jungle cat. Something about him reeked of fire and death magic—he exuded of powerful aura.

"You want us to bolster your troops with magic," he stated as they arrived at the map where tokens marked the troops they had arranged upon the plains.

"Yes," Sshkkryyahr said. "In exchange for this, you will be given possession the vagha stronghold of Valis which we recently claimed. I know you've wanted to escape the stink of the troglands for a while now."

The drider's eye twitched as she spoke to draw attention to her hands. During the course of the conversation, she also spoke in the nonverbal, secret code known only to members of the Black Forest. Sshkkryyahr told Torl about the eldrymetallum lode which Nekarthis managed. She needed the rakshasa for what they intended it.

Torl nodded slowly. "It is a different kind of stink—but the dry would improve my pelt. Besides, the Blight Tree will soon be dead." He signaled his acceptance with a twitch of his fingers and then all hands fell still.

Sshkkryyahr shot him a concerned look.

"Every year the peat from Bent Morass grows. It consumes any plant life not accustomed to the bog. Within two decades it will have reached the roots of our home; we must seek another before then. The Black Forest agrees to your terms."

The drider smiled and stabbed a finger into the map. She dropped a few new, white tiles onto the board. "This is Potshari, home of the human shamans. Queen Iluchus is most recently reported to have visited it with her entire caravan. Their children, and those unfit for battle, will remain in the adobe city thinking it safe for them."

Sshkkryyahr snatched a few of the smaller, black pawns off of the table and replaced them with white ones. One had a crown drawn on it with dark chalk. Only one stone separated them from the white crown—its symbol identified it as a small observation post controlled by the morehl.

"We will need to hurry," the drider smirked.

Shedakor checked his flintlocks and fit them snugly in their holsters. "Hurry? For what?"

"We are about to be attacked," Sshkkryyahr said as if it were all part of a plan made far in advance. She looked up at all of her companions and then raised an eyebrow at Torl. "It's good that you brought the carpets. We will need as much speed as we can muster if you hope to earn your prize. Few things are faster than mounted amazons, but few creatures are deadlier than elder monsters."

"There it is," Iluchus said, pressing her spyglass against her face. "Our next target."

The amazon army had stopped in an area that proved craggier than any of the horsemen liked riding in, but the terrain featured washouts rather than stony badlands which could damage hoof and wheel. The humans knew how important terrain was to their army's efficacy.

"There are only a few of them. Why aren't we riding in and smashing them?" Cheyamna asked. She hovered nearby. Her wagon, filled with a cadre of spell casters, followed the queen at a close distance.

Iluchus wanted very badly to do just that. She bit her lip and let Visech explained for her. The two had an obvious history.

"The ground is uncertain. Those washouts and outcroppings pose problems for the chariots. There is probably no danger, but we can't leave anything up to chance."

The queen nodded. "We've been successful against the morehl thus far because we chose every battlefield and we only engaged when we knew all the variables." Iluchus scowled into the distance. She had only counted a dozen lava elves, and that made it a tempting prize. Morehl were not plains-dwellers; lava elves didn't know what signs to look for as they searched for human invaders and the queen felt certain they'd gone unnoticed.

Visech borrowed the spyglass and observed them. "They are building some kind of lookout tower to watch for future invasions... something akin to the old vaghan towers Valis used."

"Then it is good that we came before they finished it," the queen hissed.

"Will you wait until night?" Cheyamna asked.

Iluchus and Visech looked at each other blankly. "You must not know much about the morehl... they can see well in the dark."

Cheyamna nodded sheepishly. "Would you consider a magic solution?"

"By all means," the queen said.

The oracle licked her wrists and held them in the air at her sides, feeling the breath of the elements. She called the other seers to her side and briefly consulted. Together they climbed the nearest stone outcropping and stood atop one of the table-like rises which gave them a height vantage and they remained precariously staged behind a section of boulders that provided less concealment than Iluchus liked.

Visech and the queen looked at each other nervously. "If they're seen, we're..."

A boom cracked the air followed by a ferocious shriek and rushing winds pushed by a blue drake's wings as they used their spellcraft to entice the dragon from wherever its lair was. Draconic magic could entice nearby dragons or even recall them to Esfah from whatever plane they went to after they perished here... but they could not *control* the beasts.

The morehl in the distance panicked and scattered, abandoning the framework of the tower they constructed.

Roaring, the creature sucked in a lungful of air and spat its elemental breath in an arcing line. It blasted the frenzied scouts like a hot stream of piss on a line of ants, only far deadlier. The beast screeched victoriously and flapped its scaly wings, circling around to locate and kill the remaining few stragglers who escaped.

Iluchus grabbed a nearby scout and pointed to the spell casters. "Run up the rise and tell Cheyamna to send the drake onward now so we can advance safely. Have them stay put until we send for them—I want to make sure it's safe and that we won't need to double back before we expose the Gwich'in. Morehl have been known to lay traps before."

The runner nodded and then dashed up the hill to relay her queen's orders. As soon as the notice was given, and the dragon begun shrinking towards the distance, a warhorn's peal split the air from atop the lookout post.

A lone morehl survivor blew the trumpet and continued blasting it from the uppermost level of the partially completed structure. Iluchus grimaced and snapped her reins. *I must have miscounted by one.*

She and her warriors hied their mounts and sped towards the lookout post. They had to shut him up as soon as possible. Conflict was inevitable, but the last thing they wanted was to lose whatever element of surprise their speed afforded them. None suspected that this dispute could end diplomatically.

The signalman gave a double blast as the chariots and footmen surged forward and almost reached the range of their javelins. As the lava elf hornblower dropped behind the cover of the outpost walls, morehl roared battle cries all around the amazons.

Iluchus's troops whirled around, trying to spot them, but their enemies were invisible. The whelming howl echoed through the crags of the canyon and horses screamed.

Pistols cracked and the men's screams filled the ravine and across the uneven terrain. Tainted smoke seeped from the patches of ground where the morehl hid.

The spies flung back fine weaves of cloth made by the Grotto's weavers; they had hung earth colored curtains over the mouths of caves that the crafty enemies had dug. Lava elves poured out of the clefts, kicking scree and soil as they fired flintlocks into the backs and flanks of invading soldiers.

Iluchus howled curses… *the morehl had laid in wait— they had chosen this battlefield on purpose! This was the elves' preference, not the amazons'.* She urged her forces onward so they could reposition at the watchtower they had liberated.

The Gwich'in stood stiff. A sea of enemies separated them from their battalion.

"We've got to do something," Iluchus's scout watched the battle change pitch, she yelled as she turned back to Cheyamna. Her eyes blinked, and she gulped with surprise as a blade slid across her throat. Coal-black eyes watched her curiously as the morehl assassin raked the knife against her skin.

Cheyamna only managed a gurgle in response to the scout. She clutched her neck as the cat-like human appeared behind her and dragged his dagger across the magician's collar.

She and the rest of her seers collapsed under the knives of the enemies. The last thing either saw before everything faded black was the distant, blue dragon as it suddenly turned around. With the amazons' magic dissipated, so did the arcane compulsion for it to move away from this battlefield.

Charbann shuddered as he watched Torl.

The rakshasa grinned at him with his toothy, vicious grin. Torl released the body of the murdered spell-caster and let the oracle's lifeless husk tumbled down the slope of the stone table.

The monster and his motley collection of spell crafters seemed to take special pleasure in the slaughter of the Gwich'in. He nodded skyward and cocked an ear to the distant, draconic croak as the drake announced its return. "Join with us, you and your scouts," Torl insisted.

Charbann cocked an eyebrow. "I'm no crafter," he said flatly.

"I never assumed as much," the rakshasa stated. "But we will need every scrap of power we can muster. You are morehl, after all, right?"

Charbann nodded reluctantly.

"Then you might prove useful." Torl and the others assumed whatever personal postures they preferred that put them in touch with the natural and arcane energies: that spark that connected them to Esfah, and to the Death god.

Charbann closed his eyes and relaxed. He found it difficult to focus; many of Torl's companions gyrated and convulsed as they tried to conjure that primal link. He kept quiet as they chanted and did his best to melt into the background. He didn't believe he could be any use at this, and so he was not— such is the nature of magic.

Torl, filled with eldritch energy, roared as a fissure split the air. The spell momentarily connected the draconic realm to Esfah, and he pulled a black dragon through the breach.

Fiercely territorial, the black and blue creatures locked eyes and rushed towards each other at once. They clashed like titans in the sky above the battlefield.

The morehl sighed with relief. With the dragons preoccupied against each other, they would be safe during the battle… at least, until one of the beasts emerged victorious.

Climbing onto one of his levitating rugs, Torl called back to Charbann. "Protect my students," he charged the warrior. "They will follow the drider's plan, and so must I—she needs me next below the tower."

Charbann nodded and then watched the strange arcanist fly quickly away on his peculiar mount, keeping well beyond range of any dangers of the battlefield.

The amazons' chariots whirled around, making a U shape with their backs to the now-vacant outpost that they'd attacked. Finally, they could attack the enemy forces.

Javelins streaked through the sky, sailing to their targets with deadly accuracy and frightening force of impact. Any morehl close enough to engage lost limbs and heads to flashes of kukri steel.

She and her cavalry ducked behind the carriage housing of their battlewagons which afforded them some protection from the lava elf bullets. The warriors on foot took the worst of the attacks.

Iluchus clenched her jaw and silently berated herself. *Why didn't I send scouts ahead first? I should have expected morehl treachery!*

Across the countryside, the bodies of elves and men laid strewn like chaff: her amazons peppered with wounds and leaking red, the morehl laid silent with javelins reaching skyward like standards.

The queen screamed orders at her troops. In the chaos of battle there was no way they would be heard. Her adviser would cover that.

Standing behind her, Visech waved a pair of hand-held flags to relay her commands so that she could drive. Their only hope was that the Gwich'in's magic could upset the sudden shift in the battle's balance.

Iluchus risked bruising her eye socket and pressed the spyglass to her face, searching for Cheyamna. Her heart sank as she watched the last of the oracle's cadre tumble down the embankment where they'd been left; the falling spellcaster's wrists were only bloody stumps. Two amulet-wearing trogs devoured the murdered seer's hands.

The queen roared, her heart twisting with grief. *If the Obsidian Grotto is in league with goblins we no longer stand a chance!* "New orders, Visech!"

The old man looked up and spotted the worry on her face.

"Defensive maneuvers. We've lost our support—Cheyamna is dead."

"We can't go back the way we came," he said, eyeing the gauntlet of forces that had cut them off. Returning to Potshari to regroup was the only option left to avoid total slaughter.

"It's the long way around, then," she hissed.

She ducked at a sound like an earthquake followed by guttural screeches overhead. Reptilian scales rained around her like hail the size of broomcorn ears. They bounced across the ground in a cerulean and onyx cascade.

High above them, a second dragon had engaged the blue drake Cheyamna and her casters had summoned.

Iluchus spat profanities. "As if things couldn't get worse…" She only hoped that they could somehow use the dragons' presence to their advantage.

Shedakor's eyes widened as the black dragon smashed into the blue with ferocity unlike anything he'd ever seen. Beating wings hit morehl and human alike with bursts of wind and blasts of sand.

Streaks of death belched from their throats as the territorial beasts vied with each other. Both failed to connect.

Stray streams of caustic breath incinerated the poor souls caught in their spray. Victims included both lava elves and amazons.

They collided midair again, like battle-hammers against shields, and then they intertwined and streaked high into the sky. Moving so fast, the dragons seemed to trail color behind them, as if they were comets, wrapping a black and blue braid across the sky.

Shedakor watched the amazon chariots turning away from the partially constructed outpost where he laid in wait with his riflemen, poised for battle. He burst through the main door along with his troops. "Attack!" he howled.

Morehl hammers clacked on flintlocks and a torrent of ball shot hailed upon the unprotected flanks of their enemies. Those in the back of the human army screamed and fell from their vehicles; human footmen who raced behind the cavalry stumbled and readjusted their shields.

"Tear them out, root and stem," Shedakor howled, drawing flintlock after flintlock. He slowed his deadly cadence and peered through the grey-blue haze. Far fewer had fallen than anticipated.

The lava elf general jumped back inside just as the cloud of javelin return fire streaked towards the morehl. Spears pierced his soldiers, and they shrieked and collapsed, leaking hot blood with trails of steam; many laid helpless, alive but pinned to the ground by sharp lancets.

Shedakor hissed and glanced towards Sshkkryyahr who ascended from a pit that had been dug within the outpost floor. She waited safely within the outpost and hovered within the mouth of the cave they'd dug. "Your cursed bullets are not working, Sshkkryyahr!"

She narrowed her eyes. "Of course not... they require the presence of the fire element in both user and their environment—they draw their magic from those sources."

He scowled, and she added, "I will *tell* you when they are ready for use."

With a shout, Shedakor called back what remained of his soldiers. He peered over the deep hole in the earth where the drider had come from. She stepped over the lip and crawled down into the darkness, cackling as she went. "What is down there?" he called into the black, slightly irked that he wasn't fully in the loop. *Emperor Kurlahk put* me *in charge of the army... Charbann had better not know either,* he seethed silently.

A shadow fell overhead and Shedakor yanked his head back just in time to avoid being crushed. The fanged rakshasa descended through the hole where the ceiling still yawned open and remained exposed to the elements. Torl lowered from the sky on his magic carpet and sank beneath the edge. He called after him, slowing his descent as he spoke. "Well climb aboard if you want to see it, General Shedakor."

Shedakor hesitated only momentarily and then leapt over the brink. Landing on the carpet was like falling into a hammock, but he managed to stay upright.

Moments later, they arrived at the bottom.

Torl stepped off as the carpet flattened against the floor of the massive dugout many cubits below the surface. He only walked a few steps; the landing area was not large. The floor was carved of black, igneous scoria, twisted gray basalt, and pink-flecked volcanic glass.

Shedakor followed. He could feel the heat beneath his boots and checked his pouch of cursed bullets. The ball shot glowed with ill light. The fiery elements called out to the morehl. Fire and power laid deep beneath the brittle, stone plug. He could feel it in every fiber of his being.

Sshkkryyahr stood next to a large rune she'd drawn on the plug. "Do you feel the fire?"

Shedakor nodded.

"It runs like rivers through the tectonic plates. They are under pressure and yearn to be released." She rolled her eyes back in her head and touched the rune, working her dark magic. Torl did likewise. As Sshkkryyahr and Torl chanted some fell mantra, the ground began rumbling. The rune shone red with magmic light.

Shedakor took a few steps backwards and onto the carpet. Lava elves could withstand great heat and direct flame did not faze them. They could even survive immersion in lava… for a few seconds, anyway, but few living things could survive a direct kiss from Firiel's power.

The cap over the lava flow cracked and stone splinters flew like bullets as the pressure hissed. Magma burbled up, seeping through the cracks. Everything in the vertical shaft shook with pent up energy that threatened to burst forth.

Scrambling back to the safety of the carpet, Sshkkryyahr and Torl clambered aboard and urged the artifact into the air. It plunged into the sky even as the lava flow erupted, rocketing upward with burning fury. The burning spray shooting forth sent the morehl hunkered within the outpost running. They plunged directly into battle with flintlocks and rapiers drawn.

Iluchus watched the black dragon tear out its rival's heart. She yanked the reins and drove her chariot away from the rock furrow that the massive blue drake plowed up as it smashed into the soil. It landed with its belly tore open, sloshing gore across the field. The black dragon, claws still slick with its enemy's blood, circled a victory lap and looked for another target.

The queen's eyes darted across the landscape as she searched for the largest cluster of morehl to charge her forces into. *Perhaps a pitched battle will attract the dragon's attention—if I can get it to attack a group of us, maybe the distraction will allow us to escape…*

She callously did the math in her head. If she smashed her troops into a larger army of morehl, a dragon attack would statistically do greater damage to the lava elves than to her.

Even though the dead blue dragon had stopped sliding and tearing a groove through the face of Esfah, the ground still shook. Iluchus turned and looked back. A column of flame shot into the air, reaching as high as a mountain. The quake turned violent and balls of fiery slag rained down upon the amazons.

The ground shifted and buckled, finally breaking open. Fiery walls and rivers of lava burned impenetrable barriers through the ground, encircling them. At their rear, the lava elves' cursed bullets ripped through the protection held by their shield-maidens.

Lava flows scorched the prairie grasses, and a wildfire whooshed to life, threatening to chase them down nearly as fast as morehl bullets.

Iluchus spotted a cluster of enemies gathering in the distance near the ridge where the Gwich'in died. "There! We've got to smash through that group and flee, as many as we can, back to Potshari!"

Behind her, Visech waved the flags and passed the order with a pained grunt.

She spared him a glance. A bullet had torn through his torso; she heard his pained rattle as he coughed—it looked bad. If he didn't find a healer soon, he would not survive. Visech dutifully continued flapping the flags, relaying the order despite his immense pain.

"They are attempting to break through the line, there," Sshkkryyahr said, keeping herself small so that they could all fit onto the carpet. "The lava flow is at its lightest just beyond. That is where they stand the best chance of escape; it is where the dragon will break them."

A shadow darkened the ground as the black dragon angled for an attack.

"Don't needlessly throw away our army," Shedakor cautioned. "We must defend what we have claimed from any outsiders who might seek to capitalize on our casualties. Gundakhor included."

Sshkkryyahr looked him in the face. "You can defeat them without a dragon?"

"We outnumber them two to one and your cursed bullets work now. Of course I can defeat them," he clarified.

She bobbed her head. "Good. I have other intentions on the dragon, anyhow."

Torl brought the carpet low, and Shedakor leapt off. He hit the ground running and joined his troops as the spellcasters flew up to rejoin others of the Black Forest. The thunder of human cavalry roared deafeningly at their approach, and the swelling shade of a draconic shadow lifted. Their charmed dragon swooped back into the sky and sped towards the horizon. It had been compelled elsewhere.

"Here they come!" Shedakor howled, bracing for impact. "Fire!"

Deadly missiles flew from both sides. Horses cried out in fear as they plunged through the smoke. The morehl formed a box, forcing the cavalry through a gauntlet even before they reached the river of fire.

Wounded horses slowed to a crawl and their riders engaged in melee as the troops lost momentum. The amazons on foot did likewise. Drawing blades, they were caught up in the burgeoning horde of red-skinned warriors.

"Come on! Hie!" Iluchus screamed, racing like never before.

"What do you think our chances are, Visech? Visech?"

She looked back.

Visech groaned, "I'm sorry…" Where his eye had been, a new hole was bored all the way through. Iluchus caught a flash of light through the wound as her trusted advisor fell from the speeding carriage and broke apart on the ground.

She snapped her head to the direction of his assailant and spotted Shedakor. The morehl general grinned at her, *the morehl who never misses*. Rage welled up within her—a red fury that commanded her to kill this enemy.

He was aiming for Visech… to hurt me… to kill me slow, one piece at a time! She knew it was the lava elf way, and her mind vied with her heart. One urged her to escape, and the other demanded vengeance.

Her heart won.

Iluchus roared and whirled her chariot around, charging for the devious morehl. Enemy soldiers swarmed around them, choking her speed until she arrived at her wicked counterpart on the opposite side of the conflict.

As elven rapiers tore her beloved steed apart, Iluchus snatched her spear and falchion and hurdled over the enemies. Rage fueled her and, like a bladed whirlwind, she hacked enemies apart as if some kind of battle-goddess had possessed her.

She worked her way through the expendable warriors and closed the gap with her enemy. *Visech will be avenged!*

Shedakor snarled, challenging Iluchus. Human soldiers flooded towards her, providing support and unsure if they were still routed or had decided to make a last stand.

Morehl forces were equal to the task, opening wounds and trading blow for blow. Men and elves fell, watering the ground with the blood of both races.

The cocky elf pulled his flintlock and drew a bead on the queen. He looked up at the ridge where Sshkkryyahr presided over the battle. She smiled down at chaos, reveling the abject brutality that such a conflict resulted in: a foul kind of worship dedicated to her Death god.

He traced her eyes, and they seemed to flit from him to another warrior on the opposite side of Iluchus. *Charbann.* He wielded the fancy blade of his house, inlaid with his family crest. The praetorian warrior chopped down human after human.

The new recruit from the Obsidian Grotto's ranks pressed in on the far side, separating Iluchus from her support. "War is chaotic," Shedakor whispered, concocting and rehearsing his defense. "Accidents happen."

He took aim again at Iluchus and pulled the trigger.

A cursed sphere of alchemical ball-shot whizzed past Iluchus's head. She howled in surprise, feeling it graze her hair just below her headdress. A muscular morehl warrior was about to bear down on her. Instead, he fell in a shrieking panic. Arterial blood sprayed like a geyser from his neck and steam vented skyward.

Iluchus snapped her head and locked eyes with Shedakor. *So much for the morehl who never misses,* she thought.

He squinted, wordlessly challenging her to a duel. Shedakor's hands flashed as he reached for another gun on his gunslinger's vest.

Acting on pure instinct, Iluchus raised her spear and launched it at her enemy. Both warriors were fast; the queen proved faster.

Her rotating spear tip grazed the side of his head with its leaf blade, cutting a nasty, deep line through Shedakor's face and sending his bullet wide.

"Come on! Queen Iluchus—we must flee!" her forces begged her as they finally caught up. "If we stay, none of us will survive!"

Shedakor toppled to the ground with steam leaking from his ruined eye socket. His own forces surrounded him and pressed their attack in his defense.

She roared a guttural, pained curse at him and then snatched the nearest stray horse she could find and charged for the last obstacle separating her from freedom, a river of lava that barred the human soldiers from the open field. If they could cross, they could use their superior speed to escape.

Too few of her soldiers still ran or rode at her side. Her heart ached as if it, too, had been pierced by the arcane bullets of the enemy. Her horse chortled nervously as it sped closer and closer to the lava flow, unhappy about the implications.

Iluchus growled and urged it forward.

With a terrified whiny it leapt through the air at the edge of the hellish river. *Too little. Too far.* The horse plunged into the shallow lava flow and panicked. It screeched when it landed, throwing its head in every direction and all at once. It took only four steps as it slowly lowered further into the deadly river on legs that melted like wax stamps. It screamed with horrific pain, sounding almost human as it burned alive.

Iluchus roared, looking side to side—no one else had made it this far. Only she still remained.

The horse collapsed in its death throes. She was not far from the edge: perhaps twice as far as she could jump.

Help me Father—aide me Tarvanehl!

She steeled herself, and then launched herself off the collapsing steed. Iluchus splashed feet first into the lava, two steps from safety.

From his perch above the slaughter, Torl nudged the drider and grinned through his predator's teeth. Up the slope, two morehl helped Shedakor climb the rise. Blood stained him from cheeks to waist, and he staunched the wound with a rag.

"Casualties?" Sshkkryyahr asked.

"Acceptable," the lava elf said, surveying the field. His eyes lingered on Charbann's corpse. He kept a smile from playing at his lips, even if it brought him at least as much pleasure than his victory over the humans.

"This is what you requested of me when you first came to my lair." She grinned. "Your enemy has been destroyed."

"To a man?" Shedakor searched for reassurance, still floundering somewhat with his newly limited vision.

"Technically speaking, yes." The drider's words were playful. She and the rakshasa tilted their heads to watch Iluchus take her first laborious steps beyond the lava flow—striding in the direction of Potshari by sheer force of will. Her boots had burned off, and she walked in a near-fugue upon ruined feet, fueled by duty and purpose.

"I hope she likes what she finds when she finally gets back to Potshari," Torl chortled.

Sshkkryyahr stroked the side of Shedakor's face and the turmoil in his gut finally quelled. "You have done it. You won this war, General."

With his one remaining eye, he looked up at her.

"I must now bring you into the fold, my dear. As I have helped you defeat your enemies, I ask you to help me dispose of mine."

Shedakor stared into Sshkkryyahr's sultry eyes. He nodded his head and pledged, "Whatever you ask of me, I will do."

Like weary hammer strikes against an anvil, Iluchus's feet pounded over and over. Shaky legs bore her onward with nothing more than grim determination. She walked in a haze—barely seeing, thinking, or sensing anything. She'd set her course and launched her body upon its course before succumbing to the shock.

Heat-boils covered her lower half and skin had melted from her shins downward. The quality of the ground beneath her feet shifted from sodden field to gravel. The sensation jolted her from her fugue and back into the mental trauma of her failure and to the physical pain of her condition.

Iluchus collapsed at the edge of Potshari and brushed the crushed gravel from the pads of her feet. She bit back tears and nursed her bloody, blistered, and bare feet which had somehow borne her all the way here against all odds.

Turning her head up, her gut twisted at the sight. Nothing remained of the Gwich'in city except smoldering ash and scorched skeletons. The odor of plague lingered in the air.

Tears flowed from the queen. She could scarcely rule the ashes. A shadow fell over her and a black dragon cocked its head curiously. Finally, it swooped down and took her.

More than a hundred leagues from Potshari, the sages arrived at the border.

An expanse of grass and soil spread across the flatlands, terminating at a berm which separated the tree-line and the thick foliage beyond. One of the marker stones, inscribed with a runic sigil, towered in the distance, marking the boundary of the Feylands. The stones served as warders: reminders to those with evil intent that the mother goddess Ghaeial protected what lived within.

The four sages stood beneath the canopy and peered out at the broad and expansive distance. They could feel the evil occurring beyond the limitations of their eyes. War. Bloodshed. Dragons.

Their eidolons stood just a little way behind the sages, waiting on what their masters chose to do.

"Now what?" Wehge asked. "These evil spirits may have gone off in any direction. Soon, they could be anywhere in all of Esfah."

Drokh nodded. "Yes, but I feel they have not gone too far. Whoever released them must have done so with a purpose. I do not think they will have left the Birthlands."

Wehge scowled. "I remember the journey to our Feyland sanctuary from Daur-Bor-Nin in the southern Crechelands. Such a distance is not even half the length of the continent. Forgive me if I find little comfort in your thoughts."

Drokh understood his frustration. He put a hand on the selumari's shoulder. Drokh asked calmly, "If we will not face these things, then who will?"

Wehge's shoulders slumped. He knew the dwarf was right. They would travel any distance required to stop these fiends.

Shella touched her jumpy counterpart and traced the male coral elf's tattoos with a finger. She walked onto the grass of the plains. Her armored tako followed her, walking smoothly upon all eight legs.

Lyta followed with her androsphinx striding behind her. The creature tested the grass with tentative paws; it had been decades since the thing had prowled anything but jungle.

Wehge looked sidelong at Drokh and repeated his question. "Now what? How will we Master Sages decide to act against the acolytes of Death?"

Drokh walked past him, and then kept going. "Now, we split up." The dwarf headed south, and then kept on going with his gargoyle companion walking in lockstep behind.

Wehge thought Drokh must have been joking and would turn back at any time, but the dwarf never once looked back. The selumari swallowed and then embraced Lyta and Shella each in turn. His swarm of sprites swirled around him like a tornado of lights; they gave him a feeling of confidence. He would not be alone and his eidolon would protect him when he needed to rest or felt overwhelmed. "This is it, then, the breaking of the company of Sages?"

Shella shook her head. "We will never be far apart," she insisted.

Lyta's face looked grave and she stared into the southwest. "Distance will separate us, Wehge, but I have a feeling that we shall all see each other again in the future." She, too, began walking away from the boundary of the Feylands.

Much like her vaghan counterpart, neither did she look back.

Emperor Kurlahk stood and applauded as Shedakor and Sshkkryyahr entered his dining hall. He'd insisted that they come straight away and regale the emperor and his intimate party of revelers with tales of the recently won war.

Shedakor walked towards Kurlahk while Sshkkryyahr hung near the back. She remained on the far side of the long dining table where a dozen guests were seated, all members of the ruling caste.

He strode with a cocky swagger, despite how the fresh leather thong of his eye patch criss-crossed his face. It chaffed the white, puckering scar tissue that recently formed over where Iluchus's spear had sliced him open and taken his dominant eye.

Kurlahk sat with a grin and insisted that the heroes tell them about the campaign. He leaned forward eagerly.

"There is not so much to tell, Emperor Kurlahk, except that the mighty rule over the weak. The strong lead and they take what they want by force," Sshkkryyahr said. "That is the morehl way."

"True spoken," the emperor laughed with a goblet in one hand. Wine sloshed out as he chortled. "The morehl empire is certainly the strongest. The Obsidian Grotto takes as it wills. We rule all, as is our birthright, a boon granted to us by the gods."

The drider raised to her full height, imposing her size upon the party. She stepped up onto the table and towered over the others. "Not gods… only Death. Not Kurlahk's empire, and not the morehl empire." She glanced sidelong at Shedakor and snapped, "*Our* empire. Kill him."

Shedakor snarled and snatched his flintlocks while Sshkkryyahr employed her many legs. Using their jagged ends, she attacked the guests and eliminated them in short order. At close range, the gunman fired both weapons in an eruption of blue.

Emperor Kurlahk stood to his feet; he patted his chest and checked his body. Neither of the bullets had found their mark. He whirled and flung himself for the dining hall's rear exit, quite surprised that the morehl who never missed could suddenly fail despite such close proximity.

Sshkkryyahr snarled and shot her consort a disapproving look.

Shedakor cursed a string of profanities and set his jaw. Since losing his eye, his ruined depth perception greatly affected his aim. He holstered the weapons and drew two more, firing in rapid succession while the Emperor sprinted for his life.

Both were meant to be kill shots. One bullet went wide, but another clipped Kurlahk's thigh and spun him to the ground.

While Shedakor fell upon the king with a blade, a gilded one that once belonged to Charbann, Sshkkryyahr watched her consort disapprovingly. "Hurry and finish him. The guards will be here any moment."

He plunged it through Kurlahk's vitals and casted the unique weapon aside, while the drider wiped the blood from her dagger-like feet.

The door burst open, and the praetorian guard rushed into the room.

"Quickly, he's getting away!" the murderers shouted, pointing towards the exit that the emperor had tried to reach.

"It is Charbann," Shedakor howled. "He has turned on the Emperor!"

One guard remained in the room to protect them while the rest sprinted towards the fictitious intruder.

Sshkkryyahr grinned deviously, and the room fell quiet. The crime had been perfect… almost… and now *they* would rule the Obsidian Grotto together.

Two nights later, Shedakor entered the imperial bedchamber, a spacious, lavish room that had only now become his. His and *hers*. Sshkkryyahr waited there for him, half draped over the bed with her hair pulled back, exposing her naked breasts. The room smelled like incense and hot pheromones.

He began unfastening the purple robe of his position and tossed his gun belt to the floor, eager to enter the creature's lusty embrace. He paused momentarily and pulled another slug of wine from a nearby goblet.

The last forty hours had been a debauched revelry as the Obsidian Grotto celebrated the new emperor's coronation. Shedakor's eyes looked over his consort and glimmered with lascivious intent; he had plenty more revelry in mind before dawn, albeit of a different sort.

His robe fell to the floor, exposing his red flesh to the air. "I don't know why I was ever jealous of Charbann," he confessed. Whether because of the wine or some other impulse, he did not know. He took a step towards her wearing nothing more than a smile.

"Oh. You are right to have been suspicious."

He stopped in his tracks, his hubris suddenly wilted. He cocked an eyebrow. *Did she say "are" right or "were" right?*

She beckoned to him with eager eyes.

Shedakor remained fixed to the floor. He didn't dare approach until he had clarity. He may have made her his empress, but she was still a monster, after all, and monsters could be treacherous. "The truth. Out with it," he said with a slight slur. *It was definitely the wine.*

Sshkkryyahr grinned and exposed her wickedly sharp teeth in her otherwise morehl mouth.

"I laid many plans when you first entered my lair. Now there is only one." She licked her lips—but not in a seductive way. "You were useful... *before*." She spat the last word with disgust.

Emperor Shedakor took a step backwards. His bare foot touched the cloth of his robe and the leather of his gun belt.

Sshkkryyahr snarled and leapt for him.

Shedakor whirled for his guns, drawing and firing in one fluid motion, an action he'd done a thousand times before without fail. Both weapons went off.

The drider stood tall, surprised that Shedakor still managed such speed, even when half-drunk. She cocked her head and looked down at him. Neither missile had found its mark.

"Now you see why," she said coolly, closing the gap and wrapping him within her monstrous legs.

"They will know you murdered me," Shedakor protested as the drider's legs began to crush him, popping sockets and joints. He unsuccessfully bargained. He did not attempt to beg—Shedakor had too much pride for that.

"I am the empress, now. They will believe me when I say that you simply disappeared." She sank her fangs into his neck and tore free a mouthful of flesh which she swallowed. "And once I am done devouring you, that will be the truth of it."

His nerves overloaded and pain slipped beyond him as she tore off further bites of flesh, shaking him like a rag-doll within her grip. The light went out behind Shedakor's only eye and from that day forward, only Sshkkryyahr reigned in the Obsidian Grotto.

LOVE, BLOOD & FIRE
PT. 2
DAVIAN'S IMPOSSIBLE TASK

Year 30 of the First Age

Davian Whisperwynd walked south for many days after forsaking his home. He moved slower, and with less drive than when he'd returned to Maris-ta-Sehlim from Daur-Bor-Nin. After nearly a month, he reached a great mass of water.

The coral elf basked in the salty winds blowing off the Talvat Sea. Until now, Davian had subsisted on whatever he could forage for; now he had plentiful food. The beach was strewn with all manner of kelps and edible plants and soft-bodied creatures that had washed ashore with the tide. He spent several days on the beach collecting and preserving nature's bounty and letting the gods provide for him as they were inclined, but expecting that supply to end any day.

He built only a small shelter against the elements and weaved a basket with shoulder straps. As the season turned, and the food source depleted, Davian knew it was time to move on. He shouldered his supplies, and turned East, then walked along the coast for weeks on end. He passed the Mezzoscarps and eventually came to a gulf where a rushing river emptied into the sea.

It had been months since he left his hut by the sea, and summer was high. Davian turned north and followed the river until he arrived at the dwarven city of Orelod where the Narcea River sprang from a cleft in the mountains.

The vagha were excited to meet Davian. They often traded with the selumari and had received vagha refugees years ago from Daur-Bor-Nin. From them, the dwarves of Orelod had heard tales of the great warrior Davian Whisperwynd.

He traded stories for food and provisions, befriending a vagha hero named Gundraokh who was also keen to take up an adventure.

"Have ye really forsaken your sword?" Gundraokh asked, flabbergasted by the elf's vow. He'd tried unsuccessfully for days to convince the elf hero to help Orelod repel the goblins once and for all.

"I have indeed. Even this dagger at my hip makes me uncomfortable at times, though it's never tasted flesh before."

"And yet yer still adventuring?"

"It's all I know, and it's what my heart yearns for: new sights. New experiences," Davian confessed, "But I will not kill for anyone, not for another, not for myself—not even for the gods."

"A strong vow. I may someday adventure for myself. You have inspired me. Perhaps I'll travel down to Emmira, soon… if these durngam trog attacks ever cease," Gundraokh said.

"I think I shall leave again, soon, and continue going east," Davian told him.

"For your safety," Gundraokh said, "you should head across the Duar'Bondeen Steppes. "The southerly route requires passing the Narcea Marsh and the trogs of Bent Morass, plus the red elves of Karakto."

They parted a day later, and Davian crossed the steppes. With no true purpose, he walked two months, moving ever to the east. Eventually, the peaks of the crooked spine rose up from the distance and barred his path.

Davian climbed the peaks until he arrived at the top of a mountain. From that vantage, he could see across the plains and see the ridge of the sa'Eldurim Massif where Orelod was located; further east he could see the hot peaks of Empyreanoral where they rose from the seas.

There, he built a hut and remained for a while. It was not much more than a small shack of stone and stick where he slept and kept supplies, but to him it was his home.

Davian explored his mountainside, taking ever longer trips down the cliffs as he explored the paths and gathered foodstuffs before winter. He found a gentle slope that made the way up to his home easier, though it overlooked sheer drops and precarious ledges that were exposed to the open air.

He returned to his new home from foraging and found it had been mostly demolished. A trio of giant spiders had ruined his hut and scattered his stores, destroying much of it. They howled and charged at him. Davian's hand went instinctively to his dagger, but then he released it.

"Is this how the gods test my vow?" he shouted at them. In a heartbeat, he weighed the rationale and reasons for the oath. Davian had eaten mollusks and fish on the coast. He'd feasted on venison and pork when the vagha had offered it. Did his vow extend to creatures—Davian didn't think he could be a vegetarian... that certainly hadn't been implied in his vow. Killing animals had to be allowed, but not those that had sentient thought—that included any of the elder monsters.

These spiders were the same kind of creatures that the morehl rode upon during the battle for Daur-Bor-Nin. He twisted his mouth, certain that there was likely a lava elf stronghold somewhere nearby, too.

The selumari snatched a stick and brained one of the spiders, sending it skittering off as it hissed and angrily clamped its vicious pedipalps at him. Davian jammed his pole between the arachnid's forearms, and the creature snatched a hold of it. He shoved the stick hard and high, knocking the creature to its back.

Davian whirled the makeshift weapon in a circle and swept the legs from under the last enemy. All three shrieked as they scrambled back to their feet and then scurried away, returning to their homes down the far side of the mountain. They presumably made their nests below in the Terrorwood, the dark forest filled with leafless hackwood trees. The eastern side of the Crooked Spine Mountain Range was covered in them. It looked like winter in the Terrorwood, even during the summer.

Regardless of the trouble they caused, Davian did not want to kill the pests intentionally. He preferred to send them on their way and hoped they had learned their lesson. As he watched them go, he wondered if there were more of them. If that was the case, he would need to take precautions to protect his home.

He rebuilt his shack as best as able and salvaged what stores he could. Night had drawn on during that time. In the morning, he would venture into the Terrorwoods and scout them out; Davian hoped to find any sign of a lava elf presence and the size of the spider nest. The creatures had made such a careless trail down the mountain, that it would be easy to find them again on the next day.

Davian followed the path carved by the enormous riding-spiders that had raided his home. They feared nothing, and so they did not try to conceal their trail. He easily located their nest on the far side of a creek.

The nest was near and the creatures spread sheets of webbing that hung like veils of loose-knit fabric. They crossed from leafless tree to tree, darkening whatever lay within. Some kind of light pulsed inside the shroud and Davian slipped into the water.

Gill slits reflexively formed behind his ears, as they did for most selumari. Two-thirds of them possessed the trait, and Davian was thankful to be among them.

He swam across and into the perfect vantage point. Poking his head barely out of water, he peered through the silks and identified the sight. It was a campfire and a she-elf was feeding it with hackwood logs. His eyes widened at the sight of her. She was the most beautiful creature he had ever seen; it seemed as if she'd been crafted out of his dreams. Save that her skin was red.

Davian watched her for several minutes. He barely noticed the spiders until one of them leapt upon her and dragged her to the ground. She yelped and fell.

These are wild spiders! Skin color didn't matter to Davian. He only saw a woman in need and he leapt from the river and charged to her rescue. His dagger was in his hand in an instant, and he slit an entry through the silks.

Davian crashed into the beast and knocked it aside while scooping up the pretty morehl maiden. "Come away—we must flee! There are bound to be many more of them."

She yanked her hand back, startled as much by the blue-skinned intruder as by the spider's aggression. The morehl shoved Davian back and called the flames of the campfire to her side, whipping them high and into a frenzy. They surrounded her to form a protective barrier.

She is an enchantress! Davian shielded his eyes from the brilliance of the flame. "Come away with me—I am trying to rescue you from these beasts."

"These beasts," she barked from the fire, "are my pets. I breed them for the riders of the Obsidian Grotto and they fetch me a handsome price." She let the flames dissipate and her voice softened when she recognized that he had been trying to help her. "I am sorry for the confusion," she said sheepishly as she called the large arachnid to her side and ran her fingers through its fur. "Sometimes this one gets overly playful and forgets her strength."

The morehl enchantress approached and thanked Davian. "I am Roweena."

"Davian," he responded, practically drowning in the onyx pools of her eyes.

Roweena seemed equally fixed in the shared gaze. She bit her lip, and her cheeks turned somehow redder, even.

"I would hope that… I mean…" Davian had never been at a loss for words before in his life, but he could not seem to put a full sentence together. "Are you attached to any other… I mean, are you here alone?"

Roweena giggled. "I keep my own company and always have… mainly because I've yet to find someone interesting enough to hold my attention." She stared at him with keen fascination.

"Would you like to, uh…" the sudden influx of spiders distracted him. They crowded around him like puppies and regarded him curiously. They began to clamber up his legs, and he shifted on his feet with worry.

She came to his side and brushed them off of him.

Davian noticed how warm her skin was. Heat practically radiated off her. "And you're so wet," she wrinkled her nose and then summoned a dry wind that blasted him into a state of semi-dampness.

She stood to her feet, only a hairs-breadth apart and so close that their noses nearly touched. They hesitated for a moment, and then they kissed and locked in an embrace.

"You know that I love you, Roweena?" Davian asked. She laid against him upon the bed in her home, a small cottage in the Terrorwood. His hand shifted down to the growing bump at her waist.

Half a year had passed, and he'd spent almost all of it in the enchantresses company. He spent his days preparing a garden and making a home for them here. He had kept out of sight when morehl buyers came down from the north and left with most of the spiders before winter had come. Davian kept battle far from his mind. His thoughts had turned far more domestic than they'd ever been before.

She shifted further into the grip of his strong arms. "I know you do, my pet selumari," she teased, knowing how much he hated when she said such a thing.

The tension between her race and his bothered him, if for no reason, but that it meant they could not venture into public together for fear of reprisal. Their love was considered an abomination by all of the races that considered themselves sensible. He rubbed his lover's abdomen. "You know that our child will be frehlasuhl, a gray elf." His voice was resolute, but sorrowful. "But we will always have each other. Forever?"

She reached up behind her and caressed the blue skin of his cheek. "Forever, my love. And do not fear for our children… they will be very different, but they have a strong destiny. I know these things."

"Do you now?"

"Of course. I know much of what will come to pass— don't you know that I am really the goddess of fate?" Roweena teased.

He rolled his eyes, "Oh really? Because I always thought I made my own fate," Davian said.

"I know many things," the enchantress said. "The frehlasuhl are childless, but our line will be strong. Fast and powerful—warriors born of such strong magic and mighty lineage that they will shake the world." She looked back at him. "The children of Davian Whisperwynd," she used his full name with a grin.

"What? But I never..." he had never told her his true name. He had never wanted his reputation to overshadow who he was trying to become.

"I hear much when I catch rumors from traders," she grinned. "The fame of the selumari who single-handedly filled a boat with the bodies of two thousand trogs could never be escaped," she teased. "They called you the butcher of Maris-ta-Sehlim. Defender of the north coast."

Davian laughed. "It was a cart. And the head count was less than half of that... and it was literally that. A head count. But tell me more about the frehlasuhl. I will never be a grandfather?"

"You will be," she assured him. "Gray elves can only mix with selumari or morehl," she said, rubbing her womb. "But I believe our children will be so much more than that. I know it, in fact. We are building something special, you and I."

"Are we?" Davian asked. "But the world will hate them. At least they will have a family, right?"

"I hope so," Roweena said, curling up onto her side and snuggling deeper into the bare chest of her forbidden love. "You should know that my father is stern. Certainly, he knows who you are, though you have not yet met him."

Davian cocked his head. They had never talked about extended family. The age of elves was difficult to determine, and he had always assumed that Roweena was a first generation elf, one of those formed and placed upon Esfah by the gods, like him. He hadn't considered that she might have a father. Roweena must have been amongst the first generation of those born. He caressed her body with a smile; given her appetites, however, that she may have been conceived almost immediately did not surprise him that much.

"And he does not discount me outright because of my skin?"

"How could he?" she asked. "When first you meet, I shall show him a prize that you have acquired for me. A task: a test to prove your worth to him. For a warrior of your great renown, it should prove something easy."

Davian grinned. "You give me a task to win your father's approval. I do not know him, but I imagine that it will prove difficult to win the admiration of any morehl... that I earned *yours* is miracle enough. I should not hope for a second."

Roweena sat up and faced her selumari. Her demeanor turned suddenly serious. "My father is not like you or I. And he is not like any lava elf who you have met before. But I promise you that if you accomplish this task, you will have earned his consent... and *my* undying approval."

"Then so I must undertake this quest, provided it does not violate my oath," Davian pledged. "For you, and for all our children, I would undertake any mission. Surely, you know this?"

She nodded and explained his task. "There is a cave that the lava elves call the Darkwell. It is a distance, but not too far from here, and you must take a token from it. I shall draw you a map." She began to sketch landmarks for Davian and write directions to the cave. "I know that you have already defied the gods to earn your freedom from the fates, Davian Whisperwynd... such is the tale, anyways. Your task will be to steal a piece of chalk from the inner sanctum of the morehl, a very holy place to them. Beware, the Lurker in the Deep guards it," she cautioned, referencing a tavern tale told about an elder monster said to guard the home of Lord Death, himself. "Doing this will prove to my father that Davian Whisperwynd is worthy of his daughter, and any difference in the races be damned."

The deed sounded daunting, and his vow only complicated it. Facing an elder creature without a weapon was foolishness. He asked, "And if I make the attempt and fail? What will you do if I never return?"

She frowned and remained silent for several long moments. Finally, Roweena answered honestly. "I will take the pennyroyal tea and return to my spiders in the forest. Perhaps I would return to my sisters and the life I lived before I dabbled with spiders in the Terrorwood."

Davian scowled. He knew as well as any that the herbal concoction would end a pregnancy early. This deed was important to Roweena, his beloved enchantress, and so it was important to him. "Then the task must be accomplished, and for the sake of my family line, I will succeed."

Her expression brightened. "You will? That makes me so happy," she exclaimed.

"Remember that I have made a vow to leave my sword behind, but I will undertake this quest in order to prove my love… to both you and my children. I will love them regardless of their skin color, and nothing will keep me from accomplishing mighty deeds in their honor—I will plunder even Lord Death's lair for them."

Roweena turned and kissed him. She thanked him profusely and crawled half atop him. She was not yet so pregnant that it had made movement uncomfortable. The enchantress bit his lip and embraced him, sliding her hands down further towards his hips. She intended to show him all of her gratitude, and Davian could do nothing but answer her every request.

After a tenday, Davian arrived at the area on his map where Roweena had inscribed, *the Darkwell*. It was unmistakable.

Hidden amid the crags, he found an enormous, round hole that descended into a depression. It appeared deep and rough, like a lava tube, and he knew that he'd found it. A winding set of uneven stairs jutted out from the wall, descending ever downward.

The determined selumari checked the supplies in his pack. He assumed he possessed everything he would need, other than a sword. Davian began his descent.

After a certain depth, the light from above no longer penetrated the blackness, and Davian fumbled for each tread of the stair until a new kind of light broke the monotony of darkness. Glowing lichens and fungi sprouts bathed the corridors in bio-luminescent blues and greens. Their light was weak, but it provided enough for elven eyes to see clearly.

Something buzzed near his head, and he swatted away the wasp that zipped by his face. Davian ducked his head and ran through the zone where he spotted a nest of the insects.

Tunnels branched in myriad directions and cavernous warrens spread out before him. However, he spotted no opposition. None trespassed here save one foolish selumari. Natural stone pillars of calcified mineral connected floor to ceiling and upon them were written morehl glyphs: religious symbols consecrating this place to one of the lava elves' gods... Death.

A hot wind rushed up from below and the selumari intruder smelled the sulfur on the eddies. Nearby, another hole descended deeper into Esfah's core near a cluster of boulders perched precariously at the ledge. The pit was so deep that he could not see more than a few cubits into it. He dropped a stone within, but it did not make any sound to indicate it found the bottom.

Only a short distance from the drop, a flat wall blocked the path. A simple door made of wood barred entry and the frame and wall around it were inscribed with more profane words and sigils, devoting this place to the Dark One. Light bled from underneath the barrier. Davian's stomach threatened to sour when he read the profane signs on the door. Something foul laid beyond it, he felt certain.

Quietly, Davian retrieved a tube of animal grease from his pouch and worked it into the hinges and the wrought iron of the handle's mechanism. He could not risk a creaky door alerting any sentries to his presence. The door opened silently, and Davian peered into the chamber.

Everburning torches lit the large room, which appeared to be some kind of workshop. Tools he could not identify lay upon benches; polished walls of slate stood tall where drawings and otherworldly scripts were etched upon them. Davian stared at the rows of tables and identified preserved bodies of selumari that laid open where they'd been cut apart for examination. On a workbench, alembic vials and jars contained a roiling, inky mass of black liquid that seemed to desperately desire freedom.

His heart suffered a chill, and he knew where he was. He'd heard of this place in stories told by lava elves captured during the early days after the fall of Daur-Bor-Nin. *The birthplace of the morehl—where Death twisted, bent, and recreated the elf species for his own pleasure.*

As he stared, aghast at the scene, his eyes caught movement. A long tentacle shifted as if lethargic. Davian traced it back to the fiend's body, leaning within the threshold only slightly. He found an amorphous creature with oily black skin and shaped like a giant squid, only with more tentacles. Its uppermost half ended in something that looked vaguely humanoid, but more tendrils covered where it might have had facial hair and it wore the skin of old molting like it was a shroud.

Terror lodged momentarily in his gut, and he retreated into the dark. The beast was pure nightmare fuel. Two steps back, Davian's love for the enchantress reawakened, and he hardened his resolve.

He emptied his supply bag and hurried towards the entrance to the Darkwell and located the wasps' nest. He summoned his innate connection to the magics of Esfah and drew upon a sliver of that power to cool the air around the hive, lulling the insects into a torpor. Carefully, he wrapped his satchel around it and engulfed the nest, sealing it within the sack.

Davian returned to the unholy door and unwound his length of rope, cutting it in two. He tied one length around his waist and then around a boulder on the ledge of the bottomless rift. The other rope he tied to the boulder but laced across the hole and looped around a colonnade to create a pulley.

The brave coral elf crept back to the door and reexamined the room. He spotted the object he needed on the far side of the room. Near an abandoned selumari corpse lay a few lengths of the special chalk Roweena had requested.

Only now did he make any sense of the drawings upon the slate. Scribbled in life size proportions were sketches of morehl with notes, written in the hand of Death himself. Nearby were another series of figures, illustrations of creatures, and then drawings of them merged. A kind of winged beast with felinoid features. Davian recognized sigils for air and frost, and an inverted symbol for magic, but he could not make much sense of it. The work of the gods was not meant to be understood by their creations, he assumed. Above all else, he was just glad that the lord of Death was not currently present.

His mouth turned. *This is what the gods do,* he thought, *create new life from existing life. At least, the Death god does so... he cannot truly create, only twist and corrupt what already exists.*

Davian steeled himself and clutched his spare rope; he felt the angry wasps stir within the bag as their warmth returned. He threw the sack to the far side of the room where it burst open, unleashing a cloud of angry pests. And then he launched himself into the room.

The lurker had already turned to snatch up the sack. Wrapping the nest within its tentacles only angered the wasps further, and they attacked the elder monster, making it roar with annoyance. Finally, the lurker in the deep noticed the true invader sprinting towards the far side of the room. The beast whirled its writhing limbs to engage.

Davian ducked beneath one appendage and slid to his knees. He grabbed a chunk of the mystic chalk and stashed it inside a pouch. Rolling away just in time to avoid another tentacle, he snatched the cadaver that lay near the floor and threw it up as high as he could.

The lurker seized it in a flash and yanked it closer. Its true mouth opened, splitting open a vicious aperture filled with jagged teeth. In two gruesome bites, the lurker devoured the old corpse and then locked its gaze upon the intruder, realizing the selumari's trickery. A web of tentacles spread through the room, ready to respond to any move.

Davian feinted a move. Two tentacles reacted, which would have snatched him had he fled. The lurker began ambling towards him. It would catch its tricksy prey in mere moments.

The selumari yanked on the cord in his free hand, and he heard the crumble of stone as the boulder fell. He double feinted, drawing more and more tentacles and building disbelief in his enemy. And then, a split second later, Davian disappeared. The slack between him and the boulder ran out as it fell, and it yanked him through the room with unparalleled speed.

In a flash, Davian's dagger was in hand, and he cut the rope. The elf rolled to a stop a few cubits away from the mouth of the hole. He scrambled to his feet and then sprinted for the mouth of the Darkwell. The lurker appeared too big to leave the room, but he suspected that the creature could find a way. Davian's highest concern was to flee before the master of the cave, Lord Death, returned.

He dashed up the stairs and did not slow until he was five leagues away from the stairs of the Darkwell, with his prize hidden safely on his person.

Roweena sat upon the bench of the covered wagon and looked at her prize while Davian was inside the store. She had promised Davian that he could meet her father after their child was born. Everything they did now was in preparation of that arrival.

She kept her hood low and wore gloves so that passersby could not see the color of her skin; they were in a selumari town south of Lago Rosa where the mismatched elves sometimes traveled to shop. She would not be welcome here if they knew her identity. The enchantress turned the chunk of chalk over in her hands and examined it. The white, lithic shale had more power in her hands than any could ever suspect.

A group of coral elf traders wandered down the street of a village. The traders' crier shouted their wares.

"You sir! How about some salted fish? Caught mere days ago in the Rosa Lagoon. And you, my lady… some fine fur from Hyperannor?"

Roweena refused to pay him any mind, keeping still as stone.

He kept heckling her. "What's the matter, ma'am? You don't like furs? Maybe some candied hullifruit slices? Surely we've got something you could use."

Before he got close enough to peer below her hood and meet her, Davian emerged carrying a few sacks bundled over each shoulder. He finished packing them in the wagon and glared at the trader who finally backed off. He muttered something about the silent woman's rudeness.

"If my mistress doesn't respond, it could be because she is deaf," Davian said.

The trader grumbled some more, his pride hurt more than anything else, and he returned to his peers where they'd set up a booth to vend their wares. One of the crier's friends apologized on his behalf. "If you've no need for stores, perhaps news of the realm or a tale? I hear there is a new one being sung of Davian Whisperwynd, the greatest warrior west of the Massif—how he struck down a horde of trogs to bring hope to the vagha of Orelod."

"I've no need for fiction, songs or otherwise," Davian frowned.

"News then—you know the King Edum in Farnoch has issued a bounty for any frehlasuhl. And a double bounty to bring in the parents. Trying to stamp out any unseemliness, he is. There's big money in it, too. One of the prominent merchants was caught with one of his gray bastards; the king seized all his assets and uses it to pay the rewards."

Davian refused to engage any further. His lover cradled her burgeoning belly while he steered the pony into a tight arc. He did not want to stay in this village any longer than necessary, especially with such talk. Shrugging off his outer coat, Davian laid it over Roweena.

"But I'm not cold," she said.

"Keep it on," he said firmly. One sleeve had ridden up her forearm, exposing skin between it and her glove but pulling it down would have been to suspicious. Davian risked a glance sidelong and noted how the merchants watched them depart. They discussed something intently while watching them leave. "I think it safe to assume they know you're not deaf," he said. "I'll keep an eye out for trouble."

He tried not to worry her, but before looking away, the merchants had stopped setting up and begun packing. Davian expected visitors and violence. It would come soon.

Davian and Roweena kept a steady pace all night. The selumari tailed them, maintaining a space cushion the entire time, but refusing to turn aside. Davian worked the pony all night, hoping to put space between them and disappear. In the morning they were still in pursuit. The group was ten strong and they no longer concealed their purpose.

Brandishing their swords, they began to creep slowly closer. Davian cracked the reins, and the pony charged ahead.

With the wagon laden with stores, they could not outrun the bounty hunters and so Davian kicked their cargo out the back, but it was not enough for the already overworked beast and its speed suffered. They neared the Terrorwood when they hit a ridge that nearly busted an axle. Before the cart had settled, Roweena screamed and clutched her belly. Her labor pangs started.

High overhead, the sky cracked and glowed with an ominous red, seemingly in tandem with Roweena's pain. Magmic activity sometimes flowed from the Broken Spine. Their pulses seemed perfectly timed to Roweena's contractions.

She turned between them to try to disperse the crowd with magic. Roweena was revealed. Their selumari pursuit now confirmed who she was and refused to be deterred.

Their pony frothed white with sweat and ran nearly dead on her feet as the winds of a terrible storm picked up. Stumbling, the pony turned lame, and with them on the verge of their return to safety, safe arrival looked hopeless.

"There is no way to protect us at home," Roweena insisted. "My love, you must forsake your vow and take up the sword to protect me. I have one hidden in the house."

Davian grimaced. "I cannot."

"Then do it for our children," Roweena insisted as the pony gave up and collapsed a few cubits from the river bank.

Davian pulled her from the carriage as their enemies bore down on them. She doubled over with another pain and Davian grabbed her and fell backwards into the river and swam her across. He hauled them both to the shore and past their cottage.

Crawling behind some low shrubbery, they did not enter the home and hid nearby, instead. Davian broke a stick and held it crosswise in his lover's mouth so she could bite down and fight the contractions in relative quiet.

The enemy raiders emerged from the water moments later with swords drawn. They left an archer behind with their mounts to cover the river bank and prevent any escape by doubling back. The archer put Davian's pony out of its misery, even while the hunters' horses neighed in terror when the winds picked up again.

Pounding on the door, the crier from yesterday demanded they exit the building. After a minute of silence, he took a lantern and lit it. "Then we'll just burn you out," he howled, breaking a window and throwing the brassier through.

With the cottage in flames, Roweena's most loyal spiders emerged from the thick of their webs and attacked the intruders. The selumari shrieked and turned to face them. More and more arachnids emerged from the sheaves of webbing to defend the enchantress, and one of the invaders grabbed a lump of burning thatch and flung it into the silk. The spider's home and woods surrounding them lit.

Davian's heart sank and tears streamed down Roweena's face. Everything they had accumulated was ablaze. Remembering that his small cabin and provisions remained atop the mount, Davian pulled her away from the scene. "Come. I know the way. I think my supplies will be enough to last us, though they may be stale."

As they left the shrubbery, the archer across the river spotted them and cried out. "Hoy! They're getting away," he pointed out the escaping elves who slipped through the trees. The pursuit abandoned the flaming homestead to the spiders and gave chase.

"They will catch us!" Roweena groaned as she held her belly with both hands and moved as fast as she could.

"They don't know the way," Davian insisted. "It is safe, but they will struggle with it," he reassured her, hoping he might be right. On the foot of the hill, he looked back; only half their number remained. Davian had seen two fall to spiders, and another suffered when the mighty blasts of wind threw great sheaves of fire onto him. He could not account for the others.

As the climb grew steeper, Roweena's pangs came closer and intensified. Below them, a huge swath of the Terrorwood had become an inferno. Hot winds blasted them, whipping up violent eddies that cast hot embers against exposed flesh.

The enchantress was immune to them, but they pocked selumari skin with spots of gray and black where they singed.

Roweena collapsed on a landing about midway up the climb. "I can go no further," she insisted. "Our child is coming." She felt limbs stirring in her belly. "There is more than one—I am certain of it."

Davian clutched her hand and laid her down. "Perhaps I can reason with our pursuers. If they knew who I am... who I was..."

"You must *protect* us from them," Roweena insisted. "Kill them and throw their bodies off this mountain, my love. Together we can make our home safe, and then expand it. Together, we could even take Farnoch and Lago Rosa. *You could be king.*"

Davian saw it in his mind's eye. The vision took him like a thrall. He dodged the first elf's killing stroke and disarmed him; with stolen blade in hand he cut the hunter down, and then the next, followed by the remainder of the pursuit. A potential destiny played out in the theater of his mind's eye. With an army of elves that were somehow both red and blue at the same time, he sacked Lago Rosa and struck down King Edum in Farnoch. His enchantress crowned him King of the East Coast.

The elf shook away the vision—rejecting it, even if it might have proved a potential portent from the gods. "I cannot," he mumbled. "If I don't have my word, then I have no honor."

Hot, cinder-filled winds howled against the exposed mountain trail, and Davian ducked. When he returned his gaze, two of the enemies had lost their footing and nearly slipped from the cliffs, blasted by spurts of rain mixed with glowing brands. The enemies scowled and finally began to retreat, valuing their lives above the prize.

Roweena growled behind him, returning his attention to her. "The children. They are coming!"

"Children?" Davian gasped. "You are sure there is more than one?"

She shook her head. "Of this I am certain. There are more than two moving in my belly."

The winds surged with intensity, growing more violent with every contraction and with every push by the mother. Davian delivered the children. There were five in total, but their skin was not gray. Davian had stripped down and used his clothes to lay the babes upon, leaving them on the flat stone landing which had become a birthing floor. He stared at the children, all boys, whose cries seemed somehow louder than the thunder; their skin was a mottled red and blue and their silky hair came in tufts of red, gold, and white. These were not frehlasuhl.

Davian returned to Roweena's side, and she clutched his hand to pass the afterbirth. "We have five sons, my love, but *what are they?*"

"They are strong. That is what they are. Warriors who must defend themselves because their father would not."

Davian cocked his head. He shot her a wounded look, and she looked away, to the children. Their cries had shifted in tenor, and they rocked upon the ledge, growing as they moved. A violent wind gusted through the mountain pass and flung them from the side of the cliff.

"No!" Davian screamed, watching bewildered as the whirlwind blew his strange children over the edge.

They flew back into sight upon fiery trails like comets, becoming fully grown as he watched. They looked as strong as Davian had ever been in his prime, and they took one look back at their parents, and then rode east upon the winds like fiery torpedoes.

He turned back to the enchantress. Roweena stood, looking as healthy and beautiful as she had when they'd met, only her face was equally cross and pouty. "What are they?" he asked her again. "My sons are not gray elves, so what are they? *What are you?*"

Roweena set her jaw, and her features changed. She was both colorless and filled with every color. She appeared elven and altogether not and all at once. Davian shielded his eyes, but he knew exactly what she was: Roweena was one of the three daughters of Turambar, the sisters of Fate, gods whom he had defied.

"You have been a fool, Davian Whisperwynd," her voice was as melodic as music and violent as the earthquake. Her words cut to his core. "I am disappointed that you were not strong enough to father what I had hoped to create. My sisters had said as much; I should have believed them." She reached out a hand and caressed his cheek with one final moment of softness. Her face was sad. "And I would have, had you not blinded me with such affection! I had mostly forgotten who I was, until now."

Roweena turned away. "And to think, I had offered to make you a king among demi-gods, but you loved your vow more than you loved me."

"Roweena, wait!" Davian cried.

147

She did not heed him. Instead, she withdrew the chalk that Davian had claimed for her from the Darkwell and drew a simple door on a flat patch of stone on the cliff side. It opened, pouring light both arcane and blinding. Roweena dropped the chalk and stepped inside where her two sisters embraced her.

"But our children! Tell me they will be safe?"

One sister spoke as she closed the door from the other side. "They will take selumari wives and settle in the mountains beyond the east coast. They walk on fire and air and will become a race of mighty warriors—but you will not live to see such a thing."

The door closed, leaving Davian to the darkness and loneliness of the mountain. He retrieved his chalk and wailed into the empty sky as the winds subsided.

Davian knew loneliness. For a glimpse of time, he had known great love, and despite his sorrow, he believed one had been worth the other.

Davian Whisperwynd lived in the obscurity of his hovel for decades. The years were unkind to him, and he regretted his decisions each day—wondering if he would have even met his beloved enchantress had he not made his rash vow at Maris-ta-Sehlim.

Before he passed, he left his home one final time, crossing the Duar'Bondeen and entering the Feylands. There, he entrusted his chalk to the Master Sages of Yentosh who recorded his tale for posterity. He died in full possession of his vow, and comforted by the promise that it had produced the strongest lineage that might ever live, though these Air and Fire Walkers, as he called them, have yet to be seen.

His tale might be a strange one and seem the thing of fantasy, but the Darkwell chalk is certainly real enough, and it gives the Master Sages no reason to doubt the rest.

—Master Sage Shella, year 202FA

THE FALL OF THE OBSIDIAN GROTTO
PT. I
THE GAMBIT AT GUNDAKHOR

Year 340 of the First Age

"And ye've no major regrets?" Ruthak asked, chugging another mug of ale. He'd had enough that his eyes had narrowed to half slits.

King Gundraokh Shatterfist shook his head as he quaffed his own down. He rested his hands upon the table after; they *clunked* with the heavy sound of hands that had been half-transformed to stone by mystic means. He shifted the bracelet, which he wore on his right wrist.

"Whenever I've seen what I want, I've found a way to take it." He said and stared Ruthak up and down. He had been something of a poor warlord in terms of tactics, but was an excellent fighter and he'd been a worthy drinking companion since his arrival in Gundakhor—the old city of Orelod had long since been renamed after the mighty dwarven warrior. Moreover, Ruthak's low-key hero worship of the king had made the general loyal to a fault. "And what is it that *you* want Ruthak?"

Ruthak stumbled towards the keg and poured himself another mug. "To reclaim my home. Valis."

They sat together on a terrace overlooking the city which was built into the western side of Mount Gundakhor, part of the sa'Eldurim Massif. The smaller Mount Valis had been occupied by the enemy for centuries.

"Dosenit get yer hackles up that the drider owns Valis? It's rich with precious metal, ya'know?" Ruthak insisted.

Gundraokh sipped from his own cup. "I think this may be about your pride," he said, coolly. "The Obsidian Grotto took the mountain almost two hundred fifty years ago."

"For the metal," Ruthak said. "They use it to make those enchanted weapons. Think if Gundakhor had it!"

Gundraokh shook his head. "We haven't the skill to forge it. We buy what mystic weapons we need from the gremmlobahnd artisans, same as everybody else, Ruthak."

"Made of metal stolen from vaghan mines, often as not," he argued. "We can't afford their prices with Sshkkryyahr dictating market prices on eldrymetallum and we ain't all got any of them fancy bracelets to protect us."

"I don't think you understand what these really are," Gundraokh turned the one he wore on his wrist. Each of the four was a relic devoted to one of the gods. It may have granted god-like power when called upon, but it came at a cost, like all magic. The one Gundraokh wore had already dulled his touch and turned his skin partly to stone. He would have removed this one, but his hands had turned too rigid already to take it off, and their substance had proved unbreakable.

The Bands of Turambar, brother god of the Creator Tarvanehl, were relics of legend and Gundraokh planned to pass them down to his son along with the crown. The other three bracelets, which he'd located on quests in his younger years, were safely hidden away as family heirlooms. Gundraokh hoped his son would not use them except under the direst circumstances.

Ruthak continued, "It only surprises me that they've made no move against Gundakhor in all this time. You know the drider empress has long wanted to sack this city."

King Gundraokh had no rebuttal for that. It was a valid argument.

"That fact makes me wonder all these years why ye've not struck preemptively," Ruthak said.

A bell rang on the north wall, and they watched an army of defenders run along the ramparts to respond. Beyond the fortifications, an army of trogs approached. It would be over soon and the trogs would be dead; they made such frequent forays out from the Waterblight that the entire town had become accustomed to regular invasion. They never came with enough strength to be more than a mild nuisance. The invaders barely killed as many soldiers as folk who died of simple illnesses in any given year.

The king shrugged. "I have my reasons," he said. "Primarily, I'm try'na keep those goblins at bay. They reproduce so much faster than us that it's a constant work to cull their numbers and keep 'em off Gundakhor's walls."

"Psshh," Ruthak hissed. "Goblins aren't much of a concern. They may have numbers, but they're little more'n vermin. Not a half a wit between 'em all combined."

Gundraokh flexed his stiff hand and sipped his ale again. "I hope yer right," he said, but deep down he a had a seed of doubt growing in his gut. He'd been waiting a hundred years for the other shoe to drop. The morehl in the east bothered him more than Ruthak could possibly know, but something about the trogs on their northern border had set him at unease for more than a century, and he felt certain that something would change there, and soon.

He looked curiously at Ruthak. The dwarf was on his feet and staring into the distance. "Ye got a spyglass?"

"What?"

"A spyglass. A durngam spyglass—my eyes ain't what they used to be."

Gundraokh finally saw what had caught Ruthak's eye. A dark line crawled on the horizon. Morehl signal fires flashed as they relayed orders.

The lava elves were on the move. They had come down from Valis and marched south.

"Sound the watch horn," Gundraokh ordered one of his attendants. "I want all military prepared to fight at a moment's notice."

He stared at the distant enemy and grumbled curses upon them. He would have expected a diplomatic emissary to notify the vagha that their movement was not hostile if the morehl did not want their actions so close to the border mistaken as such.

"They'd better keep to their side of the Narcea river is all I can say," Gundraokh muttered. In his gut, he knew that was not likely. He turned his spyglass back north, and his gut tightened. Typically, the invaders came in knots of hundreds, smashed themselves against the dwarven defensive line, and then retreated for a few months. Already thousands had emerged from the swamp... and more kept coming.

Under the watchful eye of the vaghan towers at the perimeter of the lands, the lava elves watched their step and made sure they did not set foot in the Narcea river. Dwarves glared at them from their towers; the morehl glowered back.

"Keep it moving," Conqueror Mokshousa yelled from atop the giant spider mount that had born him since departing the Black Forest, which he knew the vagha still referred to as Valis. Spiders were a lower casted mount, but this close to vaghan towers, he thought it best not to present a target to an opportunistic vaghan archer. The dwarves claimed ownership over all land from the north marker stones and the far bank of the Narcea River and as far south as Lyander's Pass. "No one refills a canteen until we reach our destination," he barked, glancing across the river. On the far side, a brick wall had been built a hundred leagues long from Gundakhor and half a span taller than a typical man to keep creatures from crawling from the water uninvited.

Dingarha sidled his own eight-legged beast up to Mokshousa's. The powerful necromancer was one of the strongest of those that the Black Forest had to offer, and he controlled the dark magi that had accompanied them. Dingarha had joined the battle at Sshkkryyahr's orders when the army arrived at the Black Forest.

"How long until we take Gundakhor?" Dingarha asked.

"It has been the Empress's desire since before she came to power," Mokshousa said. "It will come to pass soon, perhaps a tenday."

"But not until we cut off all of their allies," the necromancer said.

Mokshousa nodded.

They rode most of the way in silence, until Dingarha asked, "You don't fear that Empress Sshkkryyahr spreads our forces too thinly?"

"I don't think that's any of our concern. The drider queen has spent a century or more planning for this particular... refining bred stock like me in the fighting pits. We will do our part to worship Lord Death and send our enemies to meet him, shrieking in the Abyss."

The army eventually came to the edge of the Narcea Marsh, where a corps of elven engineers had been dispatched fifty years ago to build a road through it so that their forces would not bog down in the sloughs. It eased their speed along the path tremendously. They skirted the cypress growths of the Nhur-Gale, the original home of the Black Forest Cult, and soon arrived at their destination.

Midway through the marshland road, they met their contacts. A group of trogs popped out from the lichen infested trees that glistened from the humid air of the swamps.

"You are Ogekt?" Mokshousa asked.

The goblin shook his head. "No. Ogekt the shaman remains in greater Bent Morass. I am Nidjiqt. I lead the expansion force."

Mokshousa nodded. "Then lead on"

The goblin was not as stupid as he looked, and he led them to a place on the Narcea shore. A large pile of stones had been piled up nearby. They looked of the same kind and quality, indicating they'd been mined in a quarry somewhere and trucked in by the trogs. It had the looks of a massive undertaking.

Mokshousa furrowed his brow as he took it in. Whatever force had gotten into the goblin armies and organized their activities must have been a genius. He'd never seen trogs accomplish the sorts of things they'd done here.

Nidjiqt pointed to a marker on the far side of the river. "That one there… it is the vaghan boundary, and they are known to defend the other side, though selumari and humans are allowed to pass for trade purposes."

Mokshousa nodded. None of this was new information to him. And then he ducked at a shadow; a mighty troll threw a massive stone into the river, nearly reaching the far bank. It splashed with meteoric impact, and then the waters subsided. A few more boulders followed in rapid succession.

"I'm not sure I understand your plan," Dingarha confessed.

Nidjiqt's corps of monsters began laying tall trees that they'd dragged from the Nhur-Gale Forest. A few floated downriver, but those with an abundance of branches caught on the submerged network of stones they'd seeded the river with. "A floating bridge," the trog explained as his hatchet-wielding minions smoothed off the tops of the surface and then laid another section beyond.

With many trees laid end to end and lashed for support, they finally completed the scaffold and the army began to walk across. They took tenuous footsteps, but the thing held firm. The morehl and trog combined army craved blood, and they would soon get it. Their allies, led by a goblin shaman across the mountains and in the Darksteppes, had assured Mokshousa that they were pushing their mutual prey towards them.

Behind the lava elf invaders followed a massive army of trogs. They funneled towards the choke point as they trickled across. By all indications, they would taste human blood within the day.

"I don't like it," Queen Shyalou exclaimed to her commanders. She mounted her horse as the servants pulled up the tent pegs and hastily packed. "This is the second time in two days we've had to relocate. We are running out of room—soon, our hooves will be back against the Narcea."

Her consort, Cymmeron, grimaced through his thick, black beard. He didn't like it either, but it was necessary. "We are a nomadic people by nature," he began.

"Yes," Shyalou snapped, "So we can chase after game and gather seasonal crops. Not because of enemy movements." She sighed and then straightened her shoulders. "Tell me what happened?"

"Our western forces face an overwhelming army of trogs pouring from the Darksteppes," Cymmeron reported. "Heathyr the oracle barely escaped. She claims they are led by a powerful spellcaster."

The queen scowled. "But the trogs are simpletons. Surely they don't have more magic at their disposal than simple spells and tricks?"

Cymmeron shook his head. "We can no longer underestimate the goblins: neither their stupidity nor their ineptness in battle tactics."

Nearby, Jarra sounded the royal horn, giving the signal to move out. She'd long been the queen's primary aide.

Before the camp finished its hasty preparations, a rider charged towards them, flashing a hand sign to the amazon sentries. His gesture was reserved for one with urgent news for the queen, and her guards let him pass unmolested.

The charger reared up when he reached the queen. Cymmeron had one hand on his sword and grabbed the reins with his other. "State your news!"

Without delay, the rider dropped to the ground and did a quick bow to the queen. The messenger stood and reported. "We are overrun," she said. "Commander Kreelohn has fallen."

Shyalou cocked an eyebrow. "Kreelohn? But she's on the eastern hedge?"

The rider nodded. "A mixed company of trogs and morehl have come across the Narcea River!"

Shock was written all over the queen's face.

Cymmeron cursed. "This was all an elaborate trap." He pointed to the mountains on either side of them. "They've boxed us into Lyander's Pass."

Shyalou drew her spear. "Then we fight. But we must not divide our forces. Suggestions?" she asked.

"Attack east," Cymmeron advised. "The Darksteppes trogs have already established their presence and set a blockade at the pass."

"Bent Morass is a bigger territory," Jarra stated. "Their army will be larger... *and* they've got support from the morehl. I assume they've come from the Grotto, though Karakto is closer."

Cymmeron nodded. "True, but they've got a supply line problem there. Either will have to get their army across the river; that creates a choke point that would limit reinforcements. Also, if we can get east of the pass, we may be able to count on the vagha for support. If we headed west and managed to crack the blockade, perhaps we can call on the coral elves?"

The queen gave it two seconds of thought. "East it is. I don't expect breaking a blockade without help. Jarra, take a few runners. Keep to the mountain trails which the vagha maintain. Rally our support."

"To Hagrond Mount or Gundakhor?" she asked. Either community lay a hundred leagues away, either north or south.

"The smaller clans can do nothing without Gundakhor's approval," she said. "Besides, King Gundraokh has his own problem with trogs and if they have allied with the Grotto, this might be the catalyst needed to draw Gundraokh into the battle."

Jarra nodded. "I will meet you where the pass meets the river in less than a tenday."

Shyalou and Cymmeron saluted her. Jarra commandeered a small collection of scouts, and enough food for a one-way journey. The envoy departed at once.

Jarra and her companions hustled across the slope and had been making good time towards the city of Gundakhor. From their vantage, they could see morehl stationed across the river and all along the road from Lyander's Pass to the vaghan capital.

They now hurried north while led by a dwarf from one of the smaller outpost towns that mined the other mountains on Gundakhor's behalf. She and her entourage grimaced as they stopped at a towering post set deep within the stone of the peak. A braided steel zipline stretched for several leagues through the clouds and into the distance.

She looked from the thick cable and back to the gruff dwarf. "You're sure about this?"

The short and stocky miner laughed and handed her the hand truck with a couple pulleys. "Well, I'd advise ye shave your whiskers afore ye go, but you haven't gotten any. I suppose you'll be fine. The ride will save you a full day's travel or more."

"What is this upper wheel for, here?" Jarra asked, turning the pulley contraption over in her hand.

"It's a backup. In case the primary wheel wears out." He shrugged. "It happens."

Her eyebrows arched. "And if that one breaks, too?"

"Then you'll reach the ground even faster," he chortled.

Jarra shot him a squinty-eyed glare.

He merely shrugged. "Ye said you needed the *quickest* way to Gundakhor, not the *safest*."

The amazon bobbed her head and recognized the truth of it as the dwarf cinched their harnesses and showed them how to operate the handbrake and work the trolley. They'd have to switch lines at a few stations until they arrived in Gundakhor.

As the humans edged up to the cliff-side and clung to the safety rope, the vagha laughed. He kicked them over the edge and listened to them howl as they zipped away and into the misty, distant reaches. Jarra's nerves calmed and the three humans finally grew accustomed to the high speed travel. On their last trip down they took in the dazzling sights of Mount Gundakhor's eastern slope. North of the walled city, they could see the pitched battle where goblins poured from the mottled greens and ochre of the Waterblight, a swamp that rode the seam between the eternal forests of the Feylands and the rocky face of the sa'Eldurim mountain range.

More worrisome than the goblin hordes emerging from the Waterblight was the dark mass of red on the eastern slope of the plains beyond Gundakhor's boundary line. Thousands of morehl mustered into cohorts and seemed angled so they could charge on the vagha city at a moment's notice. Jarra could see them building some kind of towering contraptions. He suspected trebuchets.

They couldn't be building them here to use against humans in the south. They're building siege engines for an imminent attack on Gundakhor!

The trio of humans finally touched down on the landing above the city's main body. Jarra was simply glad that her trolley had not failed. A few dwarven guards briefly interrogated them.

"Please," she pleaded. "Time is of the essence. We've got to see King Gundraokh. I am here on urgent business from Queen Shyalou."

The dwarves waived her off and pointed beyond the curtain wall. The king's vermillion, caped mantle flagged as he swung his axe, leading his company of elite warriors. His son and heir, Eldurokh sa'Gundraokh, fought alongside him. The prince's decidedly less grayed beard flapped as he split trogs like cordwood.

Peering at the battle, the vagha commented, "He'll be done in a minute. Looks like the trogs' rear forces are retreating and leaving this lot to die." He cast a mischievous look towards a spotter on the tower. "How about we send them a little further back?"

The dwarf sighted down a rangefinder and called out distances and a set of degrees.

Just as the forward battle line of the trogs broke rank and fled, their guide called, "Now!"

The distinct sounds of a counterweight dropping caught their attention. Gundakhor was not without its own trebuchets, and they flung several massive stones over their wall in unison. The huge slabs of precisely weighed granite smashed the formations of the gathered trogs and sent them routing into the swamp and under the cover of the trees.

"They'll be back in the morning," their vaghan guide assured them. He ushered Jarra and her companions into an antechamber adjacent to the throne room where food was all being placed at a banquet table, and a few kegs of ale were set and tapped.

Jarra looked at their host. "How did you know that…"

He waved her off with a shrug. "Ain't fer you. Fighting always makes the king hungry," he grinned. The door opened as he spoke, and the king entered.

Gundraokh and Eldurokh nearly collapsed into their seats at the head of the table and began eating immediately, ignoring the humans in the room. Someone placed two mugs in front of Gundraokh and two for his son.

Jarra spoke up. "Greetings on behalf of Queen Shyalou," she bowed in a stately manner.

Gundraokh's face was dark, but he waved Jarra and her companions closer and offered them the nearest seats.

"Thank you," she exclaimed, taking her seat. "We are in dire need of support, King Gundraokh. Our defenses are overrun, and goblins have us hemmed in on both sides of Lyander's Pass."

He scowled. "As ye can see, I have goblins on my own doorstep right now. I can hardly afford to send an army out to support ye with an obvious lava elf issue whelming in the east… there's something different about *these* trogs. They're smarter. Something, or someone, is leading them." He took a huge bite and washed it down with a slug of ale.

"It's true," Eldurokh spoke for his father while he ate. "Something about the way they attack to test our defenses and then withdraw before they can take the worst of it. And they been doing it for years." He motioned to a dwarf a ways down the table who had set his spell caster's headdress aside for the meal. "Druoqe did the math and made some estimates. He thinks they've made their regular attacks to make us complacent; they been keeping most of their forces in reserves and just waited for the right timing… building a secret army."

"And now with morehl on our doorstep, too," Gundraokh shook his head. "I'm afraid you simply have to retake and hold the southern land up to Narcea. That has always been your people's duty. Trogs aren't even great swimmers. I can't see how your cavalry can't overrun some goblins who managed to cross the river…"

"The morehl are also at *our* east border—*your southern line.*"

The king dropped his fork with a clatter.

Jarra continued. "The trogs are in league with the Obsidian Grotto, we think. They and the forces of Bent Morass have built a bridge over the Narcea. If we fall, they will together pin you down." Jarra frowned. "We can no longer hold the border without additional support. We suffered heavy losses in the Crechelands during the migration, and the Darksteppes goblins followed us into the pass. Something has stirred all the four swamp kingdoms at once and unleashed a storm of goblins."

"And now the spider sends feelers out of her lair," Gundraokh growled. "A little too convenient if you ask me."

Jarra nodded. "We are in an impossible situation. We cannot stay where we are and must either loop around the Mezzoscarps or simply sail south and abandon the Birthlands altogether. Either way, we were the buffer for Gundakor and Hagrond Mount and our absence will leave a vacuum these enemies will fill."

Gundraokh frowned and pushed his plate away. He looked out the window and saw the morehl building their war machines. "Sshkkryyahr overplays her hand. She may have a massive army, but for her to reach this far means it will be stretched too thin to keep it maintained. Surely the rest of Esfah sees that she tries to claim the Duar'Bondeen Steppes, and take half the Crechelands with this move? I've no word yet if she's taken the East Coast, but we might assume the selumari have fallen."

He turned and looked at Jarra. "Return to your people. Tell Shyalou that I'll call the vagha from every city between here and the Pass and they'll come to your aide. But you must not stop once you reach her. Your riders are fastest. Dispatch messages to any other clans of your people and to the selumari. Those allied with Hagond Mount will surely respond, and I know we can count on Emmira… exactly *how much* support they will lend you depends on where Karakto stands in all of this. They've never been beholden to the Grotto; let us hope their jealousy of them has kept it that way."

Gundraokh raised his second mug and saluted his warriors. "To the fall of Sshkkryyahr the Dread. We'll put our axes up her backside afore this is over."

The battle weary dwarves cheered. "It's about bleedin' time," Ruthak quipped as the cheer died down.

"We must rally to Gundakhor," the king told Jarra. "Gather provisions and leave immediately. I've got a plan rattlin' around in me head, but I'll need all ye to arrive as soon as possible to make it work. If Gundakor falls, so will every kingdom from here to the Daurhedge—and none else will last long."

Jarra nodded solemnly. She and her escorts ate quickly and then got to work.

Wehge stalked through the shrubs. He had caked mud all over his blue flesh to help conceal him in the troglands. He kept two knit hats pulled over his head. One he had knitted, and the other was woven for him many years ago by Shella, the other coral elf Master Sage. Together, they channeled the will of the gods Ailuril and Aguarehl. Only with both caps did the fabric contain the bright glow of his eidolon protector, a swarm of sprites.

The selumari did not enjoy venturing this deep into the waterblight. He had been chasing the phantom spirit for over two centuries. And it knew that he was here, somewhere. Wehge and Surfeibese, one of the powerful totem spirits of Lord Death—*one of his faces*—sensed each other's moves and countermoves as if seated across a table from each other while playing stones.

He'd played patiently, following the enemy for a long time. Wehge sensed several traps laid for him over the decades and refused to engage. He was loath to trade his life for the removal of the great evil. Wehge knew he had never been particularly brave, but he would have sacrificed himself if Ailuril willed it. There were so few sages left in the world, and his goddess did not demand his life.

Shouldering a cold and damp shawl of burlap over his body as a disguise, Wehge entered the thick of the goblin village. He'd never gotten this close to Surfeibese, and he knew that it was now or never. Something had recently taken firm hold of the trogs' attention, and he used that to his advantage. Wehge had also never seen the goblin population so thin; only children and breeding wives remained, poking out of their dilapidated shanties. Those whelps not quite old enough to fight perched upon the rooftops and crude observation towers to watch their armies' movements.

Wehge drew close to a tent made of heavy, soiled fabrics. Skulls of foes and mighty animals adorned the posts. Foul symbols were carved into them and painted brightly. They dedicated this tent to Death as holy ground, a tabernacle for their shaman, Surfeibese.

The disguised selumari peeked around the dwelling for any prying eyes and then slipped inside the canvas walls. Fire burned in a pit in the center of the wicked sanctuary. Beyond it, a torch blazed on either side of a throne constructed of bones. A trog sat upon it, naked except for a necklace of bone that held his cape on, and a headdress made of hands; many of them were vagha and a few selumari, but there were trog hands as well.

"Ah, the sage. We finally meet at last." Surfeibese leaned forward and rested his chin on steepled fingers. He saw the intruder staring at the headgear. "Made from the hands of any who tried to lay a hand against me." He grinned, baring yellowed, half rotted teeth. "Your hands will be my most precious. We have played this cat-and-mouse game for such a long time, my friend."

"You are not my friend."

"Come now, Wehge, Master Sage of Ailuril... how long have we danced? Surely we know each other better than most lovers," Surfeibese cackled. He stood and set his headdress down upon the chair.

The goblin shaman walked slowly towards Wehge. The hairy cape, made of enemy scalps sewn together, dragged on the dirt floor behind him. "You play this game too cautiously. Why, my brothers have already been killed multiple times over by your peers, rising again each time in a new form... so I scarcely know the rules... am I winning or losing?"

He closed the distance. The trog stench was nearly overwhelming as Surfeibese lifted his arms wide and exposed his chest to the enemy. "Do it. Drive your dagger into my heart. Kill me and I will simply find a new acolyte."

"You lie," Wehge said. "If I kill you, this madness ends and I can return to the Feylands."

Surfeibese pressed his talons to his own chest and splayed his fingers as if making a target to strike. "Then here is my heart, Master Sage. Strike deep and true. Let us learn the rules together."

Wehge hesitated, unsure what trickery the cagey shaman was up to. Finally, he snatched his dagger from within the folds of his makeshift robe and stabbed it as deeply as he could into Surfeibese.

The goblin cackled and fell into the fire pit, laughing as his sickly yellow blood shot out from the wound in ragged spurts. It soon stopped altogether.

After wiping the blood clean, Wehge sheathed his dagger. He scowled.

Surfeibese had been right. He sensed the wicked one's presence far off. The spirit found a new host somewhere else in the Waterblight, and Wehge was no longer sure how he could stop this evil. The selumari ducked his head out of the black tabernacle and returned to hiding in the forest in desperate search of his next move.

Stragek shouted orders from the rear of the trog battle cluster. He wore the red hat, a slouchy kind of knit cap that designated him as the command leader of the military. Stragek was not a warrior and never had been. His strength was that of his belief in the power of Death's chosen acolyte.

Because of his communion with Surfeibese, Stragek knew how the master wanted the battle to play out. Something had changed and he no longer felt that connection. Something severed his bond.

Stragek rubbed his temples, frustrated with the sudden silence. He realized after a few moments that everyone was looking at him. Some of his underlings were shouting his name.

The goblin war commander shook his head and looked at the field of battle. Moments ago, they had been fighting the vagha a few hundred cubits from the city wall, but his army now stood in disarray.

"What do we do, Stragek? What says the master?"

He wordlessly worked his mouth and looked over the blood-splattered territory painted with trog yellows and vaghan reds. The dwarves were in rout; they'd all retreated back inside the gates. The last of them slipped inside, running at what passed for a sprint from a dwarf.

Stragek tried one last time find to find the connection, but to no avail. "Shields up!" he howled. "Prepare for archery fire." He stood just outside range, and so had no need. Curiously, no deadly bolts rained over the wall.

"The main gates are still opened," he shouted. "Charge forward! Take the city!" He was surprised by the stroke of luck; some dwarf somewhere had either forgotten to drop the portcullis or perhaps the inner mechanisms had broken.

Stragek noticed his army moved with skepticism, so he added, "Surfeibese wills it! The city is ours!"

With the kind of zeal that only blind religion can produce, goblins sprinted towards the Great North Gate of Gundakhor. They funneled into a sharp angle, ready to split the wall wide open with their wedge.

Right before they got to the entry, pairs of mammoths rushed out from within. Each pair had a spiked chain attached to their inner tusk, and they spread out as they passed the gate, dragging the deadly line of spiked iron between them. They cut down huge swaths of trogs like a razor mowing down scraggly hairs. Six sets of the beasts hacked his forward army to pieces.

Stragek growled. He had monsters in reserve; they could take down the mammoths, but they were out of place. The commander snarled and signaled for retreat, unwilling to take such heavy losses until he had a plan to deal with the mammoths.

With the trogs in rout and their dead piled in broken, stinking mounds, the mammoths turned back to Gundakhor. Dwarven missiles finally began, and without the trogs thinking to raise their shields.

Stragek howled commands, but none of his troops noticed, they were too busy fleeing the front line even as the deadly hail began. The commander stared with shocked eyes— but his connection to Surfeibese suddenly reignited. He looked up as the quarrels began pounding into dirt and flesh. He caught the sight of a warrior named Otark and noticed the unholy light glowing behind his pupils. "Otark. Otark, are you the prophet?"

The trog named Otark looked at Stragek with glazed eyes as if they saw far more than any trog could. "Otark is gone. Only Surfeibese remains."

Stragek swallowed. "My lord. Command me."

"Prepare your monsters... *and move*," Surfeibese ordered.

"Move?" The way he'd said it confused Stragek.

Surfeibese frowned as he took several steps backwards. Stragek cocked his head, still unsure of the meaning. A shadow fell over him and a split second later a massive slap of stone, hurled by a vaghan trebuchet, smashed him to paste.

Otark scowled as he searched for another goblin with a red cap, but none of them were nearby. The army scattered in disarray and fled back to the edges of the swamp, buying the dwarves at least one days' worth of breathing space before the trogs could ready their next attack.

With King Gundraokh still running his city's defenses, Prince Eldurokh departed Gundakhor. He led a small band of dwarves on ponies as they charged from around the bend of the mountain pass. They'd chosen ponies instead of riding lizards or mammoths to ensure that they would not be seen. Larger mounts would make them visible to the morehl across the river. Before the river-wall ended, they'd merged onto a trail that wound through the mountains and remained hidden from prying eyes.

Eldurokh's troops were only sixty vagha warriors, but they were each worth at least a dozen morehl, or twenty trogs.

Coming over the last ridge at a full gallop, Eldurokh howled a battle cry. Startled morehl soldiers barely had time to turn and see the slaughter that befell them as the dwarven troops crashed through their north flank at the mouth of Lyander's pass.

Without suffering a single casualty, the vagha fought their way through until they met up with the humans and bolstered the army with their meager numbers. Eldurokh was quickly met by Cymmeron and Shyalou. Jarra followed the vagha and knelt before her queen.

"Thank you so much for your aid," Shyalou said.

Cymmeron frowned, though, as another two hundred morehl filled in the gap where the dwarves had slaughtered the surprised elves. "Is this all you brought? Surely it's not enough."

"We're enough to get ye through until we punch our way through that line and escort your troops to Gundakhor." Eldurokh winked. "We dwarves are in dire need. The city will be overrun with goblins by the time we get back. They'll find the city deserted."

Cymmeron cocked his head, not sure what the vagha could be talking about. Jarra caught the confused look on his face.

"Cymmeron, Let me introduce Eldurokh, prince of King Gundraokh," Jarra said.

"Dunna worry that dainty beard on yer face, Cymmeron," Eldurokh said. "We sent ravens on ahead of ourselves." The dwarf grinned and then rushed back to the battle lines as the overwhelming lava elf forces burgeoned around them.

What seemed like only minutes later, battle horns sounded from the hills, and dwarf troops poured from the mountains. What sounded like an echo turned out to be another pocket of soldiers sent by another mining camp, and then another. Each siren turned the morehl as vagha came down from the hills and cut deeper into their flanks. Shortly after, a series of long, loud horns blew; the ground rumbled as a massive dwarf army, second only to the one fielded by Gundakhor, emerged at the south side of the pass.

Eldurokh turned his head from killing lava elves. Blood had splattered across his face and reddened his beard. "That'd be our kin from Hagrond Mount!"

Beside the prince, Cymmeron hacked apart a couple lava elves and smiled.

Eldurokh chuckled. "And ye thought me cocky enough to believe even the best sixty of we dwarves enough to kill these bastards. Ha!"

Cymmeron shrugged. "The only dwarves I've ever known have been cocksure."

The prince grinned. "Likewise."

With the arrival of the army at the south, the morehl finally had to fight defensively.

"All right boys, this is what we talked about," Eldurokh howled. "All vagha to East line—stoneskin formation!" They left the amazon army to clean up the shattered morehl lines while they stacked a horizontal vanguard of shields two units tall. Vaghan spell casters quickly formed up nearby and conjured their magic, turning the skin of the shield bearers as stony as the nearby mountains, ensuring protection from even the cursed bullets of the morehl. More vagha joined the formation as they arrived from Hagrond Mount, and the wall of protection only grew.

Any amazons not killing stray lava elves or maintaining the west battlefront against the relentless advance of trogs from the Darksteppes, formed up behind the barrier. They had finally earned a moment of respite.

True to form, the morehl in retreat peppered the line with bullets, and a cloud of blue haze obscured the banks of the Narcea River as the elves reformed with their backs to the makeshift bridge. Only the *clang* and *spang* of bullets turned aside by dwarven shields met their ears. As the smoke of so much gunpowder cleared, a hail of amazon javelins rained down as counter-fire and skewered the bulk of the army. What was left sprinted back to the Marsh at the far side.

Both dwarves and humans cheered as the enemy fled. Among the foliage of the marsh, the mixed army of trogs and morehl could be seen retreating, moving swifter with the presence of a proper road.

"I know you appreciate the breath of fresh air, Queen Shyalou," said Eldurokh, "but we must make haste to arrive at Gundakhor as soon as possible. Ye may have thought me jesting when we arrived this morning—but my father has hatched a mad plan… not just to prop up his city, but to knock that pompous drider right out of her hole, or else bring the whole mountain down upon her head. My kin from Hagrond Mount will leave a strong enough crew to batten down the pass and dismantle that bridge to secure the south in the meanwhile."

The Queen looked so weary when she turned to him. She frowned, knowing they would have to surrender the western line to the trogs. "He really risked Gundakhor for our behalf?"

Eldurokh bobbed his head towards Jarra. "She knows the truth of it. And her part's not yet done in this. Some of our birds don't have receivers in some places—namely Emmira."

"He speaks truly," Jarra nodded.

Queen Shyalou took a moment to collect her thoughts. Then she instructed Cymmeron, "Sound the signal. We ride for Gundakhor." The warrior queen stepped into her chariot and slumped her shoulders. She was so tired and knew her horses were too—but tired was better than dead. *We can always rest inside the walls of Gundakhor.*

Days ago, the goblin who had once been called Otark took charge of the army. He had finally found a trog wearing a red cap and strangled him in order to take it.

Surfeibese kept well out of the way of vaghan war machines as he directed the army and continued to soften the defenses of the northern side of the great city. He'd already redeployed ten trolls to the front where they could lie in wait in case Gundakhor unleashed a similar trick as they'd done before with their mammoths.

Two days ago, the morehl received a raven from their southern line reporting that the dwarves had come to the rescue of the humans in the pass and routed the lava elves in the pass. That surely meant that the city walls were less manned. They had begun assaulting the defenses with their trebuchets almost immediately. Most of them threw stones at the walls; some of them threw burning bales over it.

Surfeibese grinned. Though his lava elf allies had suffered great losses, the city's defensive force was wearing down. Gundraokh's splitting of their forces would prove costly.

Still, even a handful of dwarves operating from within their stronghold could prove a powerful thing, especially with strategists like Gundraokh and his kin among them. Already, on the first day, return fire from vaghan war machines had decimated most of the lava elves' war engines. The vagha had measured and aligned them for precision targeting with weighted loads and exact calculations, forcing the morehl to move their weapons closer and further after every shot to try and keep the enemy from zeroing in on them with mathematical targeting calculations. Still, the vagha destroyed the trebuchets almost as quickly as they could be rebuilt.

More weapons came from Valis. Soon they would have enough to bring down even a dwarven wall and they would rip Gundakhor from the side of the mountain. Surfeibese expected that with the vagha's attention redirected to the lava elves, they could finally press for the attack that he truly wanted.

He gave the signal and trogs poured forth, carrying shields and a massive length of tree they'd braved the edges of the Feylands in order to collect. What goblins lacked in finesse, they made up for with overwhelming hordes, and they had been building to this moment for generations.

A line of trogs rushed forward with the battering ram and began beating on the north gates. They smashed, over and over. Hot oil fell from the parapets and dwarven magic set many of them ablaze. Goblin sorcerers returned what they received and troops fell on both sides, but the gate held firm.

The assault continued for days, a dull monotony of relentless pounding. The vagha's resistance eventually dwindled to nothing as attrition whittled down the numbers and as dwarves redeployed against the morehl. The north gate was no longer defended and, sometime during the night, even the dwarven war machines had quit. Morehl engines flung their stones as if reluctant and holding its breath in anticipation of a return fire that never came.

Finally, the trogs breached the gate and their battering ram busted through. They pulled it back and readied against an expected ground assault. But it never came.

A goblin scout snuck through the fissure and returned thirty minutes later to report directly to Surfeibese. "Abandoned," he insisted. "It smelled like vagha—that stink can only be burned away… but not a soul remained inside the city. They have given it up. They didn't even bother to drop the portcullis. The filthy dwarves must have fled in terror of your majesty."

Death's acolyte smiled. "Sound the alarm. We take the city."

The goblins marched forward and two trolls pried the doors off their moorings and tossed them aside to find it exactly as described; Gundakhor was a ghost town. They walked through the outer streets with no felt urgency.

At the rear of the forces, Surfeibese paused. He sensed the selumari sage somewhere nearby, stalking him. "Advance without me," he commanded. "I must dispose of a different, nearby threat while I yet have the chance."

Goblins meandered through the empty streets of Gundakhor. They had first rushed in expecting some kind of resistance—stragglers in the street, even. Then they walked, cautious and hesitant. Now, they milled about, curious and exploring. Some played with vaghan baubles, others stole trinkets or tools before their peers could claim them.

The only noise they heard was a constant grinding sound emanating from the central castle structure, and the steady thump-crack of the siege stones where the morehl pounded at the eastern wall. Trogs penetrated deeper and deeper, thinning their forces as they spread out.

Suddenly, the air split with the peal of a battle horn from the south side of the city. The goblins stiffened momentarily and then relaxed: there was fight yet to be had in the city. And then the call was suddenly taken up all over Gundakhor. A sharp rattle came from the north gate where hidden vagha at the wall dropped the portcullis, trapping much of the army within. The barred, vertical gate smashed a troll who stood in the entry and the gate chopped him in two. A dwarven spell caster summoned Firiel's power and lit the monster ablaze so he could not rise again.

All around the city, dwarves popped out of homes and hidden cloisters. They attacked, catching the enemy off guard. Whole platoons of goblins fell until they rallied together and reformed into something of a fighting force.

[These are not soldiers,] one of the commanders yelled in the ugly speech of the marsh. [These are the woman, children, and the weak,] he snarled. [Turn and fight! We cannot lose to the dwarven dregs.]

As soon as the trogs saw the truth of it, they began flooding the city again, giving chase. And then the first mammoth stormed through the streets followed by amazon chariots as the humans and dwarves returned from Lyander's Pass through the south gate with half the forces of Hagrond Mount at their sides.

The vagha and their allies swept the streets with vicious speed as they caught the enemy off guard. Any force that tried to gain an angle on the new-coming cavalry became targets from the dwarven citizen defenders who fired crossbows from inside their homes or on their rooftops. All vagha in Gundakhor had at least some combat training for this exact scenario.

[Fall back! Regroup with Surfeibese,] the call went up.

Trogs fled for the north gate where the army pinned them against the portcullis. They realized too late that half of the army was trapped inside the walls and half outside. The interior unit was quickly mowed down by the influx of southern allies while the remainder snarled at the gates. One red-capped trog in particular hurled nasty insults and then sent much of the remaining army to join the vanguard of lava elves.

Surfeibese howled curses upon the dwarves. [Together with the morehl, we *will* sack this city.]

"What is that horrible sound?" Queen Shyalou asked, finally resting her horse in the aftermath of the skirmish through Gundakhor. The droning, grating sound disagreed with her; she and her people were used to the quiet of the plains.

Eldurokh pointed to a tower just within the inner wall of his father's keep. "Earth mover. It's an elevator system we sometimes use in the mines. The King had one set up here."

A catwalk ran from along the tower to the wall where a chained drive moved hunks of stone that poured regularly from the tower as it pulled earth from deep below. It dumped scree along the perimeter of the royal grounds. "It's all part of the plan," Eldurokh said, leading the queen and her inner circle into the keep and around the back where it abutted a cliff-side. A gaping cavern yawned open before them as if some kind of giant worm had burrowed directly into it.

Dwarven solders posted nearby signaled their relief that the prince had returned to rout the goblins. Their work had required almost every able-bodied vagha that could be found within the city.

"Our apologies for the crudeness of it," Eldurokh said. "We haven't the time for proper craftsmanship."

Cymmeron furrowed his brow as a vagha came running from around the palace. "Still, I wonder, what is it?"

The dwarven runner handed Eldurokh a fistful of tiny, curled papers: the kind that were often tied to the legs of messenger birds. He scanned them and grinned, wagging his beard. "Jarra was successful in Emmira," the prince mumbled before returning his attentions to Queen Shyalou. "I know you amazons don't typically like venturing below ground for a variety of reasons... but let me show you what we have planned."

Arriving ahead of the lava elf army as it returned to the larger battle group, Mokshousa narrowed his eyes at the commander left in charge. "How have you not yet breached the gate?" Mokshousa snapped as he dismounted from his wearied spider mount.

The forward commander stumbled over his answer. "The dwarves have been knocking out our war machines with trebuchets hidden behind their walls... how are you here? I thought you were leading the charge against the south wall so we could crush Gundakhor from three directions?"

Mokshousa glowered at the trogs which now made up a newly arranged collective of goblin battalions. *Three directions, indeed.*

"That route has become impossible… and I have been watching the battle for two hours on my approach—I've not seen a single stone fly from the city," Mokshousa snarled. "How you've managed to fail to breach by this time is beyond me. You are relieved of command—I'm in charge here, now!"

The forward commander drew his rapier with a hiss and then fell over dead. He convulsed with spasms and his skin blanched as his mouth frothed. Dingarha lowered his hands and shrugged after his spell ended with the morehl dead on the ground. "We don't have time to bicker if we are to claim the city for the glory of our lord."

Mokshousa shouted orders to the gunners aiming their siege engines. "All batteries, forget the walls and fire on those gates!"

With nearly all the artillery towers rebuilt, they fired at the barricades in rapid fire succession. Most landed close and busted against the thick walls of the vaghan stronghold. One of the stones hit the doors dead center and crushed them wholly before bounce-rolling through the inner wall and demolishing dwarven homes.

The lava elves cheered and immediately began charging across the approach to the city with their shields held high. A hail of vagha crossbow fire rained down from the barbican outposts arranged along the battlement wall.

Trolls carried lumber as they rushed to the front of the line on long strides. They would prop up the portcullis to ensure that the passage remained open.

A final rain of stone fell from the dwarven trebuchets, and boulders fell to the battlefield. They rolled over morehl infantry, crushing them to a steaming paste.

The ground between the lava elf trebuchets began to tremble and then buckled, erupting right in the middle of the lava elves' mustered forces. An enormous sinkhole opened, and a crew of umberhulks leapt out. They snapped and lashed out at the enemy with pincers attached to their massive digging claws.

Before the morehl even knew what hit them, the tunnel poured forth hundreds of dwarven warriors to secure the exit. Then the cavalry emerged on mammoth and lizard, accompanied by amazon chariots. The charging morehl suddenly faltered, and many fell to the archers on the walls.

Mokshousa screamed orders to his troops, rallying them and solidifying any slipping resolve. "Take the city, you fools! It is sparsely defended." He leapt onto his spider and whirled towards the battle, wishing the beast was one of their larger mounts so he could take down the mammoths that suddenly wreaked such havoc. "We still outnumber them," he screamed, bolstering his red kindred. "Attack!"

As the invading half of his forces passed the edge of the Narcea river, the water erupted in spray and wave as Gundraokh's selumari allies leapt into the fray. Wet, blue elves charged into the flank of the surprised lava elves. They continued to pour forth from their hiding spot where they'd secretly moved up river from Emmira on the coast with all the speed they could muster.

Towering coral giants lumbered out from the deep and stomped upon the bewildered enemy as they advanced across the battlefield, followed by armored, octopoid tako which whirled into battle with their myriad arms and walking upon tentacles. Even a scaly leviathan emerged and coiled around many of the wicked elves, engulfing several of them whole.

With the dwarves and the humans now so close to the heart of the morehl army, they tore through the belly of the invaders, causing total disarray. Those with riding mounts began to flee back towards their northern stronghold. The lava elf infantry was caught, helpless to escape the speed of the human charioteers, and the remaining trogs who had not joined the foremost vanguard slinked back into the swamp before they could be engaged. The tide of battle had shifted in favor of Gundakhor.

Mokshousa and Dingarha screeched for their minions not to flee, but most soldiers with the capacity to do so had already fled in the direction of old Valis, *the Black Forest*. Finally, recognizing the futility of remaining, they, too, turned their mounts and joined their routed peers.

Both stiffened just in time to spot the mounted dwarves charging for them. Neither had time to react as Warlord Ruthak and King Gundraokh leaned from the sides of their mammoths and swung their axes, lopping off the pair of leaders' heads and scattering the morehl into further disarray.

Gundraokh tapped the first keg and announced that a feast ought to be observed with immediate effect. The bodies of friend and foe could be buried or burned later. For now, his people needed to celebrate the victory and pause for rest.

He grumbled before slugging back the first mug, "Gods know the war is far from over. We need to mark the wins when we can and the dead will wait for us."

"Certainly, they will," Ruthak commented, sidling up alongside him with Eldurokh. "T'aint like them bodies could get up and wander back to their masters."

As Eldurokh poured his own mug, Ruthak grabbed his king by the wrist and examined Gundraokh's arm. He frowned. "The petrification is spreading," he said in a low voice.

Gundraokh nodded measuredly and mumbled, "It seems that the harder I fight, the more of me it claims."

Their human and coral elf companions had finally located the vagha leaders and gathered near. The king clapped shoulders with Reesime and Nerlov whom he'd known for a couple centuries, since his adventuring days when Gundakhor had been known as Orelod… since before finding the Bands of Turambar that now petrified his skin.

"What is the next step?" Shyalou asked.

King Gundraokh retrieved a few paper scraps that had arrived from birds sent by allies far off and away. He struggled to unfurl them; he'd lost some ability to manipulate fine things with his unfeeling fingers.

Ruthak took the messages and managed them for him.

"We must depose the drider. The Birthlands will know no peace while she still lives in the Obsidian Grotto. The smaller vaghan tribes will handle the goblins of the Darksteppes and we have the forces of Hagrond Mount at our disposal." Gundraokh frowned, "Maris-ta-Sehlim has declined to send aide at this time. They claim to be overrun with trogs of their own that are pouring out of Brackishomme… but we have the support of the selumari at Lago Rosa and Farnoch who've wanted to temper the Grotto's fire for years. If we strike, they pledge to engage from the east."

His selumari companions asked, "Will it be enough to throw the monster down?"

King Gundraokh nodded slowly. "I think… I hope… this might be just enough," he insisted. "We must harden our resolve and take the fight all the way back to that nefarious beast."

He stuck his hand in to the center of the clustered leaders; stony skin puckered slightly as he made a fist. "We make a pact, here. Let us see this thing through to the end."

Shyalou and Cymmeron laid their hands over his. Ruthak and Eldurokh laid theirs over his, followed by the selumari generals. "Until the end," they agreed.

King Gundraokh nodded slowly, though in his heart, he felt that this war was likely to claim his life by the end.

Sshkkryyahr sat upon the ebon throne deep within the Crooked Spine. Even her praetorian guard wilted before the creature that approached her. The drider rose and examined the cadaverous selumari who walked towards her. She knew what it was and had foreseen his coming.

"I come on behalf of Lord Death," said the undead warrior. His blue skin had paled many shades and his cheeks had sunken, sallow, but he looked powerful despite his condition. Everything about his nature exuded an aura of decay and the stench of the grave clung to him; if ever Sshkkryyahr met a fellow worshiper of her lord, this was one.

The drider grinned wickedly and steepled her fingers. "Hail Lord Death." Sshkkryyahr put one fist across her breast in typical morehl salute and gave a subtle bow appropriate for an Empress entertaining a foreign dignitary. "Where do you come from and where do you go?"

"I am Leisterbane of Lurneville… formerly a great city of Charnock. I am the herald of Melkior the Champion, and a true Child of Death. Where I go is my business, drider, but I bear a gift for you from Lord Death. Your army seems to be ruled by fear. It is ineffective."

Sshkkryyahr raised an eyebrow. "You know my army…"

"I have *seen* your army in action and I passed it by as I journeyed here towards the northern islands. I watched as it was routed by the dwarves and humans. Twice." He recognized the surprise on her face. "I assume you ought to be receiving word of it at any moment. It's been many days since the second loss… likely that same fear I describe has delayed the Black Forest from sending a raven."

The drider's lip curled with rage.

Leisterbane produced a glass flask of black, roiling fluid. "The gift of Death. This is the necralluvium, the blood of decay; the ichor has been growing since our lord gave it. With this, you could raise an army immune to fear. One that will never grow weary."

The undead creature placed the bottle in her hand, turned and departed. Before he made a full exit, he spoke over his shoulder. "Lord Death has favored you, and even now his four acolytes prepare a blessing in your honor. I expect you have the fate of the Birthlands well in hand to achieving our mutual purpose."

She gave him a spider-legged curtsy, and then the fiend was gone. Sshkkryyahr's praetorian troops finally relaxed. The only hint that he had ever been there was the foul, lingering odor of the dead.

Surfeibese stood beneath a shawl of hanging moss in the edges of the bald cypress where the Waterblight petered out and formed firm ground. The area formed a border near the marker stones of the Feylands and the Duar'Bondeen Steppes.

"I can feel you stalking me, Master Sage of Aguarehl," he said aloud. "But you will not claim me before Death's army is propped up and a wave of darkness advances from the Obsidian Grotto and overtakes the whole of the world."

He sneered. "Certainly you have felt it… the gods of nature propped up Champions to defend them against the coming great evil. And then Lord Death corrupted them from within and created his own Champion, a true son of the wicked path. In throwing him down, the remaining Champions sacrificed themselves like fools, leaving none to defend you against the coming tide."

With goblins surrounding him at his back, Surfeibese turned and stared into the trees, wondering if his selumari antagonist lay somewhere beyond him. Likely, he could hear the possessed trog.

"I feel the master's call," he said. "A new thing is about to happen—and by the time you understand mine and my brothers' purpose, you will be too late to prevent it." The leader of the Waterblight turned and abandoned his army, leaving the confused trogs to watch as their chief shaman simply left them behind.

Surfeibese entered the flatlands and began his long journey east through the steppes.

The Fall of the Obsidian Grotto
Pt. 2
The Knife's Edge

Blort stomped through the underbrush. His filthy feet splashed in the musty water. "Come on, Shurbnik. I don't want to get caught between villages because you're too slow to keep up."

"Aren't you an eager little minion?" Shurbnik insulted him. "You just want to be the one who carries that note on behalf of Noxigant? Yer just dying to be a hero."

"I really don't want to be killed by the ghost of the Wind Whisperer," Blort insisted. "They say he still haunts the Brackishomme, taking any poor trogs caught in the remote deeps too late at night." He gulped and looked up. Rhaudian's moonlight bathed the swamp in its pale tones.

"Children's tales," Shurbnik argued. "Are you a child, Blort?"

"I've seen bodies," Blort said. "The Wind Whisperer is a selumari ghost. He takes goblin heads to fill his horse cart and fulfill a cursed vow. Ye've never seen one of the headless bodies they sometimes find in the sloughs?"

"There's no such things as ghosts. Once yer dead, that's it, ye filthy gerk! It's to the Deadzone with ye after."

"Not true! I hear rumors of the dead rising again. Have ye not heard the news out of Charnock?"

Shurbnik glowered at him. "We ain't got time to bicker about in the thick tanglenests, ye dolt. An' I don't care who gets the glory—orders is orders, and all the chieftains need to get their note or Noxigant will flay our hides and drag us through a devilant hive."

They hurried along the marshy trail for a few minutes when a stick cracked in the foliage. Shurbnik drew a crude ax from the belt at his hip and they walked with a lighter step. Then they spotted it. The selumari ghost.

Cloaked in the darkness, pale blue ears that ended in points peeked beyond the hood. The figure stood resolute, blocking their path.

"The Wind Whisperer," Blort whispered with reverence.

"Ain't nothing but some fool who's about to become supper!" Shurbnik growled and then he charged with his weapon held high.

The selumari's blade flashed twice, and the trog collapsed face first in the mud. Both of his arms lay on the ground beside him. He blinked with disbelief when he saw them and then shrieked and thrashed in the mud.

Blort whirled around to flee, but crashed into a towering, squid-like creature. It immediately wrapped its tentacles around him and held him firm.

Pulling back the hood, the ghost revealed herself. Shella the Master Sage snatched the note from Blort and gave it a read. She frowned, and then rolled up the crude paper, slipping it inside her vest pocket.

She made a clucking noise and her monstrous eidolon held Blort out to her. With one smooth stroke, she severed his head. The tako grabbed it by the hair and flung it into the filmy water beyond and then the pair surrounded Shurbnik.

The trog hyperventilated, but managed a gasp. "You... you're real. The Wind Whisperer!"

"And I have a reputation to uphold." Shella dragged her sword across the creature's neck and then threw his head into the bushes. She cleaned her blade and sheathed it.

"Come on," she insisted to her friend. "We've got to get to the rulers of Maris-ta-Sehlim as soon as possible." Shella didn't need to talk. The tako would wordlessly follow her anywhere, but she found it helped her to retain her sanity.

"I've killed Noxigant's host sixteen times in as many decades and held the horde at bay... but I fear that I am no longer enough, and ever since the totem spirit took the warlord Kregtert as host, he's proved cagier than I can manage."

Kregtert had already been a respected and feared trog who had verged on unifying all the quarrelsome, scattered goblin families of the Brackishomme. He'd nearly gotten them all on the same page, and the letter in her pocket was a call for the thing Shella had been trying to avoid all these years: an all-out attack by the trogs upon Maris-ta-Sehlim.

If she could get to the city council in time, they would be able to prepare against the coming hordes. Luckily, she knew the fastest route to the city and, with advanced warning and the outline of the trogs rudimentary battle plan sketched by Kregtert's own hand, they would have enough notice to do some real damage.

Shella scowled as the moon slipped towards the horizon. She could feel Noxigant's foul presence far behind her, many leagues away in the goblin city. Her hand slipped to the coral box which held the mystic chalk she'd been entrusted with. *I am the spirit of the Wind Whisperer,* she mused. "This time," she told her companion, "this time Noxigant will not escape me."

Sshkkryyahr snarled and squeezed the raven in her fist until it popped with a satisfying squish. She yanked the note off its leg and then popped the bird into her mouth and began to chew.

The drider already knew what it would say, but she unrolled the note, anyway. It reported the same things that Leisterbane had told her. Her armies had been repelled from the siege of Gundakhor and regrouped at the hill of the Black Forest.

"How could they have failed?" She paced the length of her throne room. "I blame the inefficiency of trogs," she fumed.

Nekarthis hid in the shadows behind the ebon throne. "Perhaps the enemy is simply more resilient than expected?"

She cocked her head and grimaced sidelong at her eldarim apprentice.

He continued. "Death's four faces control the four strongest troglands and have been planning with us for over a century. The plan was good, but something else disrupts the web you've weaved. Some other power we've not accounted for."

Sshkkryyahr curled her lip. "We needed *more troops*." She changed her wording, knowing that they had already possessed vastly larger numbers due to the goblin hordes. "We needed *more morehl*. Perhaps if our cursed bullets could have come into play... had not Torl been murdered by a pretender who claimed his stead..."

"It is their way," Nekarthis said.

"A bleeding stupid way," she hissed. "The subterfuge of it disturbs me—his replacement is inept and a less skilled arcanist." Sshkkryyahr waved away the line of thinking. "Had we emptied the Grotto and sent all of our defensive forces so that we could uproot Gundakhor..."

"And leave ourselves exposed?" Nekarthis frowned. "King Schoyke would send his armies against the mountain as soon as he learned of it. He may have held to nonaggression all these years since his father died, but that was for the sake of his realm's safety... so he would not draw your wrath down upon him. Certainly, the safest thing for him would be to cut us from the Obsidian Grotto if such a thing ever looked possible."

Sshkkryyahr drummed her fingers against her chin and plucked a stray feather from her teeth. "We shall redouble our efforts. Gundakhor will fall. Begin the muster and send for all of our troops to report. Call half of the casters from the Black

Forest so they may redeploy from the Grotto with the army; we must not allow pieces to enter play while out of place."

Nekarthis raised a brow. He'd just explained exactly why pressing the attack was a bad plan. "But without the troops left to defend…"

"There will be troops," she promised. Sshkkryyahr retrieved a bottle of black ichor from near her throne. "I have received a visitor from Lord Death… and he granted me a boon."

Shella stood on a rooftop behind the barrier that protected the leaders of Maris-ta-Sehlim. She could sense her enemy's approach, Noxigant was among them. Shella pressed the spyglass against her eye. The sage searched the reaches of the battle line until she located Kregtert, the warrior prophet who channeled the totem spirit of death.

Goblins poured from the thin trees of the swamp and charged like berserkers. The coral elves mowed them down with bow and arrow, but between the trogs' crude shields and an exhaustible supply of missiles, they would eventually break through. So far they had kept the horde out, but it looked like the selumari would run out of arrows before Noxigant ran out of missile fodder.

As more and more of the vermin raced from the Brakishomme, the ships moved into place. On sail and oar, they lined the bay with their broadside and unleased more missile fire. The arrows distracted the trogs from the other vessels: airships crisscrossed above the edges of the swamps. Held aloft by the gas bladders that held them in the sky, selumari casters pushed the dirigibles on their courses. Crew members dumped streams of oil from the ships, slicking the approach for several leagues.

Ailuril's Kiss, the flagship of the airborne fleet, provided interference. Its decks, lined with archers, rained arrows down upon any trogs that tried to shoot down the ships. *Ailuril's Kiss* had deflated her air sacks and used wing fins alone. Her corps of casters kept the ship aloft by pure buoyancy of conjured winds. That also made it the fastest.

As the other ships cleared out, a handful of vagha casters borrowed from nearby Vhandria summoned sparks of eldritch flame in the *Kiss's* wake, igniting the flammable oils and lighting up the swamps. The conflagration charred the moors black, burning alive a significant portion of the trog army that hid there and cutting it off from those stranded between the flames and the archers of the city.

Ailuril's Kiss converged with the other ships as they descended precariously low over the battlefield and belched their sailors into the battle. With the new boundaries established by the flames, the trogs were shoehorned into a tight zone. The selumari cavalry rode out on horseback, and a few upon eagle mounts. They tore through the goblin army whose cavalry had been mostly lying in wait for the right opportunity. They'd all been burned in the inferno.

Shella watched the battle unfold with awe. Captain Gennay, who commanded *Ailuril's Kiss*, swung into the fray and hacked down fiend after fiend. She used her sword as one expertly trained in the art.

If the sage had not arrived and demanded an audience with the leaders when she did, the coastal town would be in flames right now, instead of the goblin soldiers. She looked up; Shella could feel something stirring in the ether.

Refocusing on Noxigant, she spotted the beast departing. He'd turned and left.

Shella lowered the spyglass and checked her mathematical estimates against the forces that had already been seen, and those she assumed had been burned. Brackishomme was far from emptied of trogs.

"They're routing, look!" the city administrator clapped Shella on the shoulder. "We'd have been doomed without your information." He and the other city officials thanked her profusely and offered her many rewards as *Ailuril's Kiss* came to a rest, hovering just above the rooftop where the officials had watched the battle and commanded their forces from both height and relative safety. Gennay slid down a rope and presented herself with a bow.

"If there is anything that we can do to repay you for your deeds, Master Sage…"

"There is," Shella interrupted. "I sense a growing evil in the east. You must send help. Even now, I feel the fiend Noxigant, whom I've guarded your city against for centuries, is on some new mission. I may not look it, good sirs, but I feel every year of my age. Whatever new evil the Four Faces of Death are up to, I must do my part to stop them."

The head administrator frowned. "I'm sorry, Master Sage. We sent a bird just last night. There is war in Gundakhor. The Crooked Spine is expanding their territory once again. The morehl have allied with Bent Morass and the Waterblight; even the Darksteppes have camped in the Pass and now march north. We declined their request for aide; our troops are needed here to deal with our own goblin menace."

Shella erupted, "Surely you must see that all of this is connected. Sshkkryyahr unleashed the totem spirits so that she could command the four primary troglands. *She wants* you to stay out of this fight. If King Gundraokh falls, so will all the Birthlands… and then all of Esfah, after a matter of time."

The administrators twisted their mouths, but shook their heads. "We are sorry, but we cannot spare our own safety for the dwarves' war."

"Then I must go alone," Shella said.

They argued, "But think of all the good you've done by culling the beasts from the Brakishomme. You're the next Davian Whisperwynd," one said.

"You'll find them quite manageable now, without Noxigant or Kregtert to lead them," she said as she packed up her meager belongings. "The scattered families will fall to infighting in the power vacuum that will follow. The worst you'll endure is occasional raiding. Nothing that even your local forces can't handle if they had just a quarter of their present number."

Gennay held up her hand. "I beg the council's pardon."

"Anything for the hero of this battle," an official responded. "Er… one of the two heroes," he corrected.

"I do feel that we owe it to our Sage to honor her request. I feel she is right. The goblin forces are smashed, and even if they are not, there is little use for airships against them… even if Brakishomme has produced a crop of flying harpies, Maris-ta-Sehlim's eagle riders are strong enough to handle them. No airborne threats will overtake the city. Allow me to take our airships, at least, and only with those selumari who volunteer to fight alongside Gundakhor?"

They clustered their heads together momentarily and discussed it. Finally, they gave word. "We reluctantly agree," the administrator stated. He'd obviously been displeased with the impromptu vote. "But Gennay, take care to return all our ships in good working condition. Take great care with our coral elf lives… *all of them*. I saw your recklessness in battle. Make sure each one of you returns," he scowled.

Captain Gennay bowed. "Yes father," she said with a smile. And then she and Shella climbed aboard *Ailuril's Kiss*.

As the *Ailuril's Kiss* and her four floating companions settled above the courtyards at Gundakhor, the dwarven king and his entourage came out to greet them with surprise clearly written on his face. Shella slid down the rope after Captain Gennay and spotted her old friend. She ran to embrace Wehge who stood in the company of King Gundraokh.

The coral elf sage had shown up on Gundakhor's doorstep after Surfeibese abandoned his army.

They broke the tearful hug as Wehge's sprites swirled around them. "You have it still?" Wehge asked. "I confess it has been often in my dreams as of late."

Shella produced the coral box in which they kept the artifact given to them by Davian Whisperwynd before his death. "It is safe."

They both turned at the same time. The selumari companions felt their fellow sage's presence. Lyta approached through the gate. Her face lit and she rushed to her friends and embraced them. Her androsphinx bounded along beside her.

"We are in strange days," Gundraokh said. "I am certainly glad for reinforcements from Maris-ta-Sehlim. We had feared they would send no aid."

"Thank that one," Captain Gennay nodded to Shella. "She rallied enough support to send at least these five ships, packed stern to bow with fighters."

The king offered Shella a bow. It came off as stiff with his hardened skin starting to impinge his flexibility. "Let us hope we all survive this, then." Gundraokh pulled Captain Gennay aside, "We will be planning our movements this evening. It would be best if you brought your counsel to the meeting. If we cannot defeat the Grotto's monster, she'll overrun all the Birthlands in short order."

"I shall attend," Gennay promised.

Shella, Lyta, and Wehge walked slightly away. They had played an unknowingly critical role in the world events, but they knew that their involvement was far from over. As they strayed into the shadow of *Ailuril's Kiss,* they discussed their campaign against the totem spirits.

"The enemy is on the move again," Lyta confirmed. "I had Ghastamant dead to rights. My plan was solid, and I knew I would scatter his believers again for the twenty-second time, burning their altars to the ground and forcing the fiend to begin again."

"Let me guess," Shella said. "He just abandoned everything and started walking east?"

Lyta nodded. So did Wehge.

"Something new and terrible is in the works. I do not like it," Lyta stated.

Sshkkryyahr walked through the Obsidian Grotto with Nekarthis following in her wake. She clutched the bottle with the black fluid as they approached the temple shrine dedicated to Death.

Masons had encrusted the exterior of the temple with the skeletons of the dead. Fallen enemies of the morehl were inverted with their heads buried in dishonor; their revered kin held their heads high even after their souls had departed for the Abyss.

The drider motioned around her. All dwellings nearby had taken up the decorative custom. "Behold, your army," she said as they walked further towards their Hall of Champions: a place where their most glorious dead were preserved in memorial. They descended further into the mountain where they kept slaves. Clanging sounds of smiths at the forges echoed up the tunnels.

"You will lead your army to the east and secure our borders up to the coast. Drive the selumari from their homes and burn it all. Do not head any further east than Farnoch, or further south than the Darkwell, even if the elves seem easy prey. Something deadly lives in the crags of Empyreanoral. None of our scouts have ever returned from there. My hope is that if you push the enemies in that direction, whatever lives there will eradicate them.

They arrived in the forge level of the Grotto's underbelly, where Keri bowed low to the ground. He rattled as he bent at his waist. As the Master of Keys, Keri's duty was to drive the slaves owned by the Grotto.

Past Keri's post, enslaved vagha and gnomes worked to produce weapons for the army Sshkkryyahr had already begun to create. A line of undead stretched the length of the hall. None shifted on their feet or ambled out of order. Skeletons stood erect with joints bound together with threads of necralluvium and the recently dead stood as zombie minions; some wore grave cloths and the flesh of others peeled or bloated. At the front of the line, an emaciated dwarf distributed weapons and pointed to the exit at the rear which climbed through the roots of the mountain until it emptied in the Terrorwood on the east slope of the Crooked Spine.

Sshkkryyahr poured half of the viscous, inky fluid into a vial and handed Nekarthis the jar of remaining necralluvium. "Raise your army. I have things to attend to. Our spies report that a larger alliance now mobilizes against us and I must prepare the armies." She smiled. "We do not need to venture away from home to wipe them out... that fool Gundraokh is so eager to die that he comes to us."

Nekarthis nodded. "I have heard the report. Despite this new coalition formed against us, we still outnumber them, provided these undead allow us to keep all attention away from our eastern entrance."

The drider smiled. "You are my most faithful servant, and I am trusting in you to guard the rear flank. We shall defeat this alliance upon the field of battle. And then, you and I will ride into Gundakhor and take it as our own. And who better to lead the charge against the filthy vagha than the corpse of Gundraokh, himself?"

She smiled and then returned for the throne room to make her preparations.

Nekarthis stared into the formless black and swished it around as he examined it. He loved the thought of taking the Eastern Coast by surprise. An idea struck him and he departed for a textile manufacturer he knew of.

Ailuril's Kiss hovered above them on its air bladder. The skyship had not needed any extra speed while it hung above Gundakhor during the battle's planning stages, and it provided the coral elf magicians an opportunity to rest. They knew they would be greatly taxed in the days to come.

Captain Gennay saluted King Gundraokh and the amazon queen. She searched for Shella, but the selumari sage had already departed with her friends some time ago. The captain scrambled up the rope ladder and took her place at the helm, barking orders. "Magi at your posts. Get us some serious elevation and then deflate the bladders. We've got a long distance to travel and we'll need as much speed as we can muster to make it happen."

The troops below watched the dirigibles climb into the clouds and out of sight.

"This had better work," Shyalou said.

"It'll either work, or we won't have to worry about a backup plan," Gundraokh stated as he climbed aboard his mammoth. His son Eldurokh clambered up an adjacent beast. Riding abreast were Reesime and Nerlov, the generals commanding the Emmiran forces.

As one, they began moving out. The armies marched in ranks and headed east, leaving Gundkhor behind and trampling across the decomposing bodies of fallen morehl. The flatlands between the two empires would help ease the fatigue of travel, but the distance was great and likely to take a full tenday and half again at the best speeds they expected to make.

The third night of the march drew close when the first forward scout reported to Cymmeron. "Creatures in the distance. A dark line of opposition stretches across the horizon. Another scout is gathering accurate details, but we should prepare for the worst."

Eldurokh scowled. "This was not part of the plan. Too early of an engagement takes Gennay and her airships out of play."

"I know," hissed Cymmeron. "But it's not like we have any choice. Either way, the enemy outnumbers us... but at least out here they won't have access to the magic of their cursed bullets."

Shortly after, another scout rode in and gave a follow-up report. "Good news, sir," she said. "It is a flock of drakufreet, the largest I've ever seen." On the horizon, a cluster of eldarim herdsmen approached. "There are the creatures' tenders."

King Gundraokh and Queen Shyalou rode out to meet them. After explaining their mission, they rode back before the sun set. Gundraokh grinned widely through his beard, and he clapped his son on the shoulder. "They will join us."

"The eldarim?" Eldurokh asked. "I thought they picked no sides in war... not after the purges of the Dragoncrusades?"

"Times are changing," Shyalou interjected. "None living under any banner other than that of Death will escape Sshkkryyahr's wrath. This has become so plainly obvious that it has made many strange bedfellows."

"Well, I've never been one to look a gift dragonkin in the mouth," Eldurokh said.

The king continued. "They'll ride on ahead of us for a few days. Perhaps Sshkkryyahr's spies will see the herds and look no further as they watch for trouble. She undoubtedly knows we are coming, but anything we can do to confuse her during our travels will play to our benefit."

They broke camp for some much-needed sleep. Only the occasional chirps and brays of distant dragonkin interrupted the night sounds.

Drokh could sense the presence of his enemy ahead. The dwarven Master Sage had stalked Malfeus through the swamps of Bent Morass for generations. Ogekt, the devious shaman who hosted the black spirit, had lived far beyond the expectation for a trog's lifespan. Few ever lived past one hundred forty, and Drokh had been trying to kill this fiend for nearly twice that.

He'd managed to assassinate the first host, Ogekt's master, within the first year of the totem spirit's summoning. Ever since then, Malfeus had laid the most devious sorts of traps against him as Drokh spent year after year trying to eliminate the evil from spreading beyond Bent Morass.

Drokh scowled as he remembered the last attempt in the previous winter. Malfeus had nearly been slain, and Drokh had finally developed a plan to trap the spirit so it could not find a new host, but Malfeus had turned the tables on him. He had earlier taken a harpy bride who came to his aid at the last moment. The dwarf's eidolon had intervened, but both his gargoyle and the harpy had died, leaving Drokh more alone than ever. He missed his friends and the sanctuary of the Feylands.

Using a glimmer of his connection to the magic that flowed to him from Eldurim, his patron god, he stiffened the earth along his path. Drokh hated wet feet, but more importantly, it kept his boots from sloshing in the stagnant water and alerting the enemy of his presence.

Malfeus would sense him, but since losing his gargoyle, Drokh had never let Malfeus get far enough away that the old goblin could ever feel safe and their sense of connectedness did not function like an exact range-finder. He could sneak within twenty cubits of him and the fiend would never realize Drokh was any closer than he was right now.

Up ahead, Nidjiqt, Malfeus's war commander, dashed along a soggy path just beyond Drokh's position. The vagha had been stalking him through the trees and followed him all the way to the main goblin city.

Drokh smiled. After twenty years, he'd learned Nidjiqt's weaknesses and habits: he was a jealous and vain thing. He would finally be able to exploit that weakness, and a plan formed in his mind.

[We have lost the river,] Nidjiqt proclaimed as he entered the town. [The drider's plans have failed and our forward forces were destroyed. Only a small force in our west remains, plus half of our trolls.]

The news caused a commotion as he told stories about how the sudden influx of vaghan troops had arrived to help beat them back. Nidjiqt blamed the trogs of the Darksteppes, mostly combined with the failure of the morehl. Most of the other tales seemed designed to spread his own fame, and he claimed to have killed a hundred humans and fifty dwarves during the battle.

Drokh did not eavesdrop for long. He used the cover to his advantage and slipped around to the far side of the city undetected. After snagging a bolt of crude cloth the trogs often used to make their garments, he swung it over himself as a shawl and meandered through the town, doing his best to eliminate the signature gait of a dwarf and mimic goblinoid walking patterns.

Resisting the temptation to charge directly into the mud and stick temple erected in Malfeus's honor, Drokh walked past it. He could sense the foul presence within. Instead, he went to the three huts owned by Nidjiqt. Each of his three wives had their own.

He spotted another trog he recognized in a nearby hovel. Gogjurt, Nidjiqt's brother, was addicted to the local gutchurn they fermented in stone pots beyond the festering wolds. He lay passed out with his legs sticking half out of the hut.

Drokh grabbed the goblin and dragged him deeper within his home. He conjured a spell and transmuted the dirt below to a shifting, sandy mud and formed it with his will, creating a passage through the firmament that allowed him to crawl into the home of Nidjiqt's favorite wife, a young goblin sow who was somehow considered a beauty amongst the trogs. Drokh stripped the drunkard of all his clothes and dropped him in the cot before slipping out the way he'd come.

True to fashion, a few minutes later, Nidjiqt presented himself at the temple gates to report to Malfeus. While there, he called for his wives to prepare themselves to tend him. Before the goblin leader could emerge from his temple gates, the commander's brother emerged from the hut, fully nude and shaking of the grog of inebriation.

Nidjiqt lost his composure. Screeching insults, he flew after his brother with murderous intent and pummeled him with his fists. The gathered crowd watched with rapt interest until the violence spilled over into the crowd and turned into a riot that rippled through the community.

With his ax readied below his filthy shawl, Drokh waited by the doors, expecting Malfeus to emerge at any moment. As soon as they opened, he would deliver a killing stroke and spin Bent Morass into chaos without the guiding hand of evil that had guided the denizens of the swamp to become a regional power in the land.

The doors never opened and the turmoil nearby was finally beginning to calm down now that Nidjiqt's brother lay in mangled repose with his skull cracked open against a rock. Yellow blood and chunky gray matter leaked from the gaping head wound.

Drokh knew he could not wait much longer or he would be discovered. Against his better judgment, he opened the door and slipped within.

A few steps into the shrine, the first trog leapt for him, snarling with animal rage. Three more came from the other corners of the room. He hacked with his weapon and chopped them to pieces until the temple fell to complete silence. The sage scanned the shadowy interior, looking for his enemy.

Finding nothing, he reached out with his senses and felt that Malfeus was on the move. Just as Drokh had used the distractions as cover for his movements, so had his enemy. Malfeus had left the area and seemed intent of departing Bent Morass.

Escaping the city right now would prove no small feat, and Drokh doubted he could catch his enemy. He scowled. He would have to try. Whatever Malfeus was up to now, Drokh had to stop it. Even if he lost his life fighting against the fiend, his fellow sages had to know what he had devised: a way to finally end the threat of the four totem spirits.

Nekarthis stood on the slope of the Crooked Spine. He'd set local slaves to exhuming whatever graveyards they could find and piling the corpses in the Terrorwoods. It took only a single drop of Necralluvium to animate the body.

He swished the black material around in its container and felt certain it had increased in size, like a slow rising yeast. The necromancer had already ripped all the decorations from the local buildings and revived the corps of fallen morehl heroes from their death galleries. His army swelled to a couple hundred thousand. Each had been outfitted with weapons for warfare and the gremmlobahnd had been set to work forging simple scythes and bucklers.

Equipping his army would prove the most difficult task. Morehl troops had raided the gnomish supply for whatever weapons were available to outfit the soldiers. The undead were far less picky. They had no need for clever weapons of warfare; they would march in to battle equally confident in the efficacy of shovel or sword.

Nekarthis had no need to feed this army. They stood in wait of his command as he bolstered their forces with the long-dead troops who died during the wars of previous eras.

Finally, morehl textile makers walked through the army that stood among the bare branches and thorny bracken of the Terrorwood. They cut swaths of sackcloth and burlap long enough to drape over the undead and conceal their true identity.

Wearing bolts of cloth, his army stood like two hundred thousand formless lumps. They had no need of vision; they did not see with their eyes. In fact, very few of them had anything resembling freewill at all, save the ranking members of the army and those dedicated as spell casters.

Nekarthis draped a shroud over the skeletal steed that he'd been brought. Signaling them that the time had come, he blew a note on his horn. The sorrowful note echoed through the dead forest and they followed him as he led their slow march away from the Obsidian Grotto. Nekarthis let the signal horn of his command hang over his neck; it rested next to the eldrymetallum ocarina slung around his neck.

With any luck, the selumari would not know who or what this army was until they were already upon them. Just as Nekarthis had planned.

The drakufreet had marched with them now for two days. Gundraokh watched the creatures as they intermingled with the alliance troops as they advanced across the plains. They'd just passed the crevice ramps of the trench which yawned away from the main approach to the Grotto. The army would arrive at the enemy's doorstep by the next day; they already rode in the shadow of Sshkkryyahr's mountain.

"Magnificent beast," Gundraokh stated from atop his mammoth. The dragonkin mount ridden by the eldarim herdsman was tall enough that he could easily meet the dwarven king's eye level.

Yarrow, the herdsman, patted the creature on the neck and rubbed his skin in the direction that the scales ran. "That is one of the four largest we have. Champions we call them, when they get that big." The big one nearby had scales that shimmered with a cerulean hue; it rose the height and a half of the mammoths.

Gundraokh raised a brow and noticed Eldurokh's covetous glance. The dragonkin champions were nearly the size of the smallest dragons and he knew their hide was thick enough to stop most missiles, including flintlocks' ball shot. While still a far cry from a legendary white dragon, the draconic creature Yarrow rode was nearly three times the length of a mammoth.

"When all this is said and done, is there any way we could get some of these magnificent creatures for our cavalry? Your champions would come in especially handy."

Yarrow kept a neutral face. "I'm afraid that is not how it works. The drakufreet can be magically enchanted, summoned, or a bond can be built with their kind. If I were willing to sell any of these dragonkin, I would not be worthy of the bond I've built."

They rode a little way further in silence as the vagha watched the eldarim's bonded creatures. The drakufreet trotted on four legs, though the champions also possessed wings, as did a few smaller ones. Some of the dragonkin walked on two feet and towered taller than even the selumari as they walked. They were as varied as any other race, it seemed. Truly, an army facing the armored beasts would find them a formidable opponent.

There were thousands of them. Despite the bond and affection Yarrow felt for them, still he ushered them towards a battle and certain doom for many of them. *Perhaps even the eldarim realize that Sshkkryyahr is a cancer. Left unchecked, the drakufreet would be bent to her will or destroyed.*

Gundraokh realized that Yarrow studied him as much as he watched the herdsman's creatures. He stared at the band around the king's wrist.

"Is it true—the stories?" Yarrow asked.

Gundraokh laughed and rolled his eyes. "Which ones?"

"They say you took the bands of fate and ripped them off the arm of Turambar himself."

"It wasn't nearly so exciting as all that…" he trailed off and twisted the enchanted bangle as he thought it over. It only twisted with some effort.

"Did you really take them all?"

He shrugged. "There was just the one I found at first. I spent many years collecting the remainder in my younger years. The other three are locked away in my family vault. Truly, I'd have taken this one off years ago if it were possible."

Yarrow looked amused. "You say there were only four?"

Gundraokh raised a bushy brow. "What are you saying?"

"Nothing," Yarrow waved the question away. "My peoples' legends sometimes differ from yours, is all. Will you tell me about finding them? The eldarim have a special reverence for Turambar, besides Mother Ghaeial and Father Tarvanehl and all their children."

The king grimaced. "Perhaps another time. It's not a short tale and we must arrive well rested for the battle tomorrow."

Yarrow nodded, and the army broke camp, but kept no fires this close to the expected conflict.

For the first time, Gundraokh thought that their alliance finally stood a realistic chance of victory, and he his fingers itched to throw the drider from her mountain. There would be blood all around on the next day, but he figured it would at least be let in equal measures, now.

A murmur rippled through the camp in the morning's infant light. King Gundraokh jumped to his feet and looked for the source of the trouble. It was immediately clear: Yarrow and all the drakufreet had abandoned them.

He muttered every cuss word in all the languages he knew and quickly followed them up with every prayer he dared hope could be answered. Silently, he cursed himself, thinking he may have insulted Yarrow during his conversation on the previous night. *Would he really have convinced the other herdsmen to abandon us completely... or perhaps they were in league with Sshkkryyahr all along, and this was some kind of psychological game? Will we arrive at the Obsidian Grotto's gates to find Yarrow and his beasts on the opposite battle line?*

Gundraokh looked towards the mountains and spotted a distinctive, dark line at the base of the mountain. The morehl army was already arrayed against them and just waiting for the enemy to arrive. He knew that, by the afternoon, one side would draw first blood.

As he crawled atop his mammoth, Eldurokh blew a signal horn. Other horns greeted him from the distant companies that followed their lead into battle. Eldurokh blew another, pulsed call in two spurts as asked after their allies in the sky. None returned the signal; the airships couldn't yet be spotted.

The lava elves had come out of the caves and arrayed themselves for battle. They formed up defensive lines to go on the offensive and prevent a siege. King Gundraokh had proven canny enough in the past that they arranged the vanguard to be adaptable. They refused to yield him the foot of the mountain for fear of some trickery he could engineer.

Gundraokh raised his ax. "Right where we want them! Charge!"

The amazons raced ahead with their chariots. Dwarven and selumari casters fired magic into the battle as they raced forwards and closed the distance. The two forces collided with thunderous impact. The largest hell-hound any vagha had ever seen leapt from a cave and tackled Gundraokh's mammoth, knocking the king to the ground as the beast tore the mammoth's throat out.

Eldurokh whirled to rescue his father, but Gundraokh waved at him. "Lead the army. I'll take down this pup," he roared, brandishing his ax. The bracelet on his wrist shone with a bright glimmer as he charged at the monster, pummeling it with the strength of the earth god, Eldurim. With a mighty swing of his weapon, the blade cleaved the hound in two.

Gundraokh panted and reached for his flask as the battle raged around him. He frowned. His grip would not release from the handle of his weapon. The king shook it in frustration. He had heard of warriors acquiring a frozen grip, but this was altogether different. Gundraokh examined the hand nearest the mystic band. It had turned almost entirely to stone. He said nothing, but flung himself back into the fray.

Screams, the cracking of bone, and gunshots echoed through the canyons and washed over the flats on the foothills of the Obsidian Grotto. Both forces duked out their hatred of each other, spilling blood and sweat.

It devolved into a brutal slugfest. Neither side possessed a great terrain advantage. In Sshkkryyahr's hubris she sacrificed that element so that the mighty Gundraokh would know that she had beaten him at his own game. The morehl needed to be closer to the mount for their cursed bullets to activate.

Both sides shed blood and positioned against each other for hours on end in a contest of strength and grit. Morehl fell and others replaced them. Vagha and their allies took wounds and shrugged them off, bolstering themselves with the fire of inner determination; there were no more of them to call upon for reinforcements.

On the crested ridge above them, three sages rode upon wild drakufreet they'd charmed for mounts. The sages had arrived only a little in advance of the army as they pursued the source of the evil they felt; that sense had led them to the same place. Shella, Lyta, and Wehge paused on the rocky trail as it wound around the surface of the Grotto. They watched the battle unfold below.

"Things look dire for our allies," Lyta frowned.

The others nodded, agreeing with her discouragement.

She looked up again and then stiffened, recognizing a familiar form. Drokh stood only a little ways down the path. Lyta leapt from the mount and ran to embrace him.

Drokh winced at her touch but then leaned into it.

"You're wounded?"

"Mere scratches. The pain will pass," Drokh said. He'd earned scars both old and new since they'd seen each other last. "I practically walked through the depths of the Abyss to get here."

"You are following Malfeus?" Wehge asked.

Drokh nodded. "Apparently they've all been called here for some vile purpose."

"Your eidolon?" Shella asked, searching for her friend's gargoyle.

Drokh measuredly shook his head and frowned.

Shella gritted her teeth. "I think the forces of nature need every troop that can be spared against Death's worshipers." She closed her eyes and whispered words of encouragement into her tako's sensory organ. The bond between sage and eidolon did not require words—speaking them were for her benefit. Together, they sent their monsters to the battle below.

"Do you think we shall see them again?" Wehge asked.

"It is in the gods' hand, now," Lyta said.

Drokh crooked his jaw and watched the massive battle rage down the mountainside. Something in his gut twisted. "I am uncertain we will see much of *anything*, past today."

Far to the east of the Terrorwood, Nekarthis led his tireless army across the moors as they sloped down to the coast. They had already come to the outlands surrounding Farnoch. They'd taken care to use no lanterns and travel at night, circumventing all towns and dales that dotted the lands of the East Coast.

After traveling all night upon tireless feet, they continued towards Farnoch, the selumari capital city east of the Crooked Spine. Nekarthis smiled when he saw the army of coral elves already arrayed for battle.

Nekarthis grinned. Their observation tower had already noted King Schoyke's army gathering in preparation. "Farnoch would have attacked our east border as soon as the dwarves arrived on the west."

His sackcloth lumps plodded behind him without a sound and with the reek of their rotten flesh constrained beneath the bolts of fabric. Farnoch's army stood at the ready and merely awaited orders. "At least they are not complete idiots," the eldarim said. "But they have no idea what they face."

Their armies were roughly equal in size, and the necromancer had no doubt that Farnoch would fall. He heard a rumble in the south and saw the glimmer of steel plate in the morning light as the selumari army from Lago Rosa approached to reinforce and flank.

Nekarthis held up a hand and his silent army stopped. He rode ahead of his army and waited in the space between the two vanguards, waiting for representatives from the other two armies to join him in no-man's-land. Two armored coral elves rode out from each army and met him.

The younger one from Farnoch gave him a disgusted look from underneath the heavy armor. Nekarthis wore nothing but his black robes, which made his skin look all that much paler.

"How dare you march into our lands?" he spat. "You commit an act of aggression while wearing your lounge robes?" he scoffed with enough haughtiness that Nekarthis suspected he was the prince.

The selumari from Lago Rosa proved more level-headed. "Sir, we outnumber your troops two to one. You cannot take this field of battle. Even if your numbers were thrice what you brought, you could not win the day. The morehl that you've obviously hidden beneath those shrouds will find little victory in our lands. Your fabled 'cursed bullets' have no effect here."

The prince snarled, "Take your red-skinned abominations back to the drider while we still let you leave."

Nekarthis stared at him defiantly, and then turned his horse and whirled it back again to face them. He did not honor them with words. Instead, he sneered and put the eldrymetallum ocarina to his lips and played a phrase from a selumari song.

In full view of all the armies, all four of them fell from their mounts, stone dead and dragged to the dirt by the weight of their heavy armor. At the distance, none could understand how the enemy had killed their commanders, only that he did. His methods would not matter.

Nekarthis spurred his mount back towards his army, blowing his horn before the hail of selumari arrows could be released.

Responding to the battle horn, the undead threw off their shrouds and revealed themselves for what they were. A wave of stench rolled off them and a deep, unsettling terror rippled through both armies as an army of the dead charged for them.

"More souls for you to harvest today, father," Nekarthis said as his minions rushed past, melee weapons brandished high.

Many mouths opened on the side of the Sshkkryyahr's mountain where tunnels exited to the slope. She perched on the overlook hanging off the one leading to the main upper hall of the Obsidian Grotto. Sixteen of her praetorian guard stood behind her at attention.

Keri, the Master of Keys approached from the rear of the corridor. He held one end of a chain that attached to the torc hanging around the chief gremmlobahnd's neck.

The drider spoke aloud, but mostly to herself. "The battle is pitched, and it seems no clear winner will emerge this early," she said. "Let them think that. Let the vagha and their foolish allies believe that they stand a chance of victory." A twisted smile tugged at her lips, and she relished the thought of breaking Gundraohk's spirit. She wanted to see his face when the rest of the morehl troops suddenly took the battlefield and the famous dwarf lost heart. Sshkkryyahr searched the battlefield for him.

"When we take the field," she promised her royal troops, "then the *real* battle begins. Not one single invader will escape."

Her eager eyes finally located the vaghan king, and she pointed to his general location. "There is our target. His son, Eldurokh, fights beside him. Kill *him* first, while I engage the father. Let Gundraohk witness the end of his lineage before I cut him down."

Sshkkryyahr turned to the gnome. He presented her with two blades that he'd expertly crafted of the mystic star metal, eldrymetallum. "These are *dawn blades*," he said. "Your enemies shall not see another dawn."

The drider slung the scabbards over her back in an X pattern and drew one. Light played across the blade and its keen edge sliced even the refracted light along the metal as she sighted down it. It shimmered like a mirage along the grain of its dividing line.

"They are very sharp, mistress," the gnome informed her. "So sharp are they, that a dawn blade does not merely kill. It severs the ties to even the gods and banishes the soul, trapping it for all eternity inside the star metal. Eldrymetallum can be used to create tiny pocket dimensions, similar to the massive one where the dragons were banished in the Dragoncrusades. The edge of a dawn blade has such a pocket to steal the souls of its victims. Never have I created a more devious weapon." The gnome's voice wavered between pride and sorrow for it.

"I would deny even passage into the Undying Lands for you," Sshkkryyahr hissed and pointed the tip at her enemy. "You stand upon the knife's edge, King Gundraokh. And finally, I am ready to push this battle back across the blade, and there will be blood."

She slid the impressive weapon back within its sheath. Quillon clicked against locket and she nodded to Keri that he should return the gnome to its work station.

"I will cut off this army's head and scatter their allies so that we will pick them off more easily." She emerged from the cave and into the daylight. "Let us finish this."

THE FALL OF THE OBSIDIAN GROTTO
PT. 3
THE END OF GUNDRAOKH SHATTERFIST

Gundraokh and his forces were wounded and weary, but they had managed to beat the enemy back to the foot of the mountain. He looked up, and his heart sank. Tens of thousands more lava elves poured out of the side of the ridge, and their numbers showed no signs of slowing.

The monstrous drider led the charge. He met Sshkkryyahr's eyes as she began picking her way down the side of the steep slope. All through the canyons, they heard the cheers of the lava elves who expected an immediate victory.

And then the bells began clanging: morehl warning signals. The Grotto's advance slowed. It did not stop, but the bells permeated the topmost theater of the battle nearest the peak where Sshkkryyahr's reserves had been pouring from.

Cymmeron and Shyalou pulled their chariots alongside Gundraokh and Eldurokh who now shared the same mammoth. They turned their eyes up towards the sky.

"Do you see them? Have our reinforcements arrived?" Cymmeron asked.

Reesime and Nerlov urged their horses towards the command team. Nerlov's chest had been torn open by morehl ball shot. Green tinted blood trickled down his blanching skin. The way his chest heaved left no doubt as he lifted his eyes to the sky: Nerlov would not survive until the end of this battle.

"There," Nerlov pointed to the clouds overhead. "I see them."

The *Ailuril's Kiss* turned a lazy arc above the east side of the Crooked Spine and the Terrorwood. Spindly trees reached skyward like skeletal arms grasping for the clouds from beyond the grave. Through her spyglass, Captain Gennay watched over the edge of the ship. The selumari of the East Coast faced off against some enemy below.

One of the magi aboard rested a hand against the captain's head. She helped clarify the range and clarity of the picture in her telescope, giving her arcane concentration. Gennay gasped as the undead threw off their cloaks, revealing the undead forces that suddenly surged for the blue-skinned armies gathered at Farnoch.

She gasped when she recognized zombies and the skeletal forces. They overwhelmed the selumari of the East Coast.

Before Gennay could even process the implications of the battle on the eastern front, they spotted their four compatriots' ships. They were waving and pointing to the battle below.

"All winds, push us into view!" she barked.

With their dirigible bladder inflated, they moved more slowly. But it had been part of the plan. The casters needed to be fresh for battle and so they had charted a course and speed, saving the last two days of their journey to travel at a slower pace and with the balloon inflated to allow the arcanists to refresh themselves before the battle started.

Gennay ran to the bow and hung over the forward tip with her telescopic lens extended. She gasped. "The battle has already begun—and it goes poorly for our allies," she shouted. Her stomach soured as she remembered the decision to inflate the bladder on schedule, despite knowing a headwind had been brewing and that it could affect their travel speed with the dirigible module up.

Morehl forces were flooding down the west side of the mountain like an avalanche of red death. She collapsed her monocular lens and stuffed it in her belt and then began scrambling for the foremast. "You two, you're with me," she sent them for the main and mizzenmasts.

"Orders captain?" her first mate called as Gennay began climbing.

"Charge into battle—we follow the plan. Signal all other ships to follow our lead."

The officer's eyes widened as he realized what Gennay was up to. Inflating and deflating the dirigible bladder took time—precious moments they did not have if they were going to have any effect on the outcome of this battle.

The officer ran through the ship, shouting to all the magi aboard *Ailuril's Kiss*. "Up! Up, we'll have need of you in seconds. The Captain is cutting us free!"

Moments later, Gennay sliced the ropes on the foremast and *Ailuril's Kiss* lurched, pointing the bowsprit precariously downward as the bladder detached at the front. The other sailors on the next two masts cut their lines and freed the ship from its blimp. *Ailuril's Kiss* suddenly plummeted from the sky with no backup support. The magi summoned the winds to fill the side sails and control the free-fall, turning it into a speedy dive bombing maneuver.

The other airships followed suit and all five coral airships strafed the side of the mountain as they zigged and zagged across the western slope at high speeds. The sailors fired arrows with reckless abandon, raining a deadly hail of arrows across the unsuspecting morehl.

Ailuril's Kiss drove straight down the enemy's gut and drew the enemy return fire while her sister ships crisscrossed back and forth over the enemy forces in her wake. Morehl ball shot tore holes through her wind catcher sails, two of them ignited, and *Ailuril's Kiss* careened down the slope and crashed, plowing a furrow near the mountain's base. Selumari leapt from the ship and into the fray while the other airships continued their pincer maneuver and harassed the enemy flanks, converging on the thickest part of the enemy.

Firecasters from the Black Forest hurled flaming missiles at the ships, targeting their sails, which frequently caught flame and then extinguished in a burp of smoke as selumari casters summoned water to put them out.

Captain Gennay crawled from the wreckage of her ship and tried to shake the ringing from her ears. She watched the sky battle, knowing the conclusion was foregone. It would only be a matter of time before the other ships would land of their own accord or they surrendered to the flames of attrition and crashed as she had.

But we have bought precious time for the vagha and our troops can still bolster the alliance. She took momentary comfort in the amount of damage their sneak attack had dealt to the lava elves, and then something slammed into her chest and knocked her from the busted wreckage. Gennay landed hard on her back with the wind knocked out of her.

She touched her chest and pulled her hand away from a ragged hole that spurted green blood. Some random sharpshooter had plugged her with a morehl flintlock. Gennay tried to move, but could not muster the strength. She laid on her back and stared at the sky. High overhead, Esfah's clouds rolled by, indifferent to the wars raging below.

Whatever those fiends were east of the mountain... I hope they cannot make me into one of them, she thought.

Captain Gennay stared, becoming one with the clouds. Her eyelids did not close, even when the next selumari airship ignited into a hot blaze and plummeted into the heart of the battle on the slopes of the Obsidian Grotto.

Sshkkryyahr snarled as the coral elves' airships began unloading their missiles upon her armies. It may not have been a decimating maneuver, but it did significant damage. More importantly, it shifted the winds of the battle.

Before the drider could fling herself further into the battle, she heard her name called from behind. And then she smelled them. Trogs.

Sshkkryyahr turned to find the summoned totem spirits of her dark god. Malfeus, Noxigant, Ghastamant and Surfeibese. They had emerged from one of the many tunnels emptying out of the mountain. "Lord Death favors you with a gift," Ghastamant stated.

"No longer do we work alongside you as acolytes," Surfeibese said, "but in you and through you—a communion of wickedness."

"Take. Eat," Malfeus and Noxigant said in unison.

Sshkkryyahr approached the four. Behind her, she heard the cacophony of the battle intensify. And then she fell upon the trogs who stood still as she tore them apart and feasted upon their hearts. Finally, she turned back to her praetorian guards. None dared flinch as she approached with forearms splattered with the yellow blood of her servants. Her chin and chest were likewise slicked with its sickly hue.

"I have never felt such power," she said as the dark energies coursed through her. "I could contend with the dragons," she hissed. "I could single-handedly smite the gods of fate and install myself in their place. From today onward, I decide who lives and dies."

Sshkkryyahr drew the swords from over her shoulders and reemerged upon the hill as a second airship went down in flames. The drider leapt over the edge and flung herself into the battle. She hacked and cut her way forward, chopping down selumari and vagha alike as she set her eyes on King Gundraokh and fought her way towards him.

She struck with such power that she sliced through enemies with ease. Enemy movements seemed to have slowed around her as she moved and reacted with supernatural quickness. Sshkkryyahr threw a gob of webbing across an area like a net and ensnared a crew of dwarves and an amazon chariot. The horse reared, and she punched it in the sternum, burying her arm up to the shoulder in gore and horse flesh.

"Such power!" she cackled. With a flick of the wrist she decapitated the eight soldiers caught in the snare, and then she set her eyes upon King Gundraokh.

"Back to the battle!" Devin screamed at his fellow selumari who tried to flee. "We cannot surrender this line or those bloodless creatures will take Farnoch—I will die before I let them reach King Schoyke." He yanked the coral elf back towards the battle.

They were immediately cut down by a massive death knight. It stood two full cubits taller than Devin. The bulky warrior swung a shimmering bastard sword, which Devin barely evaded. It seemed to crackle with mystic energy as it cleaved the air above him.

"To me! To me!" Devin yelled, rallying any nearby soldiers to his cause. Devin blocked the next attack with his shield and counterattacked. Two of his comrades hacked at the knight; one stabbed him in the chest.

The death knight cackled and whirled aside, tearing the sword from the elf's grip, and bringing his own to bear. He chopped through the elf like a scythe through brush and then whirled back to strike Devin with a killing blow.

Devin's shield splintered and fell apart under the ferocity of the first stroke. He fell backwards as the knight brought his impressive blade crashing down again. The selumari hero blocked with his blade and that too broke under an attack from the death knight.

Devin's squire leapt for the fiend as he delivered a final blow to the coral elf hero. The squire hacked cleanly through the death knight's forearm and the blade dropped to the dirt.

The knight whirled with his remaining arm and smashed the squire's head in with a bony fist. Both helmet and skull broke apart under such force.

Devin scrambled to his feet as he snatched the bastard sword and brought it to bear, slicing vertically through the knight. Its keen edge easily cut through both armor and bone, splitting the monster in two. It collapsed into busted pieces as the halves clattered to the hard, coastal scree, and the undead knight's segments broke apart.

He tried to rally the troops, but Devin's victory was one small win amongst a sea of failure. All around, the undead swarmed over the coral elves. Lago Rosa's soldiers were already trying to retreat into a position where they could flee to Farnoch as soon as morale finally broke—and that was a foregone conclusion. Devin roared as he attacked creature after creature; he knew that moment of morale failure would come any moment.

Across the battle, he spotted the man who had led this bloodless army from the Terrorwood. The pale eldarim in black cloth rode a warhorse that looked as dead as the rest of his army.

"He is the key!" Devin screamed, pointing the archers to the necromancer who commanded them. "Kill him—all forces target that one!"

No sooner did Devin yell, than Nekarthis turned his gaze upon him and sneered.

What few selumari archers remained that still had their wits nocked arrows on bowstrings. A pack of fenhounds snarled and dashed from among the hordes of undead. The beasts resembled mastiffs that stood the size of ponies and were twice as fast. They glowed with an eerie light as they leapt for the archers. Two fenhounds fell as the coral elves redirected their aim at the monsters. The remaining seven beasts fell upon the archers.

"Archers! Magi! Someone!" Devin howled as he hacked at the enemy that seemed to swell with an even more overwhelming force than ever. "Everyone! Target their eldarim leader!"

Before any could heed Devin, two monstrous worms screeched with an otherworldly sound as they revealed themselves. The carrion crawlers reared back and thrashed, scattering filth and greenish blood as they tore open whatever brave selumari dared to remain at the front. The pale yellow aberrations shook their tentacle-like proboscises.

And then the selumari broke and fled for the city of Farnoch. Devin grudgingly turned and joined them, not wanting to die alone on the battlefield, but also knowing that the city could not hold out against this new threat.

The sages continued exploring, searching for their escaped trogs. They came to a rocky clearing on the mountain path with a smooth stone floor. Flat rocks protruded from the ground and formed a kind of walled section that shielded them from prying eyes. Connecting to the mountain, a tunnel burrowed into the Grotto on the one side.

"Stop," Lyta said. "We must stay here."

Wehge looked at her skeptically.

"I feel it too," Shella said. "A premonition from Aguarehl. I suspect you each feel the same?"

Drokh nodded. After Wehge calmed his nerves and searched his feelings, he did likewise.

"Evil tries to emerge—to display its dominance for all of Esfah before it materializes and devours all that live." Lyta's voice was pained. "Only *we* can restrain such a force... four such forces."

They sank to their knees on the four corners of the smooth stone underfoot and entered a meditative trance. Drokh felt especially constrained... something powerful drew his interest. He was the Master Sage of Eldurim and he could sense that he was not the only person nearby channeling the power of his patron god.

All four instinctively knew their roles, and they stretched out with their power—their connection which tethered them to the gods. They used it like lassos, wrapping up and restraining the four Faces of Death. Together they bound the totem spirits and refused to let them unleash their power upon the forces of nature embroiled with the morehl down below.

Drokh's eyes fell to Shella, and he noted the bulge in her hip pouch. The voice of a god echoed within Drokh's mind—though not the familiar sound of Eldurim which he'd heard before. This one spoke as a god, but one whose voice he did not yet know. *The ultimate destiny of Davian Whisperwynd will finally come to pass. The fruit of his life shall prevail and bind the evil that would otherwise conquer this day.*

The dwarf looked from face to face on each of his peers. None of them showed any indication they heard the same thing. Without breaking the trance he spoke, knowing that his peers would hear him. "When the time comes, I have a plan to stop the spirits—but we must each play our roles."

Sshkkryyahr charged down the last length of the slope and used the weight and girth of her body to slam into the mammoth bearing Gundraokh and Eldurokh. The mammoth flipped to its side, trumpeting with surprise, and then it howled as the eight-legged monster crawled upon it and plunged a blade through the shaggy mount's ribs and stopped its heart.

Eldurokh struggled to pull himself from beneath the bulk of his dead mount and the drider crawled towards him like a spider to a fly in her web. As she raised her sword, Gundraokh swung his ax and warded the fiend off while his son extracted himself. The king battled Sshkkryyahr while Eldurokh turned and faced down a host of elite lava elf guards wearing the royal guards' armor.

As the prince battled the praetorian guard and eliminated one whenever he could isolate a soldier, Sshkkryyahr whirled both of her star metal blades and tried to take down Gundraokh. The drider's speed and strength nearly overwhelmed the king, and she drove him backwards on uneasy footing. Ash and cinder floated up from the pyres that littered the battlefield.

Sshkkryyahr drove the famed king towards the wreckage of *Ailuril's Kiss*, where she hoped to pin him to the flaming craft and decapitate him with the cursed blade that would rob him of glory in the afterlife. Gundraokh's footing faltered and Sshkkryyahr sliced with a killing stroke. The king barely got his arm up in time and Sshkkryyahr's dawn blade hacked through the haft of the vaghan ax, lopping off the dangerous end and leaving Gundraokh with no weapons.

She raised her blade to deliver a final blow when a voice roared from the flames. Warlord Ruthak barreled through the leaping inferno on the back of a lizard mount and crashed into the drider before she could strike. The reptile screeched as the two collided in a tangle of legs and bodies.

Gundraokh got his bearings again as the Drider crawled to her feet and slashed one of her blades through Ruthak's midsection, splitting open armor and flesh. He fell to his knees, and with her second blade, Sshkkryyahr took his head.

"No!" Gundraokh howled, charging for the monstrous creature. He clenched both his fists tight and channeled energy from the band at his wrist. Knuckle to forearm solidified to stone and the dwarf's body glowed with a godly, golden energy as he pummeled the drider like a pugilist.

She slashed and stabbed at him, but his skin deflected her blades. His entire body had turned to stone, and he struck with the strength of a landslide as he channeled Eldurim's strength. Her blades flew like a maelstrom of damage, but Turambar's bands had made him impervious to wounds.

Gundraokh snarled and delivered a leaping uppercut that connected like thunder. The force of the impact knocked Sshkkryyahr from her feet and she lost the grip on her gnome-forged blades. They clattered into the distance.

Roaring, the stone-form dwarven king walked towards the drider with menace in his granite eyes. He prepared to deliver a killing blow as the dazed empress tried to pull her wits back about her and retreat.

She called upon the power of the four totem spirits inside her, but her body still reeled from the shock of such a grievous blow as the living elemental force approached. She suddenly realized that she hadn't felt the power coursing through her since engaging the dwarf... something was wrong with her connection to the spirits of evil. They still crawled beneath her skin like maggots, but offered none of their power. Something was blocking them.

Gundraokh's steps slowed, each one stiffer than the last, until he stopped altogether. His body had become one with the forces within him and he'd become fully encased in stone. The glow radiating from his bracelet faded and then stopped altogether.

Sshkkryyahr finally clambered to her feet and caught sight of Eldurokh retrieving her dawn blades; the praetorian guards nearby lay dead by Eldurokh's hand. The prince noted the terror that played across her eyes when he gripped the handles of her swords and approached. He looked at the weapons and both knew that Eldurokh understood there was some significance to the swords... and that Sshkkryyahr feared them being used against her.

She turned and put some distance between her and Prince Eldurokh. Her forces still outnumbered the invaders by a large margin—but she was not willing to risk her own hide when there still remained countless minions she could send to wear the vagha warrior down with. She would wait until the throes of exhaustion finally took her enemies... and then, she would strike.

The battle dragged on and wore down Prince Eldurokh as he wielded the exquisite blades. More and more lava elves seemed to keep pouring from the mountain to replace those that had fallen—and the vaghan alliance had no such reinforcements, and they felt every bit of exhaustion as it crept into their numbers. He realized what Sshkkryyahr had planned: to let them burn themselves out until they were too weary to continue... and then deliver a coup de gras.

He saw the drider lording above the battle. She'd moved to the fringes to keep some distance between her and the keen blades that Eldurokh had stolen from her. Instead, she used her other abilities to trap enemy soldiers in her gobs of webbing to make the prey that much easier to cut down.

Eldurokh beat back the nearby red elves and stood erect, trying to catch his breath and take stock of the battle's flow. They'd fought valiantly, but the coalition of selumari, amazons, and vagha was doomed to fail and Eldurokh knew it in his gut.

He muttered to himself, "Sshkkryyahr must have abandoned the eastern slope. It's the only way they could have so many troops present." Eldurokh wondered why the selumari from Farnoch had not honored their commitment to siege the eastern slope and split the Grotto's forces? It had been a crucial part of the plan, and King Schoyke had committed to the war. He spotted the drider again as she moved through the battle lines; she towered taller than the other monsters in her vicinity.

The dwarven prince scowled at her and promised himself he'd see her thrown from the mountain for her role in so much bloodshed. He turned his eyes and spotted his father's statue nearby, standing proudly upon the rubble with his fists balled and clenched for battle. Never had he seen a finer monument.

"I will meet you in the Undying Lands, father," he said aloud, still daring to hope that it might not be today.

Before despair could fully set in, a brassy trumpet called to the south. A sister siren called to the north. They continued to blow as they grew closer and the ground trembled with the rumbling of many thousand troops that felt like heavy cavalry.

An army of dragonkin arrived and poured over the ridges and crevices. They crashed into the morehl as a second wave against the shore, hitting like an unexpected tsunami.

The flames of hope stoked in Eldurokh's belly. "They didn't abandon us," he realized. "They were rallying even more of their kind to the cause!" *There must be twice as many drakufreet as when Yarrow and his troops slipped away.* There were more eldarim, too, he realized.

Two large dragonkin champions thrashed at the edge of the battle, blasting lava elves with hot breath, and then smashing them with jagged claws. Red-skinned enemies flew through the air as the scaled beasts split shield and buckler. The drakufreet horde continued to swell and the armies of nature raised a cheer.

Yarrow and his army laid waste to Sshkkryyahr's troops and the vagha prince suddenly realized that, for the first time, they outnumbered the morehl forces.

Eldurokh caught Sshkkryyahr's eyes as she ordered the retreat. She snarled at him, and Eldurokh caught the glimmer in her eye. Sshkkryyahr still believed that she could win—though her backup plan must not have been ideal.

The dwarf knew that, if they retreated into the Obsidian Grotto, the morehl would be difficult to expel. Any warrior in their home stood a greater chance of victory, and the terrain would certainly favor the lava elves—not even the thick hides of the drakufreet would save them from the morehl's cursed bullets once they were inside the mountain. They stood a chance to kill Sshkkryyahr if they acted quickly and smartly, but they were not likely able to expel the entire race from the mountain.

The vagha troops had rallied around Eldurokh and his father's stone figure. "The drider must die, today! If we do not finish this here and now, the scourge will only return like a sickness."

A weary cry of agreement went up from the vagha who caught their breath and prepared to venture further into the mountain to sanctify as much of it as they could by spilling morehl blood.

"If we lack the strength to take the Grotto, at least we'll seal it up and lock the morehl away long enough for the rest of the world to recover from their blight—but only once Sshkkryyahr is gone," he yelled his stern declaration. His kinsmen shouted a reinvigorated response of agreement.

Eldurokh took his father's hand and snapped it off at the wrist. He'd been transmuted to stone the whole way through and the rock crumbled like wet shale where the golden band dedicated to Eldurim had been. Eldurokh took the bangle and slid it over his wrist.

Before leaving Gundakhor, they'd had letters from Farnoch. Though the East Coast selumari had pledged support and remained to be seen, the prince dared hope that they would still meet on the field of battle. *Perhaps they've already breached the Grotto—they must have left barely a skeleton crew for their eastern defenses.*

He raised his two dawn blades and growled, "By Eldurim, today the gods will punish Sshkkryyahr the drider!" The vagha rallied behind their leader and together they stormed the gates of the Obsidian Grotto as dwarves, dragonkin, eldarim, amazons, and the few remaining coral elves from Maris-ta-Sehlim and Emmira began the invasion in earnest.

Devin hurried through the streets of the city. Only the centrally located royal keep had walls and gates. The better part of the city had no protection from the invading horde. Farnoch's bells rang as someone urgently pulled the rope to warn the citizens of danger.

Undead dogged Devin's heels as he scrambled. Everywhere he looked, people fled their homes and ran for the keep. Most of them were not fast enough and were swallowed by the hordes—some of them quite literally; zombies and fenhounds tore bites of flesh from screaming victims.

The coral elf kept his stomach in check and refused to lose his composure. An elven child struggled with his dog. The pet would not come and barked at the approaching bloodless, refusing to go with the child who struggled to keep the animal in check. Devin scooped up the child and cast off the leash.

Screaming, the child reached for his pet even as it rushed into the approaching army. It quickly squealed in pain and then went silent.

Devin looked down a street and to the docks. Ships cast off into the sea, their captains likely praying that these fiends could not swim. He spotted undead soldiers clinging to the stern of at least one ship. Most of the crafts would contain civilians— and even one of those creatures could wipe out the entire crew.

He made it inside the main doors of the keep just before they were closed and reinforced with thick beams. Devin released the child and shooed him away. He had no time to deal with helping him find his parents. Command officers were difficult to find, and someone had to organize the defense of the castle.

Scrambling up to the parapets, Devin shouted orders at any who would listen. They fired arrows into the advancing mob with precision accuracy, but most of them did nothing to slow the undead. "The eldarim," he shouted. "There is an eldarim that I suspect is controlling these creatures... perhaps killing him will stem the tide of these bloodless fiends. It is the same commander who killed the prince before the skirmish."

Devin scanned the horizon, but could not spot the eldarim he'd seen on the field of battle. The buildings were too densely built in Farnoch to give them clear sight lanes. Devin scowled; he'd been telling his commanders they needed to insist that King Schoyke expand the walls for years now. Today, his citizens paid the price while the King remained safely within his walls.

A few of their selumari casters began having some luck on the far tower, flinging bolts of ice and lightning. Four of them suddenly tipped over stone dead and fell from the wall. The attackers utilized their own foul magic. A line of elves posted on the wall began to scream and fled their posts. Their face and eyes were covered with leaking pustules and boils.

Devin sprinted along the wall, searching for the enemy he thought was the key to all of this. One of the enchanters tried to run away, and Devin blocked his path. "Stand and fight! There is nowhere else to retreat to, and if you turn your back to the enemy again, you'll find *my* blade in it!"

The spell crafter gulped and then resumed his duties.

"Someone locate that damned eldarim commander!"

Nekarthis stood on the battlefield while his army pursued the routing selumari. He bent low over the dead where they littered the grass beyond Farnoch and put a drop of the black fluid upon many of the corpses. They shuddered and then returned to a state of animated unlife.

A raven landed upon the saddle of his skeletal steed and cawed at him. As the new members of his army moved towards the city to rejoin the fight on the stronger side, Nekarthis pulled off the note attached to the raven. Sshkkryyahr's battle had soured. She faced an additional foe they had not accounted for and had been forced back into the Grotto and required the undead to aid them. The halls of heroes and any corpses of any value had already been tasked into service by the eldarim, and so she could not make her own undead soldiers.

Nekarthis put a drop of necralluvium onto the lips of thirteen defeated selumari. The final body he willed to take a second life and granted the creature its own autonomy. It blinked at him with gray eyes. She had been an evoker before taking the wound across her neck, and so she would be more greatly attuned to the forces of magic.

The eldarim took her by the hand and stared at his newly dead army of twelve. "I need an escort and we must make haste. Their flesh weighs them down." His voice shifted as he channeled the dark arcana. His new minion added her black magic to his, and he blasted the flesh from their bones. The skeletons bled with rivulets of red except where joints tethered to each other by stringy fronds of the inky necralluvium.

Nekarthis placed his vial into the palm of the creature he'd made and gave free will to. "Make a new army from the corpses littering the field. They will obey your commands. You must send them to the Obsidian Grotto and drive out those who do not belong to Lord Death. Do not delay."

He turned and crawled into the saddle of his skeletal steed and gave one last look at his army in the city below. They would follow their instincts and his last set of commands in his absence. Either would eradicate Farnoch.

Moments later, he rode across the plains of the east coast at land-speeds no other creature could attain. His undying guards sprinted alongside him, running at a tireless pace and with speeds enhanced by cursed magic. These fiends would never need rest and obeyed his every command.

Nekarthis planned to make the journey in record time, and the eldritch forces he dabbled with would make it so.

With red skin flush from the heat of battle, Doqmarra and Viennay scrambled through the tunnels. The two morehl had both run out of ball shot and saw the tides of battle shifting within the Obsidian Grotto.

Longtime friends, they'd abandoned their posts together and swiped whatever spendable valuables and supplies they could raid from theirs and their neighbors' homes and then dashed for the nearest exit.

"I know of a lesser-used passage," Viennay exclaimed. "It leads up higher on the mount so it is less likely to be overrun by those nasty dragonkin or vagha."

Doqmarra looked over his shoulder. Another morehl fusilier, whom he'd trained for the military with, screamed behind them as the invaders cut him down. "Lead the way," Doqmarra insisted.

They scrambled into a tunnel and followed the path upwards. It splintered into several directions, winding and merging with larger veins like varicose capillaries of the mountain. It soon branched off again.

Doqmarra and Viennay were not the only lava elves who seized the initiative to make themselves rich. They traded embarrassed glances with one praetorian guard who kept his nose down and took a different path; the imperial guard had an armful of treasure taken from the empress' horde.

"This way!" Viennay led him deeper and up a steep incline.

Doqmarra asked, "What will we do when we escape?"

"Besides avoid being mauled by drakufreet? I can think of plenty of things. Probably the best bet is to head along the Spine until we can cut across to Karakto. We may need to purchase supplies at some of the smaller strongholds in the outliers." Viennay wrinkled his nose, "Whatever we do, let's avoid Bent Morass. I'd hate to survive the sacking of the Grotto and fall prey to the Trogs. They may plan to betray our alliance."

"You think they would?"

Viennay shrugged as they walked. "I think, with the Grotto fallen, all bets are off."

They exited the final portal and walked out into the evening air atop the mountain path and nearly stumbled when they encountered four enemy creatures. Two selumari and two vagha sat in some kind of prayerful position. Their eyes were closed as if they were taken in some kind of trance.

Doqmarra looked them over. "I recognize those tattoos that they wear. These are sages, like the kind we nearly eradicated at Daur-Bor-Nin: eldarim trained mystics and lore keepers."

"We didn't get 'em all last time, I see," Viennay grinned and drew his dagger slowly from his belt.

"What are they doing?" Doqmarra asked, amused as he noticed the twitching faces and rapid eye movement behind their enemies' eyelids.

"Praying. Communing. Who knows? The Sages claimed they could feel the instructions of the gods." Viennay laughed as he walked towards the female coral elf. "So much for the power of the gods," he said. "There is only one god above all others and that is Death, the void-child of Selurehl."

A low growl suddenly got Viennay's attention. He turned too slowly to see Doqmarra fall to the ground as an androsphinx leapt in a flash of color. It snatched him by the neck and locked its jaws into morehl flesh before dragging him down over the cliff with a trailing scream. Steaming blood splattered the smooth stone and marked the direction Doqmarra had been taken.

Viennay clutched his knife and snarled as he rushed to the selumari who refused to open her eyes. He raised his knife and found it immobilized. He turned and faced an enormous sea monster. A tako towered above him and wrapped the morehl's wrist with a tentacle. The creature's armored carapace had been cracked and several parts of it broken off to reveal the wounds it bore; a few of the creature's many limbs had been severed completely, but it had more than enough strength to deal with a murderous red elf.

The tako lifted Viennay off the ground and curled a sinewy tentacle around each limb as the morehl screamed. And then the protective eidolon pulled on each one with one violent, jerking motion. The tako spilled the elf's pieces over the edge, and then returned to where it hid as a protective sentry and warded the sages as they continued to bind the full power of the evil spirits possessing the drider. Without the sages, Sshkkryyahr could potentially win this war by her own strength.

"We're saved!" Devin shouted from the wall when he spotted the water rippling in the marina. Four coral giants strode out of the depths and began approaching. But half the undead horde continued beating on the gates of the keep, and the other half turned and intercepted the giants before they could reach the keep. They piled up as they overwhelmed the reinforcements. One by one the giants fell as if they were locusts being overwhelmed by stinging devilants.

"No, no, no..." Devin yelled. Not only did the giants fall, but more undead gathered outside the city, and these wore selumari armor; some had been soldiers he'd trained or fought alongside in the past. Despair had finally begun to set in his gut. *There is no way to survive... Farnoch will fall and we'll all die here.* He swallowed hard, knowing that by this time tomorrow he'd be a part of Death's army.

The horrible banging from the main gates hadn't shifted tone yet—at least they remained solid; the door's integrity withstood the battering ram. King Schoyke had made sure his home was well defended, at least, and these creatures had no siege weapons. Devin bit his lip and wracked his brain. Even though the doors would hold for some time, the closest army that could help was Lago Rosa, and most of that army was already within their walls... what remained of it, anyway.

Most of the soldiers had manned the parapets already, and the civilians huddled in the main court below. Some of them screamed, and Devin searched for the cause of all the commotion.

The mausoleum doors leading to the royal family's crypt had been blown open from within. A carrion worm had burrowed beneath the keep and emerged in the house of the royal dead. The six corpses inside had emerged covered with black blotches of necralluvium carried by the segmented wretches.

"Breach! Breach!" Devin howled, pointing to the invaders. "Someone cut those bloodless down."

As sentries ran towards them, more carrion worms burrowed their way underneath the main wall, creating tight portals where the dead crawled in. Brave soldiers rushed to intercede, but the corpse of King Edum, Schoyke's father, threw the barriers free and released the gate latches, opening the main entry to the dead.

In the east, fire and thunder cracked the sky and flames enveloped the cursed Empyrean mountains where they rose from the sea. As the deep reds and flashes of lightning scorched the sky, Devin growled, "This is it. Even nature conspires against Farnoch." He drew his sword. "Then we shall die resisting Death."

The selumari hero swung his newly acquired weapon and hacked the dead apart as they flooded through the gates. He whittled them down only to watch them rebuild and reattach limbs. He chopped the head free from a ghoul; the eyeless face stared back at him, smiling with a permanent rictus grin. The cadaver did not get back up.

"Sever the heads—chop off their heads and they don't get back up," he yelled, knowing that the knowledge had come too late.

And then the sky lit vermilion and yellow as meteors began to fall from the crimson heavens. The selumari took cover as much as possible, but none of the burning missiles struck the coral elves as they rained down with precision too exact to be meteorological or celestial.

A whooshing sound sucked the air out of the atmosphere, and then Devin saw them. Blue skinned warriors streaked through the sky, trailing fire as they rode the winds and hurled flaming balls at the undead. They crashed to the ground with landings that cracked the soil beneath them.

"Firewalkers," a warrior next to Devin whispered, staring at the sky in awe.

The creatures looked like selumari, but they were not. While they had blue skin, they did not have the pointed ears of their kind, and their hair fell in crimson, gold, and white locks that framed their blazing eyes. The muscular warriors wielded tridents and short swords as they hammered against the enemies.

Flames rose from homes in the city as Farnoch burned. Cinder blasted the battlefield like bombs, igniting the firewalkers' shields. All around, the tides of the battle shifted. Undead soldiers flailed as the fires lit them like torches, spread by the newcomers whose shields blazed like brands. They pinned zombie and wight with their forks and then severed heads from shoulders before their enemies could wriggle free.

One of the warriors streaked to ground upon a tail of fire and looked for whoever was in charge. He locked eyes with Devin. "Cousin selumari," he said. "Your lands are overrun by Death and its minions defy the empyrean gods. The enemy has mocked the procreator and must be destroyed."

"We have a common enemy," Devin said.

The empyrean nodded stiffly and then rushed into the fray.

Devin did not know half of what the newcomer meant, but the firewalkers' assistance meant they would not all die today. He rallied the selumari forces and then rushed into battle on the heels of the fresh reinforcements.

Cherluch yawned. The morehl had been at his post in the observation tower for weeks now without relief. The tiny outpost was built atop the drider's mountain. His small brick facility contained a giant contraption built of mirrors and glass lenses. It looked almost like a lighthouse, except that it monitored, rather than warned.

Every two hours, Cherluch was supposed to send a status report to the throne room by way of the vertical tube that emptied far below, near the Obsidian Throne. So far the war had been an overwhelming slaughter and the lava elf had neglected his watch. As interesting as seeing their enemies ripped apart was, his true interest was in his art.

The morehl sat in his chair and easel, where he spent most of his time sketching and painting tasteless nudes of the varied races of Esfah. As he finished his current piece and laid down his brush, he took his seat at the machine and dialed in a set of coordinates to swing the lenses to the western slope where he planned to check in on the battle. He expected to report on the final moments of the vaghan alliance. The last report he'd sent was to announce the engagement on the eastern front where the Grotto's undead army overwhelmed the selumari. They'd wiped out nearly fifty percent of them in a matter of thirty minutes and seen the forces retreat towards the inner walls of Farnoch.

Cherluch focused the lens with a mechanical dial and scanned the torn battlescape in front of the Obsidian Grotto. Bodies lay strewn everywhere. Cherluch squinted; there were far more morehl dead than he expected, and the ratio increased dramatically the closer he scanned towards the main gate. Wild drakufreet roved all over the front of the mountain slope.

He grimaced, unsure what it meant. At first, his heart jumped at the thought that the home forces could have been overrun. Cherluch shoved the notion far from his mind. That couldn't be: Sshkkryyahr's army was the strongest in the region, and the largest, too. He sighed and convinced himself that the dragonkin must have been attracted to the dead bodies and feasted upon them, even though he'd never known them to be carrion creatures before.

"The army must have returned to the Grotto to celebrate," he told himself. Cherluch swung the telescopic controls back to the edge of Farnoch which lay at the furthest reaches the equipment was able to spy upon.

He focused the picture as best as he could. This far out, the image was still fuzzy, but Cherluch could see that huge portions of the city lay in flames. He maneuvered the subject area around in a sweeping pattern until he found movement. A horde of undead selumari had been raised and was headed towards the Grotto. Blue-skinned warriors that looked similar to coral elves, but were not, laid waste to the undead.

Cherluch did not know much about the battle, or the tactics, but as he scanned the landscape, it was clear that his side was losing. Most of the undead forces had been terminated; corpses lay with heads severed and coral elves and their hybrid newcomer friends were on the cusp of victory.

He searched the field in a panic for Sshkkryyahr's pet eldarim. Cherluch was instructed to keep an eye on him and report any problems immediately.

The morehl watcher fretted as he scrambled to get a fresh sheet of paper while looking at the timepiece. He had to report… and should have done so hours ago. Cherluch hoped all would still go okay—he'd gotten so wrapped up in his art that the eastern front had fallen, and the drider had no advance notice of it. She'd killed servants for lesser failures. He noted the deep crimson hue on the horizon and watched as soldiers dropped from the sky.

Your dark eldarim has fallen in battle. The undead are overrun by some new selumari trick: magic I've never seen before coming from Empyreanoral!

He stuffed the note into two halves of a metal ball and twisted it shut. Cherluch dropped it down the chute and listened to it tumble into the depths. Returning to the scene, many of these fiery, new humanoids pointed directly towards Cherloch and the morehl's mountain.

They concentrated their energies as if mustering magic from the core of Esfah as Cherluch had seen so many spell crafters do, and then a battalion of the warriors erupted in fire and blasted off from the ground, scorching the field and flinging themselves through the air with incredible speed.

Scooping up his precious paintings and art supplies, Cherluch raided the stores and dumped whatever he could find into a travel pack. Between the wrath Sshkkryyahr was sure to show, and the impending attack from these firewalking creatures, he had no intention of remaining at his post.

Cherluch fled down the mountainside, aiming for new beginnings as far from the Obsidian Grotto as his legs would carry him.

Sshkkryyahr barked commands at the forces within the Grotto. They'd pulled back as many of their morehl as possible and fortified their positions, but anarchy flooded the halls. Eldarim drove their dragonkin to barbarism, and the vagha hid behind the armored creatures and struck when targets presented themselves.

The drider shifted tactics and had her summoners conjure lava flows through the tubes that wormed their way through the mountain. Dwarves had some resistance in their common heritage with the goddess Firiel, but they were not fireproof... and a flood of lava could wipe out much of the drakufreet, humans, and selumari.

Dwarven thaumaturges bent the tunnels, transmuting the bedrock of the mountain into new channels and halls that let them avoid magmic attacks. Meanwhile, any corpses the lava elves could find had been stacked like wood inside the throne room.

Sshkkryyahr searched for any members of the praetorian guard to put in charge of the battle. Finding none who remained, she grabbed the nearest soldier she could locate and barked orders at him. "Hold this line! I will be sending reinforcements in a matter of moments."

She hurried out of the tunnel and made for the throne room where she'd instructed her minions to the pile of corpses. Sshkkryyahr round a corner and a startled morehl soldier bounced off one of her eight legs.

He stiffened when he realized who he'd encountered.

Sshkkryyahr snarled. The soldier's flintlock was slung over his shoulder where he could not use it; his arms clutched a pile of gold ingots and traveling provisions.

"You dare flee?" she shrieked.

Without attempting to answer, the frightened elf dropped his supplies and turned on his heels to attempt an escape. In the distance, others sprinted away from the battle who were beyond her reach.

Sshkkryyahr speared him with one of her sharp legs, plunging its speared tip through his chest. The morehl fell limp as a rag doll, leaking a wisp of steam from the bloody wound. She dragged the body the remaining distance to her throne room and dropped it alongside the others.

He was the first one that she spared a drop of necralluvium from her vial. The inky fluid was eager to attach itself to the dead, and they rose again. Sshkkryyahr counted them. Barely sixty troops of mixed races. *It's far too few... I need more!*

The drider searched the pits of her black heart for the connection to her death god. "Where are you? I summoned you to my cause, totem spirits of evil. Malfeus, Noxigant, Ghastamant, and Surfeibese, your power is required—you claimed to imbue me with strength and magic... your power has proved impotent!"

She listened to the void. No response came, even for direct insults upon the aspects of Death. "Everything is falling apart," Sshkkryyahr growled. Then she noticed the message orb lying near the throne of black glass, and she snatched it greedily.

"Finally, a message. Nekarthis must be nearly arrived with a whole army of the dead. They will eradicate the invaders." Both the forces of the Grotto and the vagha were so exhausted, that the undead had become the only hope for her to assure a victory. Once they struck down Gundakhor's alliance,

Sshkkryyahr knew it would take two generations to recover, and she would need to convince the trogs of Bent Morass to provide support in the meanwhile... she did not relish the thought of their odor in her halls.

She scanned the note and shrieked with rage. *Nekarthis is dead. My army is smashed by some secret race from Empyreanoral... and they are coming.*

Sshkkryyahr snatched the weapon from the nearest undead unit. It was a far cry from one of her gnomish dawn blades, but she did not have time to go in search of anything better.

"My army, head below, and kill anything that is not an ally of ours." The undead shambled out of the throne room and left it silent. Wadding up the note, she cast it away and headed towards the tunnels that ascended to the exits. She knew the deserters had been right.

With another impending attack, she had to escape before the troops from Empyreanoral arrived and put the final nails in this coffin. The Obsidian Grotto was failing, and she could not remain within and keep her life. "I can build again," she told herself. "I rose from a pit to the black throne once before... I will do it again. This time, I will do it quicker." She grinned as if this had all been part of her plan since the beginning. "The wars have depleted my enemies' ranks, and I have a solution of my own." Her hands touched the bulge in her hip pouch to make sure her container of necralluvium was still there.

She made her way quickly through the halls before emerging into the dying light and a crimson sky blistering the evening horizon. Blood had been splattered across the stone floor and she spotted two vagha and selumari sitting on the four corners of the landing. As one, they opened their eyes and stared directly at her. "They are here," all four stated in a shared monotone.

Momentarily, Sshkkryyahr felt the surge of power return to her as the Faces of Death coursed through her again, unrestrained. She felt the strength of the black god reinvigorate her as they released their mystic hold that strangled the totem spirits' power. She snarled, "So it was *you* who have denied me my birthright! Your meddling cost me this victory—for that, you must die!"

Just as quickly as the monster lunged for them, the sages sprang to their feet and into action. Shella tossed Wehge the piece of chalk from her sacred box and yanked her sword from its sheath. She crossed swords with the drider and growled her opposition.

Sshkkryyahr pressed her back with the incredible strength she again channeled. "You cannot bind the power of the Dark Lord! You are not the gods' chosen Champions—they are all dead!"

Lyta jumped to Shella's defense as Wehge ran a circle around them, dragging the chalk along the smooth stone underfoot. He dove through the drider's legs and kept the writing tool pressed upon the stone, keeping the shape correct.

Overwhelming them with the strength of the daemons inside her, Sshkkryyahr threw both Shella and Lyta aside. They landed next to Drokh, who used his magic to work stonecraft upon the four stones he'd snatched from the side of the mountain trail; he flattened them into perfect tablets. Whege completed the chalk circle and looked up in horror.

The monster raised her blade high for a strike that could cleave through all three of them. Lyta's wounded androsphinx and Shella's tako leapt from their hiding places with enough force that it should have toppled her easily. Instead, Sshkkryyahr bit the sphinx in the neck and shook it violently enough to sever its spine while she sank her talons deep into soft flesh of the tako's body. She snatched the thickest legs by their trunk and lifted the eidolon over her head.

"Now you will see the power at my disposal," she yanked and pulled the final of the sage's defenders apart with a sickening *sklorping* sound. His two halves remained connected by entrails and tissue as the drider flung them aside.

Shella screamed at the brutality of it.

Sword in hand, Eldurokh emerged from the tunnel and set his eyes upon the drider. Wisely, he kept his distance, unsure of what he was witnessing as the sages battled with powers far beyond the dwarf prince's understanding.

"Wehge—the chalk!" Drokh demanded.

Sshkkryyahr turned to face the selumari hiding behind her, but failed to catch the arcane, clastic rock when he threw it.

"Now, everybody!" Drokh scribbled a foul sign upon each of the four tablets, one for each of the fiends that amplified Sshkkryyahr with their god-like power.

The four sages channeled their energies into the tablets and siphoned out the spirits of Noxigant, Surfeibese, Malfeus, and Ghastamant. The spirits' host collapsed to her eight, spiny knees as the energies left her body and became bound within the four stone tablets, each bearing the sigil of the totem spirit imprisoned within.

Wearied, and weakened back to her originally powerful state, Sshkkryyahr rose back to her full height and traded blows with the two dwarves and the selumari woman who struck at her with all the contempt of someone who'd just lost a close friend.

Sshkkryyahr grabbed the vial of black fluid from in her pocket and frantically reached for the bodies of the two guardians she had just killed, seeking immediate reinforcements, but Lyta and Shella crashed into Sshkkryyahr and knocked her backwards, refusing to let the monster lay another finger on their dead eidolons. They knocked the glass vial out of her hand and it landed unseen in the nearby grass.

Drokh kicked the writing utensil back towards Wehge who snapped up the chalk given to them by Davian Whisperwynd, who stole it from Death over three hundred years prior.

At four equidistant places along the circle, Wehge drew a symbol with the chalk. Each different sign represented the four elements. The sages took their places at each of their signs where they were drawn and held out their hands.

Sshkkryyahr leapt for the nearest sage, but bounced off a wall of pure force. She could neither touch nor harm her enemies while trapped within the bubble they had summoned. She beat at the walls of the mystic prison and snarled like an animal, flinging spittle and bruising her knuckles.

"Give her to me, good Master Sages," Eldurokh shouted from the rear. He clutched the dawn blade in his fists. "She must pay for her crimes—and I hold the proper tool to administer justice."

"Nay," shouted Drokh. "She has defied the gods and they have a different punishment in mind for her."

The drider tried to break the sages' hold over her, but was helpless to escape from the power the four wielded. "What is this sorcery?" Sshkkryyahr screeched.

"Magic stolen from the Dark Well—from the chamber of the death god himself," Lyta gloated. "You have defied the gods and they are cruel in their judgment of you—perhaps none more so than Fate. She decrees that you have a greater role yet to play in Esfah's future, on behalf of her cousins, the elemental gods represented by we sages."

"No! No... my followers will release me—they are many, and you are only four. Empowered by the gods or not, they will find and release me, no matter what the prison."

"They cannot free you... not where we are taking you," Shella spat the words as her eyes glanced aside to her dead eidolon.

Wehge's eyes blazed, and he spoke with authority. "All Esfah will remember the glory and sacrifice of King Gundraokh. But a few will even know the name of Sshkkryyahr the Dread." Mystic chains crawled up from anchor points on the chalk circle and bound themselves to her. They dragged Sshkkryyahr into the shrinking circle. There came a flash from within the magic circle as a wayfare spell activated. And then nothing remained but a steaming slab of stone.

Eldurokh rushed to the center of it and turned a slow, silent circle. "It is done. It's finally over," he said, picking up the four stone tablets, intending to secret them away so they could never be used to release the evil within them.

Nekarthis abandoned his skeletal steed some distance up the eastern slope and peeled back a sheaf of moss to expose a hidden entry that led to the depths of the Obsidian Grotto in a round about way. The eldarim ducked through the portal and entered the secret tunnel with his skeletal chargers in tow.

He hurried through the halls and peeked around corners, but it was clear that much of the Obsidian Grotto was overrun by the enemy. "Sshkkryyahr will be holed up in the throne room as a last resort," he muttered to himself. "We will need to rebuild and begin again. Likely, nobody is protecting our most precious asset." He shuddered to think how they would fare against the army headed for them from Farnoch. The firewalkers would be impossible to resist, even if they repelled the western forces in league with Gundakhor. "The Obsidian Grotto is lost."

Nekarthis skulked through the obliterated sections of the halls and descended into the quieter depths of the morehl city. The jails and factories would not be raided until the later as they sacked the city.

He left his skeletons to stand guard and entered the lower halls at the foundry level and found the gremmlobahnd still hard at work, oblivious to the war that raged on their doorstep. Under the din of the hammers striking and forges blowing, Keri the Master of Keys approached.

Nekarthis pulled him aside. "Gather the strongest of the slaves and direct them to gather all the eldrymetallum and bring it here. Follow my lead and be quick?"

"Sir?" Keri raised a brow.

"The Grotto is under attack," he replied, keeping his voice low. "The gnome workers who can work the star metal are too previous to let slip into enemy hands." He frowned. There was no way they should have lost this war. They'd been winning it for hundreds of years, *and for it to have turned so rapidly and violently against them?* Other forces must have been at play.

Keri nodded and did as he was bid. He grabbed the only remaining weapon in the gremmlobahnd's arsenal of completed weaponry, a vorpal blade: a weapon that could kill its victim with a mere scratch. Nekarthis scowled when he saw the fine weapon in the hands of such a rapacious morehl, but he said nothing.

Nekarthis yanked the chain of the gnome who had been so long in his master's possession. "Gremmlobahnd, I know you had been working on folding the void in your 'dawn blades.' You had another project, I am told. Have you harnessed the power of the void?"

The gnome reluctantly bobbed his head and offered a puzzle cube.

"Open it," the eldarim commanded.

He did as he was told, and the cube opened up. It disassembled into a kind of linked chain, but the opening remained, somehow creating a massive storage space in a pocket dimension.

Nekarthis nodded to the pile of star metal. "How much of this can we preserve inside the cube?"

The gremmlobahnd blinked as if the question were odd. "All of it."

"And the cube will not gain any weight?"

He shook his head.

"Excellent," Nekarthis ordered it all be shoveled into the opening. When it was done, the thing coiled itself back into a cube shape, much to Keri's bewilderment. Nekarthis stuffed it into his pocket. "Everyone, follow."

With a chain gang full of gnomes, they climbed the stairs cautiously and then ventured further into the ascending halls in search of the drider. The skeletons ran ahead of them and secured the hallways so that they traveled secretly and safely.

They paused in the throne room. None of the others had been inside the Obsidian Grotto's royal sanctum before. As they looked around with wild eyes, Nekarthis found the crumpled note. He skimmed it and cursed, understanding that she must have already fled, having received word about the Empyrean army's approach.

Nekarthis heard the footsteps behind him and dodged the blade that he had long suspected was coming. He turned his accusing eyes to Keri and saw the greed in them. The Master of Keys saw great potential in setting up his own forge. Uncontested, he could profit greatly off the arcane weapons crafted by his slaves.

The eldarim side stepped the next two strokes of the fine weapon and then raised his ocarina to his lips and blew a trio of notes. Keri collapsed in a trembling heap and then gasped his last. Blood trickled from his ears as his body laid on the floor near the throne.

Nekarthis snatched the vorpal blade and looked up to find the gremmlobahnd had all fled. Only one remained, the first gnome they'd taken whose chain remained around his neck. The gnomes were a crafty race and had picked their locks in a matter of moments once Keri maneuvered in for the kill. "You did not run?" Nekarthis still clutched the instrument and stared down his nose at the short gnome.

"I know you could kill my kin with a few notes and they wouldn't make it mor'en another few cubits if we all went. I will remain in your care; I only ask that ye let them escape with their lives."

The eldarim cocked his head. "You know I can track them down in the future."

Nodding slowly, the gnome replied, "Aye. And you may do that, but it'll be worth it to me if my deed secures them another few years of freedom."

Nekarthis nodded and then took the gremmlobahnd's leash and led him up to the exit he planned to flee by. They emerged from the tunnels to the last, dying gasps of light on the horizon. The sky burned redder than ever as the firewalkers verged on arrival. There remained no doubt that the Obsidian Grotto was doomed.

After taking two steps along the path, Nekarthis's toe tapped something unnatural. He bent and retrieved Sshkkryyahr's bottle of necralluvium. He knew some unfortunate end had found her. "We must go."

"Where to?" asked the gremmlobahnd.

"We shall return to the home of my youth, the mountains of Dereh'Liandor. I remember tales were told there of hidden temples and godly relics in the mountains." He smiled, momentarily sentimental. "We shall bend them to my will and change the course of history."

The two turned and began heading south along the mountain road.

Eldurokh stumbled down the slopes and headed back to the main gates of the Obsidian Grotto, which hung busted open. The dwarf felt wearier than he'd ever been before, and the light of Soll had begun to creep up over the western horizon as dawn broke.

With much of the Grotto cleared, the battle had petered out, and the invaders had begun retreating to the camps set up on the main battlefield in front of the gates. There they regrouped and could breathe in air that didn't smell so strongly of sulfur. Eldurokh spotted Reesime and approached the coral elf who stood amongst his diminished group of selumari.

"Spoils of war?" Reesime asked, nodding to the stone tablets cradled in Eldurokh's arms.

"Something like that. These must go in the strongbox of Gundakhor where they will be safe." Eldurokh looked around and only one of the airships from Maris-ta-Sehlim appeared operational, though it had run aground atop a cliff. Elves stitched patches upon the wind-catching sails. Without the dirigible bladder, he had no idea how it could gain the necessary elevation to launch. "Captain Gennay?"

Reesime shook his head and frowned.

They spotted Queen Shyalou sitting nearby. She'd sustained many wounds that had bled all over, but they appeared mostly topical. Heathyr, her oracle, stitched shut as many as she could. Shyalou would live and had earned many scars for her participation in the fight.

"Where is Cymmeron?" Eldurokh asked.

"Fallen," Shyalou stated flatly. "Many of the enemy possessed weapons that our shields simply could not contend with."

Eldurokh took one of the dawn blades and turned it over in his hand. He offered it to the amazon queen.

She nodded and accepted the gift. "Star metal," she said, examining the sword. "I've never seen such fine craftsmanship."

"The morehl have been routed," Reesime confirmed. "What are your plans for the mountain you have claimed? Will you hold it?"

"I haven't the forces to hold it. We'd be driven out sooner or later as the Grotto's allied towns come to her aid. The drider is gone now, and that was the goal." He scowled at the mountain. Finally he spat, "Let the morehl have it. It will never again see its former glory."

"You could ask those warriors from the east for help... the Empyreans?" Reesime ventured.

Eldurokh shook his head. "They were already beginning to return by the time I left the rubble behind. They had the same goals: deposing the drider and eradicating the undead. It looks like all the walking corpses have been destroyed." He shuddered. "I saw only a few in the halls, but they were unlike anything I've seen before."

Queen Shyalou agreed. "Then the only thing left is to raid whatever supplies we can take for the journey back home... *King Eldurokh.*"

Eldurokh nodded. "I suppose you are right." He extended a hand and helped the amazon to her feet, and they soon marched west, back to their homes.

EPILOGUE

Year 447 of the First Age

Thus, did Eldurokh depart from the Crooked Spine Mountains and return to become the true king of Gundakhor and continue protecting the realm where his father had left off, establishing the vagha as one of the true protectors of Esfah.

In the wake of such decimation, the amazons reclaimed much of the territory they had lost at the Duar'Bondeen Steppes. Within one generation, the morehl surrendered Valis back to the forces of Gundakhor.

The Dawn of War came to an end, though wars were far from over. Dawn had passed, and now the full light of it had arisen. As long as worshipers of Death remain, peace shall likely never last. The intervention of the sages may have stemmed the spread of evil, but their kind grows rarer and rarer, and following the burning of the Library of Yentosh, much that was once known is lost forever. New pupil-sages may have been trained by those sages who remain, but meeting one is a rare thing and it is said that they live in seclusion of the Feylands dedicated to the service of the Great Trees.

Whatever grudge the firewalking empyreans hold against the undead has not been made entirely clear, and they remain a reclusive race, although some of their kind have been known to leave their homeland. The firewalkers hold a special reverence for the selumari hero Davian Whisperwynd, though they are generally a tight-lipped race and have only recently begun to trade with the outside countries. They are often seen along the East Coast in selumari towns.

Rumors of darkness still persist in Dereh'Liandor and many new weapons of the mysterious eldrymetallum, also called star metal, have made their way into greater circulation.

Whatever impact this will have on the world, and on the state of its many wars, remains to be seen. These weapons will either amplify the death and destruction, or deter them by forcing diplomatic solutions. Esfah remains forever hopeful.

Tal the Righteous: The Book of the Land, 1st edition

APPENDICES

GLOSSARY OF TERMS

Abyss - the home of the Void, a realm where silence reigns aside from pockets of terror and chaos where unknown gods reign. This is a similar concept to Greek myths of an underworld.

Ailuril - the secondborn of the Esfahan gods. She is represented by the color blue and has power over the air elements.

Aguarehl - the fourthborn of the Esfahan gods. He is represented by the color green and has power over the water elements.

Amazon - the race of mankind said to have been deposited whole upon Esfah as one of the few races created by Tarvanehl himself. Amazons are the warrior caste of human race.

Areosa - commonly known as the frostwings, a frigid felinoid, winged race with magic resistance.

Bloodless - another common name for the undead.

Deadzone – synonym for the Abyss, except from the point of view of the trogs or morehl. Within their respective religions, versions of the afterlife differ wildly and as often as they align in geopolitical goals, neither could imagine spending an eternal afterlife in the company of the other.

Death - the half-brother god who is the child of Nature and Void.

Dragons – these beasts come in two forms: Drake and Wyrm. Drakes have wings, and wyrms do not. Though the dragonkin are a kind of subspecies, they are not the same thing, no matter how similar they are. They used to live hidden across Esfah, but were nearly eradicated in the Dragoncrusades. Dragons have eternal spirits and when they die, they return to the plane where they now dwell. Dragonmagic came in two forms and it summons them from this realm or from nearby (the older form of this magic which has now been forgotten since these mythic beasts have largely gone out from Esfah.)

Drakufreet - the dragonkin come from the same realm as dragons and appear as a type of draconic hybrid race.

Eldarim – a human-like race that emerged over eons from Esfah's primordial soup and predated the gods-made races. The Eldarim are versatile and have proven the capacity to breed with many of Esfah's races. They are called Eldarim, meaning "from the earth."

Eldurim - the firstborn of the Esfahan gods. He is represented by the color gold and has power over the earth elements.

Efflorah - the race of treefolk.

Esfah - the world and one of two planets revolving around Soll.

Empyrea - known commonly as the firewalkers, a war-loving mercenary race.

Faeli - commonly known as scalders or steam dancers. These creatures are fickle and capricious and were once captured and tormented by Death.

Firiel - the thirdborn of the Esfahan gods. She is represented by the color red and has power over the fire elements.

First Age - everything from the beginning of creation to the year 863.

Frehlasuhl - also called the Forsaken or Mudbloods. They are the offspring of Selumari and Morehl unions. They cannot breed with each other to have children, only with one or the other race, but they are rejected wholesale by both.

Ghaeial - the mother goddess known more commonly as Nature.

Ghwereste - called the "feral folk." These are a hybrid of animal and man created at the dawn of the Second Age.

Gwich'in: "the people of the land" a group of human magicians gathered for study and knowledge (the closest English word might be "coven.")

Leguin - a sister planet to Esfah that also orbits Sol; it can often be seen in the night sky appearing above the horizon like a bright star.

Lich - a powerful undead spellcaster. Lichs often possess necromantic capabilities, though their created undead are maintained by force of will, rather than by other means, such as the Necralluvium.

Morehl - commonly called lava elves. They have red skin in addition to their elf-like features and their blood is said to smoke when exposed to air.

Necralluvium - a kind of magical potion with a seeming life of its own. This black filth can kill the living. The dead that are exposed to it become animated.

Rhaudian - the name of the moon. It circulates Esfah twice in a daily cycle.

Sarslayan - commonly known as swamp stalkers. These snake-men emerged in the Second Age as a result of Death using magic to twist the creations of his half-brother Aguarehl. They create more of their kind through magic conversion rather than by reproduction.

Second Age - everything after year 863 of the First Age. This began when Ghaeial walked the face of Esfah and surveyed the damages of the myriad of wars. The 864th year is year 1 of the Second Age.

Selurehl - the name of the second god to emerge after Tarvanehl, usually known as Void.

Selumari - commonly called coral elves. They have blue skin in addition to their elf-like features.

Shara – what the Eldarim people refer to themselves as when they communicate with each other. It means "little god-in-the-making."

Soll – the sun.

Tarvanehl - the creator god who came first, according to all mythology and story; he is often known as Father Time, or simply The Father.

Trog - a synonym for goblin. Trogs much prefer to live in boggy areas and tend to pollute the land.

Vagha - commonly known as dwarves.

Void - sometimes used interchangeably with the Abyss or, the power or person of Selurehl who is frequently referred to as Void just as his son Malgrimm is more widely regarded as Death. Context determines the meaning.

Warchief - a title of rank among the Vagha. Below the king is a Warchief who leads Warlords and Warcommanders under them. It might commonly be understood as a sort of general.

TIMELINE

Included is the general time line of major world events in Esfah. Please note that, during the time before the Mother, Ghaeial, became a goddess and the First Age began, prehistory spanned a scope of time measuring eons, and in that time, verily, only Time *existed. Despite the sage's attempts to capture much data and ancient knowledge, they did not begin tracking time and dates until the first passing of the Daybringer. The first three years of history might very well have been hundreds or even a thousand years as the gods (and the earliest race of eldarim) kept time differently.*

Prehistory N.D.

Tarvanehl exists and creates within the realm of Void/Abyss and Esfah and Leguin are born; Ghaeial realizes she is a goddess and falls in love with Tarvanehl.

Turambar courts Leguin

Selurehl, third of the brother gods grows angry

Eldurim the firstborn (earth) god-son of Ghaeial and Tarvanehl is born

Ailuril the secondborn (wind) god-daughter of Ghaeial and Tarvanehl is born

Firiel thirdborn (fire) god-daughter of Ghaeial and Tarvanehl is born

Aguarehl fourth born god-son (water) of Ghaeial and Tarvanehl is born

Malgrimm cursed bastard son (Death,) conceived and birthed after Selurehl's violence upon Ghaeial

Eldarim are birthed by Esfah and slowly emerge from the mire of her lands and water, evolving over long periods of time. They call themselves the Shara in their own tongue

The First Age

03FA the Daybringer Comet passes Esfah for the First Time, the Sisters of Fate are birthed of Turambar and Leguin, Dragons and the Drakufreet are created during the schism of the god-children

04FA Earliest creations of the gods: "monsters" are formed

15FA Selumari are created

16FA Vagha are created, Trogs are created

17FA Morehl are created

19FA The Dawn of War. Morehl invaders overthrow the first Selumari

22FA Humans arrive on Esfah via Tarvanehl's intervention

28FA Davian Whisperwynd leaves Maris-ta-Sehlim

32FA The proto-empyreans are birthed in the whirlwind

42FA Gundraokh Shatterfist finds the Bands of Turambar and renames the city of Orelod to Gundakhor

96FA Sshkkryyahr the Dread rises to power

103FA Malgrimm attempts to create a new powerful, destructive force within the Shadowlands, but the Areosan's magic resistance helps them maintain mild independence from the Death god and he abandons them to the frost plains

143FA Undead created, Melkior is defeated upon the Raithlan Plains by the gods' chosen Champions

167FA Dilution of the Eldarim race and the reduction of the Dragon population via the Dragoncrusades that eliminated nearly all the natural dragons of Esfah; the spells that compelled natural dragons that still remained in the realm became forgotten after this date in favor of those drawing eternal dragons through the interplanar rifts

341FA Existence of the Empyreans is discovered when they aid the elder races in the first major Undead uprising

447FA *Book of the Land, 1st Ed.* is published and immediately begins revisions

520FA Morehl city of Karakto falls to the selumari

532FA Morehl discover cursed bullets and retake Karakto

544FA Large load of Eldrymetallum discovered on the Karakto slopes

562FA Final version of *The Book of the Land* completed after 23 quintennial installments

836FA The Magestorm Wars erupt with the tectonic cataclysm that opens the Netherwold and nearly splits Dereh'Liandor in two; the Arcana Veil stiffens

842FA Disappearance of the gremmlobahnd and the genocide of the drakufreet

863FA Final battle of the Magestorm Wars ends the first age, the faeli are birthed in the Firequags and captured by the forces of Death and subjected to torments in the pits of the World Wound.

The Second Age

01SA Ghaeial walks the earth and surveys the damage of the elder races

03SA Ghaeial creates the ghwereste

79SA The plagues of the World Wound at its evils continue and the first of the sarslayan emerge from the nearby Snekdenn Bayou

153SA The areosa race emerges from the Shadowlands. They are known mostly as rumors, but their existence is verified to the outside world

209SA Whether the faeli escaped the torments of the World Wound or were released, none know, but they were so twisted by the centuries of abuse that they have become more children of Malgrimm than Ghaeial

233SA Under Ghaeial's wishes, the sylvan efflorah, existing as trees since even before the humans came to Esfah, picked up their roots and first emerged from forest and grove

829SA Zephras "Thunderfist" dies in Cyrea defending Balgavarr from a dragon

967SA Geril sa'Guhren "Dragonsbane" born

1021SA Geril sa'Guhren rules in Balgavarr

1082SA Coryn Sa'Geril is born

1119SA Daybringer Comet makes its pass by Esfah

1122SA Kholkoro Wicebrow writes her commentary *Kholkoro's commentary on Book of the Land*

1127SA The famed "Adventurer King" Hy'Mander sa'Meril is blinded

1139SA Melkior is revived

1142SA Daybringer Comet makes its circuit

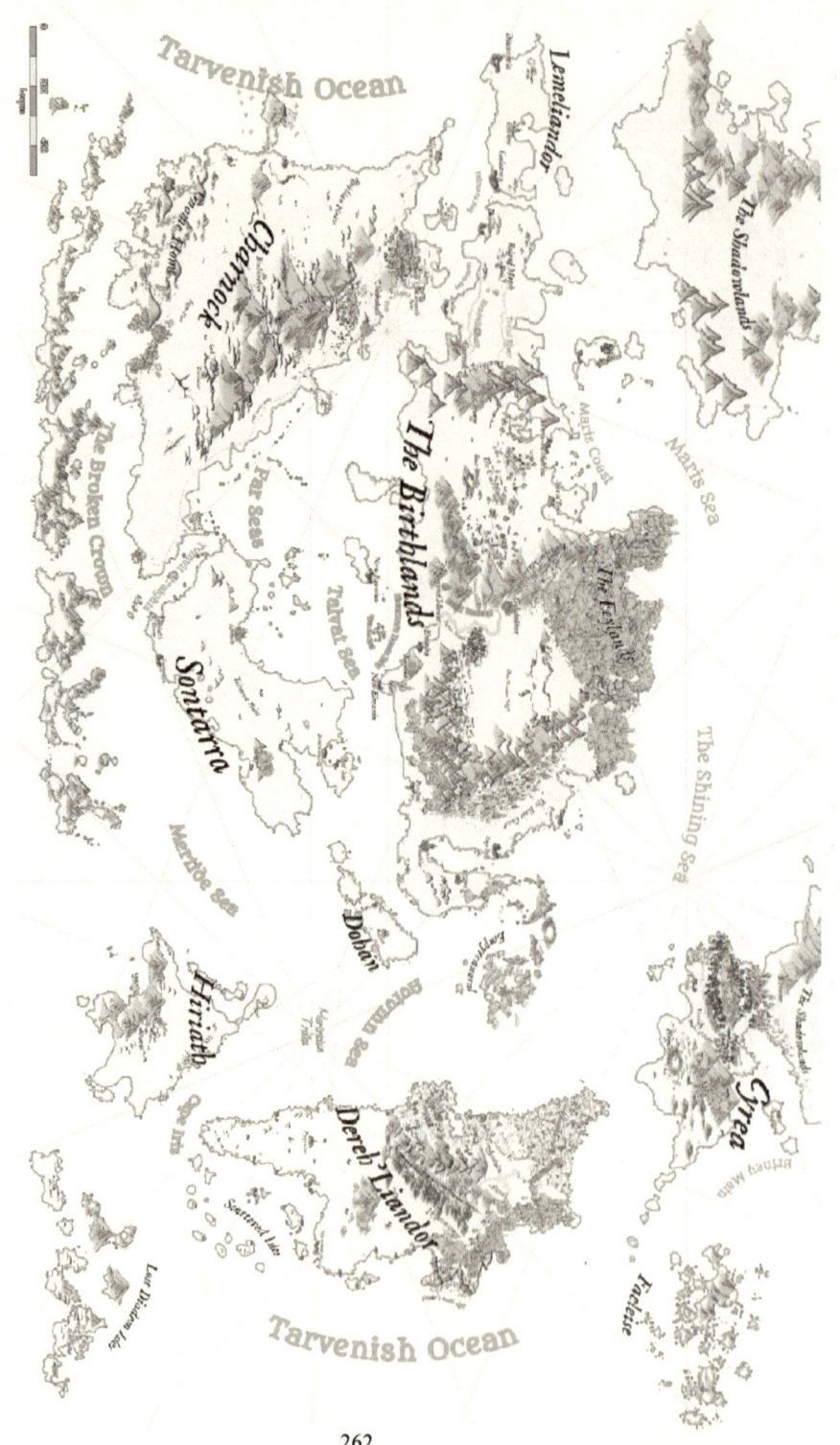

BOOKS
IN THE DRAGON DICE UNIVERSE
OF ESFAH

Rise and Fall of the Obsidian Grotto
Cast of Fate
Tome of Tarvanehl*
Heart of Stone and Flame*
Ashes of Ailushurai
Rise of the Champions
Drakuwar
Chill Wind
Eye of the Storm
Secrets of the Shadowlands
Army of the Dead**

*These two short books were the first produced by TSR and are included inside the re-released (2020) version of Cast of Fate, which was originally produced in 1996.

**This book was scheduled for release by TSR in the late 1990s but never published. A version of this book was released in 2003 but should not necessarily be considered Esfah canon and unless it is rereleased should not be considered part of *the Esfah Sagas*.

About the author:

Christopher D. Schmitz is author of both Sci-Fi/Fantasy Fiction and Nonfiction books and has been published in both traditional and independent outlets. If you've investigated indie writers of the upper Midwest, you may have heard his name whispered in dark alleys with an equal mix of respect and disdain. He has been featured on television broadcasts, podcasts, and runs a blog for indie authors... but you've still probably never heard of him.

As an avid consumer of comic books, movies, cartoons, and books (especially sci-fi and fantasy) this child of the 80s basically lived out Stranger Things, but shadowy government agencies won't let him say more than that. He lives in rural Minnesota with his family where he drinks unsafe amounts of coffee; the caffeine shakes keeps the cold from killing them. In his off-time he plays haunted bagpipes in places of low repute, but that's a story for another time.

He has a special offer for readers on the following page.

You can connect with him via the following links:
http://www.authorchristopherdschmitz.com

Follow me on Twitter:
https://twitter.com/cylonbagpiper
Follow me on Goodreads:
www.goodreads.com/author/show/129258.Christopher_Schmitz
Like/Follow me on Facebook:
https://www.facebook.com/authorchristopherdschmitz
Subscribe to my blog:
https://authorchristopherdschmitz.wordpress.com
Favorite me at Smashwords:
www.smashwords.com/profile/view/authorchristopherdschmitz
My Amazon Author Profile:
amazon.com/author/christopherdschmitz
Follow me at Bookbub:
www.bookbub.com/authors/christopher-d-schmitz

SPECIAL OFFER:

As a special bonus for you, I'd like to invite you download FIVE ebooks for free as a part of my Starter Library.

To get your free Starter Library, simply visit this link:
https://www.subscribepage.com/p1o9c9
Enter your email address and then collect your books as they are sent to you. It's that simple!

FREE STARTER BOOK LIBRARY

If you like Sci-Fi and Fantasy, you'll love these books, subscribe now to have them delivered right away.

DRAGON DICE

Dragon Dice™ is SFR Inc.'s core product. We are constantly working to create a quality game that everyone can enjoy. Dragon Dice™ was originally created by Lester Smith and produced by TSR© in 1995. After several years, TSR, now owned by Wizards of the Coast, had put Dragon Dice™ on hold to work on other projects. In October of 2000, SFR Inc. purchased the rights to Dragon Dice™ and now will continue to support and create NEW! products for the game.

Dragon Dice™ is strategy game where players create mythical armies using dice to represent each troop. The game combines strategy and skill as well as a little luck. Each person tries to win the game by outmaneuvering the opponent and capture 2 terrains. Of course eliminating your opponent completely is another acceptable way of winning.

Get online today and "Roll your way to victory!"

http://www.sfr-inc.com